LIGHT

Timothy O'Grady

LIGHT

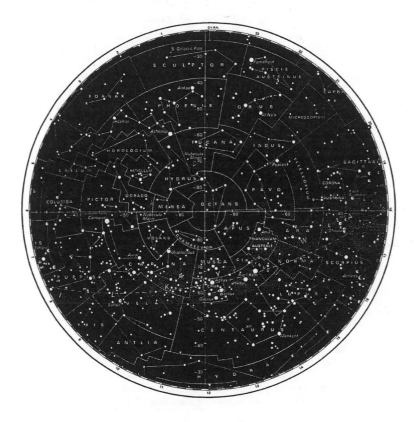

Secker & Warburg
LONDON

Published by Secker & Warburg 2004

2 4 6 8 10 9 7 5 3 1

Copyright © Timothy O'Grady 2004

Timothy O'Grady has asserted his right under the Copyright, Designs
and Patents Act 1988 to be identified as the author of this work

First published in Great Britain in 2004 by
Secker & Warburg
Random House, 20 Vauxhall Bridge Road,
London SW1V 2SA

Random House Australia (Pty) Limited
20 Alfred Street, Milsons Point, Sydney,
New South Wales 2061, Australia

Random House New Zealand Limited
18 Poland Road, Glenfield,
Auckland 10, New Zealand

Random House (Pty) Limited
Endulini, 5A Jubilee Road, Parktown 2193,
South Africa

The Random House Group Limited Reg. No. 954009
www.randomhouse.co.uk

A CIP catalogue record for this book
is available from the British Library

ISBN 0436206420

Typeset by Palimpsest Book Production Limited

Printed and bound in Great Britain by
Mackays of Chatham plc, Chatham, Kent

For Aoife O'Grady

The longing to behold harmony is the source of the physicist's inexhaustible patience and perseverance.

Albert Einstein

PART ONE

I

In the Café Voltaire

I met him under the green awning of the Café Voltaire in a corner of the Stary Rynek in Krakow during an early evening in the month of September in the year when my sister Renata took ill and a train out of Gdansk went off its rails, leaving forty-two dead. Already the air was cooling after a hot summer. He was wearing a long black cashmere coat with the collar turned up. His hands flew about like startled white birds when he spoke. In his eyes I could see many things – curiosity, panic, irony, qualities of both empathy and aloofness, an intelligence that may not have been instinctive enough to be truly useful to him. I do not believe that his face had met with a razor for at least three days. On his lap was the book *Physics and Philosophy* by Werner Heisenberg.

I had come to the Stary Rynek to listen to the trumpet calling from the high steeple of the Mariacki church and to take a glass of Zubrowka. In the morning I had travelled to Krakow and passed the afternoon with my sister while she waited for the morphine that would remove the pain of the disease that was eating her bones. In the evening I was to return to her, but now I was taking a Zubrowka. To think of the cities of the world where I have searched for this pale green drink!

He was at a table in the corner, the wind blowing around him. If you look at the men who sit alone in the cafés of this square you will find them motionless and composed, their backs like washboards as they lean into their chairs, their eyes blinking as slowly as tortoises', their fingers just touching the sides of their drinks which rest on the tables before them. I was among them in my green woollen jacket and English hat, all of us timid and decorous, all of us liking to think of ourselves as enigmas, all of us knowing each other's fraudulence. None of us could keep our eyes for very long from the turbulent man in the long black coat who sat alone at a table in the corner. He was a small cyclone, the red wine leaving his glass in great gulps, his tapping foot, his reading of Werner Heisenberg and the little notes he made in the margins of the book having the look of a desperate race against time. Who or what had forsaken him? With what instrument had the world cut the lines into his face? I thought, Young man, why is it you carry about you the look of an abandoned church?

In April I reached seventy-two years. I have swum great distances in the pale blue waters of the Pacific. I drank wine from a goat-skin in the streets of Tijuana. I picked cherries with Mexicans in the orchards of Oregon. I saw a man bisected vertically like a block of cheese by a sheet of metal that fell from the sky. I look now at these scarred hands stained brown by the years, at these feet which ache in the morning. These are the days when I ride the rails of Poland and pay visits to graveyards or to those soon to make their homes in them. I can sit in a chair and for two hours listen to the conversation of my neighbours' children through the wall. I persuade myself that I have a special interest in international athletic competitions and read accounts of them in the newspapers. At night, alone in my bed, I wait for a sleep which rarely comes. Pictures from long ago drift in. There is father in his tram conductor's uniform, snow on his hat, buttons polished, his tie a little askew as he reaches out for me when he comes from work through the door of our home. There am I, arm outstretched, eyes closed, wine running down my neck and on to my shirt. Beside me a mountain man from Zakopane. About what were we laughing? And there is Renata at eighteen with a look which says she will not be denied. I think of her coquetry and her schemes, of her rapturous face as she rode our uncle's mare through the high trees of Puszcza Piska, of the cold and hungry way she stared from her bedroom window. Now she takes her food from a spoon held by another's hand.

If I have anything at the end of seventy-two years, it is time. Truly I am not taking so badly to old age. I have not as yet an exclusive obsession with the observations of doctors. I like to take my bicycle and search for mushrooms in the forest. I go to the library and read the encyclopaedias. I take pleasure in the feeling of the sun on my back. I think to myself, Will my sense of taste increase while my eyesight diminishes? Sometimes I set myself tests. Sometimes I provoke my tongue with an anchovy.

When I went to the Café Voltaire that evening I knew nothing of Werner Heisenberg or of the world which he struggled to understand – that tiny world of atoms and their particles that makes up all that we can see. But then that evening in Krakow the young man spoke of love and ruin and physics. How unlikely it all was, and yet how compelling. So now before I wake I am already dreaming his story and when I sit in the library I read not about generals or the great religions or the rivers of Africa, but rather about light and momentum and the structure of the atom. I look for him, for how he moves in this strange world of the infinitesimally small looking for an answer.

'When I lost her, I began to read about physics.'

That was what he said. Strangely, I understood him.

* * *

There are events which detonate in memory and reveal with their light what went before as well as the moment itself. It is as though time itself begins to slow as the moment approaches. I remember seeing Angelina for the first time as she turned a corner of the stairs in the house where my colleague Pawel had lodgings in Berlin. I remember her hand on the dark wooden railing, the folds in her grey dress as they followed the lines of her loins, her downward glance and look of private amusement, the dark hair falling around the sweeps and hollows of her neck. That was a single moment in the course of a dark German night in November 1955 – the only moment that mattered after all, for thereafter nothing was as it had been. But I remember also the seconds just before – the man in the blue metallic suit who passed by slapping his newspaper on to his open palm, the smell of his cheroot, the piercing call of the red parrot which the caretaker kept in a cage in the hall.

In the Café Voltaire that evening a gust of wind rose and blew out the candle by which the young man was reading his book. I remember the feeling of eagerness and servility with which I rose from my chair. I remember reaching for the lighter in my jacket pocket. I remember a thin man at a neighbouring table lifting his spectacles on to his nose and looking at us, a bicyclist ringing his bell, a Russian prostitute standing under the arches helpless with laughter. I lit the candle and the young man looked up at me. He could have thanked me for the light and returned to his book, but instead he extended a hand and invited me to sit. The men around us watched, as still as rooks on a fence. He called out to the waiter for a Zubrowka and more wine. There was in his gestures something which seemed to tell me that in the anonymity of our short encounter discretion would not be necessary. The candle flame in the green glass flickered in the wind and he moved out of its range. In the shadows he seemed composed of shades of blue and quicksilver, like fire or ice or something mined from the earth. I could not immediately find him. Then he reeled around again and leaned forward into the light and began to speak. He spoke for eleven hours through that night of the woman he loved and lost and never really knew. He barely paused in the telling. What did I see when the light struck his face? His pain, his amusement.

What was his name? He said it once, but I didn't catch it. I shall call him M., for Michal, a name I have always liked, though of course it could not have belonged to him.

'I watched her,' he said. 'I could never get used to her. I'd have watched her all day if it weren't so embarrassing. I knew I was living the days of my life and I wanted to keep them with me. That was bad luck, for I did it too well. I know her voice, her movements, the grain of her skin. I think I know what's inside her. But I don't know the facts. She didn't speak in facts. She made up things, about people sitting at another table, about me, I suppose about herself. I went along with her in this. She liked doing it. It was a kind of . . . what? Maybe a kind of seduction.

'Suddenly she vanished. I don't know why. I've been trying to find her. I've driven all around Europe looking for her. I'm heading for Finland now, a city called Turku. There might be something there. But really there's no trail. There are only her stories.'

He turned away and I heard him laugh into the darkness. 'Ridiculous,' he said. He took a drink of wine, and then his face entered again the pool of light.

'Did you ever read classical physics?' he said. 'It's so wonderfully clear and knowable. Everything written down in simple, indisputable numbers. There was a time when they believed that nothing could escape these numbers – not the past, nor the present, nor even the future. As long as they had the formulas and the data, they believed they could know absolutely everything. Nothing could get away from them. They had the feeling of absolute clarity. Imagine. Nothing was uncertain.'

One by one the men of the Café Voltaire returned to their homes that night and the last waiter sat in a chair and listened forlornly to the radio. From there we went to Krzysztofory, with its students so grave and important over their chessboards, and then to Pod Baranami. At the end we made our way like men maimed in war down the stairs of a bar unknown to me where the walls were painted black and where the music sounded like rain falling into a barrel. At this point the light of the following day could not have been far away. Through all of it – the Czech baritone shaking the walls of Pod Baranami, the girls with their little shorts and long boots flitting like mayflies around the dancefloor – he drank his wine and told me about that woman of transcendental beauty who transfixed him and left him broken into tiny pieces, as tiny, it seems, as the pieces of atoms. He drank the last glass of wine, he arranged his long white fingers around the empty bottle before him, and he said,

'Her hair was fair, a pale, muted gold. She parted it in the middle and it swept in around her neck under the line of her jaw. It was a little shorter in the back. She was very careful about the way she fixed it. Her eyes were green. Everything in her face moved slowly, the drop of her eyes, the way her lips parted. Her voice was very soft. It seemed to fold around you like an embrace. She had a gift for thinking logically. She knew remedies for things. Her laughter could be out of control. She told stories. But these things aren't any use. They don't bring her here to you. I don't know how to do it. Her beauty shook me. I couldn't get used to it. People stopped to watch her pass. Children especially. Her eyes were a little too prominently set. If she was off her guard and thinking about something they could look cold. But you also felt that there was a whole world there, that if you went down into it you might never come back. She was slender, graceful. Very elegant in all the things that she did. But her feet were long and flat. Sometimes she seemed to be walking on small skis. She didn't like the way she walked. I don't know how to do this for you. It's like trying to describe colour. It was all the things about her that made her a woman. Her silence. The softness of her voice. The slowness of her movements. She had mystery. She had it the way some people have good eyesight, or long fingers. I tried to get behind it but I couldn't separate the elements. Here. Look at these photographs. One of her on a boat, one in winter, and then this one. Just look at her face. Can you get it? She made me think of miracles, genius, wondrous things. She could make the rest of the world go away.

'With her I was alive. Everything around me seemed newly made. I miss the way she could make me feel this way and see these things. I miss the world she made for us. And I miss her beauty, like it was a separate person.

'I drive around in my car looking for her. There aren't many places left. I sit in hotel rooms with a glass of whiskey and I think about her. I try to put together the pieces of the story. I try to think of what she could be feeling. But I can't get it. Why did she go? Was it real? Did it happen at all? She seems to be around me sometimes then. I get the feeling of being near her skin, her voice seems to come out of the stones. Then I see her face.

'I go to bed with this and I wake with it. Sometimes I think I should destroy it. Sometimes I try. But I can't do it. It was a gift I got. I never had anything like it. Maybe it's something you get only one time in your life.

'I lost myself when she went away. I can't get hold of the idea of who I am. If I look in the mirror I seem to see the wrong face. And the sounds I make seem wrong. I look into the windows of places and I see people talking and laughing. They're moving around. But I don't seem to have anything to do with them. Nothing is familiar.'

The night was at its blackest when finally we came up out of the cellar we had found when everywhere else was closed. Inside, the lights had come on, the grille come down over the bar. There was that sound a little like night insects as the till printed out a record of all the money that had been taken. The girls with the slender bronzed thighs and the expectant looks were putting on their coats, their eyes narrowed now. They look so different when the night comes to an end.

We had passed through drunkenness by then. I remember him calm and clear as we stood facing each other in the street. He had emptied himself yet again of his story, as sinners do to their priests. He did it whenever he could, with whomever would listen. His eyes were bright under the lamplight. He shook my hand. He thanked me. He apologised for his long speech, an apology he said he had grown accustomed to making. I have the self-absorption of a child with an earache, he said.

Here in this room there is that same deepened darkness of the hour before dawn. I hold my finger up to the tip of my nose but I cannot see it. This is an hour well known to those of us who are old. I open the curtain and look out the window. Nothing moving. In the faint glow of the streetlamp the grass looks grey and the building opposite as though it's been painted on the air. Somehow I am also on a street in Krakow in September. More there than here. It's like the held frame of a film. Then it moves on.

He walked away. I watched his back, the black coat billowing a little. I saw a flag grey with age stirring on a wall. He looked up at the buildings to either side of him as though interested. Then he rounded a corner and was gone.

I stood in the street. I heard his footsteps moving towards the car that was his home. Celibate footsteps, I thought. He'd driven across Europe looking for a phantom. What will become of him? Can the physicists help him? Can I? I looked at our national flag. Forgotten there by an attendant who was to have brought it in for the night. Forgotten there probably every night. The Heart of Europe, we call ourselves. Here we have been flayed to the bone and then broken. Then broken again. Perhaps it's a privilege to have seen so intimately the very worst that man can do. It distinguishes us somehow. But in certain moments M.'s suffering is not lighter. I know some of the colours of this spectrum. When a woman leaves you when you do not wish her to it seems she spits into your soul.

And just as I turned to take home with me all that I have heard through this long night the thought of Angelina hit me like a mad wind. It staggered me. I should have expected it. But I never do.

Days pass. The nights come in just a little earlier. Someone else, it seems, is performing my actions. I get up, stretch. I pass through the verse of a song in a whisper. I leave the trace of my breath on the window when I look out. I go to the kitchen and swallow a spoonful of oil for I am told that it can help ease the pain in my bones. Look how I am. My knees have no spring in them. Little pouches of skin like the coin purses of old women hang over them where the muscles have collapsed. The skin is so pale you'd think there was no blood running under it at all. But in my head I am as I have been for nearly the past half-century –

since that day in the hotel room in Erfurt, Germany, when I became myself at age twenty-four. About this I will say more later. Now I think of M. and his lost girl. I seem not to be able to avoid thinking of this and I do not entirely know why. I try to see him in his German car, the green lights of the driving instruments moving over his face. He beats out a rhythm on the steering wheel. He shifts a little in his seat. He turns on the radio and passes through a succession of sounds which have no meaning to him. He carries clothes and documents and a little food. Sometimes he stops in a bar. Sometimes he goes into the back of his car and lies down and goes to sleep. He would like to think with purpose, to focus his mind, but the little Czech cars which sound like mowing machines, the whoosh of the trees, the small vacant towns all distract him. Inside him, nothing is at rest. This is a pain that nothing has prepared him for and that nothing can stop. His head aches. He cannot eat. Waves of uneasiness fall over him. He hopes that time will cure him, but he fears that it may not. If he thinks of her lips moving over his, the warmth of her breath, the look of her as she rises from bed in the morning, he may not be able to stop himself from weeping.

Why am I doing this? I have listened to stories of actual human wreckage all through my life and remembered little in the morning and nothing at all just days later, not the facts nor the faces as the stories were told. Why does his persist? It must surely have to do with what happened with Angelina near Miedzyzdroje among the sand dunes of Wolin Island in the summer of 1956. Two stories, his and mine, hideously twinned – the disappearance of the women inexplicable, the ending absolute, the rapture something we had never known before and never would again. So I look at him not only with pity, but a pity felt by one whose wound has been the same.

But there is something else, no? Something that connects me

to him. What is it? Something in his eyes – their nervousness, the ruin they carry, the excitement. I hesitate here. It seems so foolish, so grandiose. But who is listening anyway? I had the feeling that what I saw was myself looking back at me. We are of different times, different worlds. We would not know how to live each other's lives. That is clear. But listen. People are born into this world and if they have the fortune are then born again when finally they discover who they are. This can happen slowly, like the healing of a wound, or as fast as a slap you do not expect. But whatever way it happens and at whatever point in your life it comes to you a lens is formed and it is through it that you will look at the world for ever more. Can it be that the flame that passed through me in the hotel room in Germany when I was twenty-four years old also passed through him somewhere else, that though he is from the West and I from the East we were somehow delivered into the world and marked in the same way? Is that what I saw in him, a birth in common with mine? And the ache I felt as I listened to him, was it recognition, nostalgia? For I too became lost once.

Now the world is his enemy. He feels alone on the dark roads. Even the thought of food makes him sick. His time with that woman of elegance and stories has made him forget who he is. Maybe the cruel truth is that this self which he once discovered will stay lost to him for ever. But it is there for him, nevertheless. It endures. This much I know.

It is when I am dressing and reach into the pocket of my jacket for a pencil that I find there M.'s photographs of his beautiful girl. Idiot! I have the urge to run out and find him. I try to think of a way of getting them to him. It happened when we were leaving that final bar after he showed them to me and I lifted them from the table rather than him. I was just a step behind him as we moved through the people but he didn't hear me as I held them up and called to him. So I put them in my pocket. I only wanted to keep them safe until we got up the stairs and out into the open air. Then there was the ceremony of farewell. I have all three of them, all that he had with him. Double idiot! Drink on top of old age and then a person can't think at all. Well, at least me. How many times each day did he look at them?

2

Hanna

M.'s story has taken up residence in my mind. I can feel it moving and there is a pressure inside my head. But I do not quite know what it is. It is a kind of organism hidden from me by a bank of cloud. I try to clear this cloud and coax it out. I want to see it. But it remains just a pressure, with the colour grey.

Each day I try to get out before noon and take a turn through the streets looking at all the people. Already the weather has turned and I've locked my bicycle in the janitor's shed. I walk for three kilometres through this city where I have no past and then I call in to Mrs Slowacki's shop. I buy bread, a block of white cheese and a nice ripe tomato. I smile at Mrs Slowacki as she hands me my change and tells me that at our age we need to be eating prunes.

I return home and prepare my food. If there is a bite in the air I will take a bowl of soup. I place my food on a little metal tray and sit before the television watching the breakfast news which arrives by satellite from America. So many doctors offering remedies, so many lawyers with opinions, so many women doing exercises! I lie on the sofa and M.'s story turns like a troubled sleeper in my mind. I listen to the birdsong and the shouts of children and the sighing of lorries. I call Renata. I go to the café. I go home again and get into my pyjamas. I offer a short prayer and I go into my bed hoping that I will sleep. Always his story, insistent yet out of reach.

Sometimes I have awakened from a dream and felt a great thought form in my mind. Sometimes I have run to the table to write it down. I cannot describe how terrible was the banality which the morning light would reveal when it fell on those pages. Now the nights are cold in Poland. I do not like to leave my bed in the mornings. Still less do I like to leave it at night when I feel the call of nature. But words which I do not understand form in my mind and will not go away. Cherries. Air. Baboon. Sea. What is that? They push through the clouds, they rap like a bailiff's knuckles on my head. I look at them. Whenever they seem to reach an end they start again at the beginning. Nothing can move them. Finally I know that sleep will not come until they are taken from my mind and let out into the world, towards M.

One evening last summer when I was in Krakow visiting Renata a man in a black suit was singing like a wounded animal beside the Mariacki church. A sign at his feet said FORMER PROFESSOR OF FRENCH LITERATURE. I stopped to watch him. He sang nearly to the end of a verse, slowed and then halted. He pinched his nose, grimaced, and began again, but once more wound down and stopped. He looked all around the sky and then began for a third time. I dropped fifty groszys into his cup. He gripped me by the arm before I could pass. 'Give me two zlotys and I'll tell you a joke,' he said. I told him I did not think a joke would suit me that day. 'Well, give me one zloty and I'll tell you something you may not know.' I gave him the money. He looked a little surprised. I don't think he had anything ready. His Adam's apple went down into his throat like a bucket into a well. Then he spoke, his eyes wide. 'You must know your song well before you start singing,' he said, and his head swooped around and away from me like a diving bird.

M. was dreaming. The sun had turned the surface of the sea bright blue and chrome. The wind was blowing. He was standing in the bow of a round-bottomed boat, eating cherries. The currents in the air carried the smell of pine trees. A baboon was trying to reason with him. He was very happy.

A roar like the foghorn of a liner crashed through his head. The earth shook. The red dust of Spain swirled around him and caught in his throat.

He woke up in a lay-by. He could not quite get the picture. Everything in his limbs was heavy, the warm webbing of sleep still holding him. He saw the back of a lorry as it receded from him into the settling dusk. He remembered that his father was now a frail figure lying in his bed in Ireland and that he was about to begin work as an interpreter in the trade delegation in Barcelona. He had been travelling for two days, and now he was just thirty kilometres from his destination.

He drove into a small town he had never heard of before. He bought a newspaper and chocolate. A man in a wheelchair sold him a ticket he said could bring him a fortune. The last of the day's light ran like water from a broken dam down the street where he was standing.

He turned from the man. Across from him was a bar. He moved back towards his car, but then stopped. The element of chance in this moment was high. He could see nothing except the particles of dust in the flooding light.

He crossed the street and went through the bead curtain of the bar into the darkness and the smell of stale beer and agriculture. He waited for a moment until his eyes adjusted to the change of light. He saw a man – he seemed a giant – standing before an electronic poker machine, blue and green light passing over his face as though through sea water. There were more men at the bar, heavy and still. On the television was a programme about the wild scavenger dogs of Africa.

He sensed something luminous to his right, and he turned. This was when he saw her. He sees her now in his long night, his tyres singing like wasps on the wet Central European roads. She was behind the bar in a single pool of light, standing very still and looking right at him. The men and their aromas and the African dogs faded away into the void. She was dressed very demurely in a kind of alpine pinafore and a white blouse trimmed in pink and buttoned to the neck. Everything immaculately pressed. Pale golden hair. She was almost off balance, with her hand raised as though she had stopped in the midst of doing something, her mouth open a little, the light glimmering on her lower lip. Her eyes were wide and green and they seemed to be asking him for something. His mind at this moment was empty. But he felt something strange and powerful, a deep visceral explosion, warm and breathtaking, that sent its waves out to the ends of his limbs and upwards in a column into the core of his brain.

He did not recall what it was he intended to do in this place. He was still held somehow in the dream of the boat. He sat with the men at the bar. She took a step towards him and stopped. Then she continued. She did not look away from his eyes. She leaned towards him. She took his order. 'Caña,' she said after him. A small beer. She had a slight accent which he could not place, a voice full of music and intimacy that moved through his head like a vapour. He could feel her breathing. What was she thinking? In that moment it seemed that everything was possible.

On the morning that M. set off on his journey he sat on his father's bed and took him up in his arms and held him. He seemed light as a cloud. Could it be that he would not see him again? He had not thought this before, but now the idea possessed him. 'Are you afraid of anything?' M. asked him. He looked at his father's eyes. They were large and round and already they seemed half in another world. 'No,' he said. 'I'm not afraid of anything.' He did not say this to reassure him. He said it as if M. were not there.

He sat at the bar and he watched her move – the way she leaned forward to open the bottles of beer, the way she held her hands up and shoulders back as though surprised when she punched the numbers into the till, the turn of her ankle when she stepped forward. She stopped for a moment to take an order, her hands leaning on the bar. A beam of light fell on her ring finger and he saw a slender gold band. It had not occurred to him that she could be married. He thought it tragic and unjust. He did not wish to think of the man who gave her the ring or the ceremony where it happened, but he could not stop himself. He pictured him lying across a sofa with his boots undone, her on the floor looking up at him in awe. Now there in the bar M. saw her hair fall across her left eye. Had the man across from her told her a joke? A smile broke over her white teeth, a smile full of the knowledge of folly and of pleasure. He thought, The man who is loved by this woman is blessed. But he did not wish him well.

He stayed in the bar that night for four and a half hours. He did not think of the man from the trade delegation in Barcelona who had prepared a bed for him. He placed her gold ring away outside his consciousness. He felt there was nothing greater than his need to gain knowledge of this woman whose name he did not know. She tended to the men. At times she became very still and turned to him. Or she would speak rapidly to him in a voice just louder than a whisper. She gave him the impression that she wanted nothing from this night except to be with him, but that something she could not express to him held her. She told him very little about herself – something about a boat out of the Baltic, a dart thrown at a map which pierced the name of this little town. It only deepened the mystery. There was urgency in her eyes, some kind of music crescendoing in his head. It all seemed just a breath away.

A man arrived to collect the money and lock the door. The lights went on. M. blinked a few times, sat upright on his stool. He waited until the man went into the back room and then he asked her what her name was.

'Hanna,' she said.

'Would you like a lift home, Hanna?' he said.

She looked startled, and a little unsettled. Then she said, 'No.'

'Do you work here regularly?' he asked.

'Yes,' she said. 'Four nights a week.'

He bid her good-night. If he'd had a hat he'd have lifted it to her. He got into his car and drove towards Barcelona with pictures of her wheeling like a flock of birds in his head.

I take out her photographs and lay them out on the table. Have I the power to draw her up from that paper – to find the way she looks when she combs her hair, the inclination of her head when listening, the pitch of her voice? Where does such a power come from? How is it found? I would like her to fall over me like a soft rain. Is that how a painter would find the face of an angel? It's a long time since I have seen intimately a woman who is in her best years. I will have to use memory.

She stood before M. washing a glass. She had a faint smile meant to suggest that this was not her calling. She had been with the men, patting their arms and wagging her finger at their jokes. She had played a hand of poker on the electronic machine with the giant. Now she was before him, with her hands in the water. She seemed to be searching for something. Then she held up the gold band which he had not noticed was missing, and dried it. She placed it on her finger, moving it back and forth so that he could see how loose it was. She leaned forward. He could see the skin on her chest rising and falling as she breathed.

'This is something you need in this job,' she whispered. 'I borrow it from the woman upstairs.' She turned the ring on her finger. 'She's a little overweight.'

He did not allow himself to think about any of this. There was something about her that did not admit calculations of debit and credit. He just held on to his dream, the dream he nurtured each time he drove out to this little town. He built his weeks around the nights she was there. He didn't miss any of them. What did she do the rest of the time? He didn't know. He didn't ask. He watched her move around behind the bar. There was a silence to her movements, like a current of air through grass.

He watched the men leave, one by one. He knew them by now – the car dealer who bought her perfume and invited her to race meetings and trips to Capri, the farmer who boasted of the wonder of his aubergines, the gravedigger who told her dirty jokes. They will think of her in their cars and in the darkness after they have gone into their beds next to their wives. They all hated him. He had unsettled their nights. They hated the silent looks between them, their urgent whispered conversations. He was taking her from them and they were angry. 'They've complained to the owner,' she told him. There was a silver-haired man who wore a black T-shirt with the sleeves cut at the shoulders. He seemed made from concrete and sat each night behind piles of coins and glasses of beer, his foot going up and down on the bar stool like a piston. Each time he saw M. his knuckles went white. When once M.

sat next to him he heard the man's teeth grinding, saw the muscles move in a spasm across his face. 'Watch him,' she told M. 'He's not long out of prison. He carries a knife the length of your forearm.'

Finally the men were gone and it was M. and her and the giant sleeping by his machine. Her movements slowed and became more rounded. She turned down the lights. She sat behind the bar facing him. She reached into a cupboard and poured him a vodka flavoured with blackberries, and then one for herself. She looked at him over the glass. He saw her parted lips through the rose-coloured liquid. She raised her glass and said something very softly, a smear of letters. He didn't hear it very well.

'What's that?' he asked her.

'It's a toast,' she said. 'You learn many in this job.'

For the first time it was just M. and her, face to face. She leaned back in her chair, turned away. The silence boomed like a vast heartbeat. He could have reached across to touch her hand but the bar between them seemed huge, dark, cavernous.

He heard a movement by the machine and the giant called out the name Ascension in a small, high voice. Then he fell to the floor, bringing two chairs and a table with him. Hanna went to him and knelt beside him. She cleared the hair away from his eyes. He nodded and smiled. He lifted his hand to her face. She righted the chairs and got him to his feet, whispering to him all the way out into the street, like a nurse leading someone away from a train crash.

She came back, sat in her chair. She took a small sip of vodka.

'His head is full of torments,' she said. 'They come out sometimes when he sleeps.'

'Who's Ascension?' M. asked.

She seemed about to answer with a shrug, but then stopped. She lit a cigarette, smiled, looked up to the ceiling. It was a look he would see again, and already he feared it – serene, far away, without need.

'Ascension was his younger sister,' she said. 'She was pale and blue-eyed and had something wrong with one of her feet. The bones were short. She had to wear a special shoe. There were no other children in the family. They went to their house in the country and one day when he was supposed to be minding her she fell into a pond and drowned. She was three years old. He'd been reading a book and hadn't noticed.

'After that, he couldn't live with himself. He thought he shouldn't be seen again by anyone he knew. He ran away. He wanted to be invisible, but of course he couldn't be because he's so big. He keeps moving from place to place. He lives in his car. He's very brilliant and has a powerful memory. It's curious the things he knows about. He knows about guns and diseases of the skin and about people who live in extremes of cold and heat and darkness. For company he most likes people who haven't homes.'

'How do you know this?' M. asked.

'He told me,' she said. 'He tells me everything – his regrets, his desires. When he doesn't want to talk we play the machine together. It's difficult for the machine to beat him. He can almost make enough money from it to eat.

'He's very kind, very generous. Yesterday he brought me a present, a book. He made it himself. He brought it in in a plastic bag and he handed it to me. It was quite big, like an atlas. The covers were made of wood which he had painted. There were shapes made from latex on parts of it and around the edges he had glued things. There were small pieces of rusted metal, the spine of a fish, also some skin from a fish. There were feathers mixed with the paint, and earth. There were tiny white things which he said were teeth from a snake. Some stones and pieces of egg. And there was black hair. He said it was from someone he knew who died. She was a very good friend of his, he said. She had bullet wounds in her side.

'When you opened the book there were just ten pages of paper. Really beautiful paper, of an ivory colour. They were blank. He said I could write on them whatever I wanted. It was for me. His head was turned a little to the side, like a bird's when it's listening. His mouth was open. Poor man, he seems to forget about parts of himself. He can appear with only one shoe. You don't see him smiling very much, but that's what he seemed to be doing, the kind of smile that people can have when a thing shouldn't make sense but somehow does and they want the other person to know this. Just a little twisted at the corners. The lips wet, like a simple person's. One eye squinting a little and the other very big just then – dark, maybe black. You had to feel something for him when you looked into those eyes.'

She was quiet then.

She got up and put a little jacket on over her dress and told M. that she had to close the bar. She didn't say good-night. He went out into the street and waited for her while she locked the door. She leaned over to the lowest of the locks. Her dress was short and moved up her leg. She pulled down at the hem. M. looked away so that she would not feel his eyes on her.

He found that he was looking at the place where the man in the wheelchair had sold him the lottery ticket just before he passed through the bead curtain of the bar with his newspaper and chocolate and discovered her standing in the light. He knew that as long as her opaqueness and beauty remained with her the men of the world would make offerings to her. How much of his destiny lay in that moment when he entered the bar? Could there be any peace there? Was he about to win his fortune? He could not know.

He walked along with her through the streets of the town. How would it be in that place? The howl of a cat, the insect-like whine of a motorbike, the sigh of an old man turning in his bed? A brief, hot wind loaded with the smell of wild herbs from the hills? I can't sense this very well. I know this country where all these things happened to M. only from pictures and stories and what was told me by an old man in the Café Lara who spent half his life's savings on two winter months in a hotel room high above the Mediterranean Sea. I see a light from a window fall on the long line of her leg as she takes a step. A pulsing, moonless sky. I see the bones move in her hand as she takes the hair from in front of her eye. Her skin has reddened a little from the sun. Her hands have a look of intelligence.

They walked slowly towards the edge of the town. She did not speak and neither did M. She was looking down, her face inclined towards his, as though waiting for him to speak. A breeze stirred in the branches of the palm trees and the air drifted past him. It had the feeling of silk.

They arrived at a tall wooden door, a wonderful door with deep red tones in a large house at the end of the street. She stopped. She seemed not to know what to do. She looked into the trees, then up at the sky. The air seemed so brittle to him now as to be made from glass. He looked at her from the side, this woman just on the verge of becoming herself. He tried to imagine the forces of her life that were making her as she was. 'I love you,' he told her in his mind. He looked all around him in silence trying to find a way to reach her. Then he heard her say, 'Good-night.' He turned and saw the big wooden door closing in front of him. She was gone.

When M. was alone he thought of her. He looked out over the rooftops of the city from his apartment and tried to take hold of some idea of who she was. Her face, her gestures, her voice, they were like stray notes from an unknown piece of music. He tried to fit them all together. But he couldn't.

Here in this room I have the same thought. I am like M.'s ghost.

She was before him at the bar, her eyes down. She placed the top of a bottle of beer into the mouth of an opener, then pushed down slowly. Her arms pressed into her sides. Her long neck opened to him as her body moved down against the bottle, her feet splayed, veins erupting briefly in her forearm and neck. Her eyes moved up, fixed on his, and then moved on.

She left him there for a long time. He drank his beer slowly.

'Another?' she said then, moving past him. One brow was a little arched.

She shuffled and dealt from a deck of cards, her hands like a chef's opening oysters. When she sensed that M. might have an advantage in the game they were playing she stiffened a little and concentrated. Sometimes she bit her lip just at the corner of her mouth. He watched the flesh sink beneath her tooth. When she held the advantage, which was nearly all the time, she pressed ahead and looked at M. with a trace of sorrow.

The men sat in a corner of the bar growing hysterical in front of a television broadcasting a football match. M. and Hanna played twelve hands of cards and M. lost eleven. He would know later that there was not a game involving memory at which he could defeat her.

He told her a story about a mathematician attending a conference in China. One night the mathematician had to speak with the professor who was chairing the session the following morning. A woman answered the telephone at the professor's house. She could not speak Farsi or English, which were the mathematician's languages, and he could not speak Chinese, which was the woman's. The mathematician said the professor's name and she replied at some length without him understanding a word. Nevertheless, he was able to memorise everything she said, syllable by syllable, telephone a bilingual colleague and repeat what he had heard. In this way, he discovered the whereabouts of the professor.

Hanna seemed to like this story. She had a laugh when she liked something, brief and quiet, which started in her chest and finished high.

'What is the first thing you remember?' M. asked her. He had hoped to catch her in a moment when she would answer without thinking. When finally he said it it sounded strange, as though in the wrong language.

She looked up at the ceiling, then at him. She smiled. He saw again that distance and serenity he had noticed before and recognised somehow as inimical to him, even if he could not understand why.

'I remember my mother dancing through trees,' she said.

The men got up from their chairs and came to the bar to order drinks. They were in surly humour, their hands flying upwards, all of them speaking at once. She watched them.

'In a forest?' M. asked.

'What?'

'Where your mother was dancing.'

She put a hand on his arm.

'Wait,' she said.

She poured drinks then for the owner and his wife, for the car dealer and a customer with whom he was trying to ingratiate himself and for a young mechanic M. hoped she would not linger before. She poured drinks for the men until they forgot the lost football match and began to tell jokes about the mayor. Their voices rose, and then fell. Finally they went.

She lit a candle in the corner of the bar and sat before M.

'They're getting used to you,' she told him.

'You think so?'

'Yes. I saw them say hello to you.'

'It's true.'

'Tell me something,' she said. 'And don't laugh.'

'I wouldn't,' he said.

'Good. Do you think the whole of a person's life can turn on a single moment?'

She looked at him. He could not tell if she was serious. He would have liked the answer to this question to be yes, but he did not say so. He did not say anything.

She told him then the story of her past.

3

Two Convicts and a Virgin

I turn on the light. The Virgin with her gold celestial halo looks like she will drift out from the frame and enshroud me in her blue robes. My sister Renata's little granddaughter Basia gave me that. I could not refuse to place it where she directed. The Virgin's eyes are wide and sleepy and a little delirious. The mouth has a slight twist in one corner. The salt of irony. Was the painter having a little joke? On the table next to the bed are two bottles of pills, one for dyspepsia and the other for circulation. A spoon serving no purpose. Three newspapers, a pile of books and a radio. I must put some order there. Across is a piece of furniture with drawers made by Czechs lacking measuring instruments. Above the bed a dark circle on the wall where my head rests when sleep is hopeless. I pad out into the living room in my slippers. They drag a little. The sounds of old age. There are times when I fill with contempt for myself. But they pass.

There's my teapot, my umbrella ready beside the door. On the wall a map of Europe and a photograph of the Polish national football team of 1974. I could not have brought M. here. I would not bring anyone unfamiliar with the claustrophobia of this life. It would be like opening my shirt to display a surgical wound.

I sit on the sofa and turn on the television. Across from me is a table with a drawer and if I had anything at all to remind me of Angelina – a letter, a photograph, a gold chain – it is here that I would keep it. But of that time nothing remains. Sometimes I can think I've nearly forgotten her. A long time seems to pass without my thinking of her at all. But then again later it will come rushing in, her voice, her touch, the way she put on shoes. Still I turn the whole story of what passed between us over in my mind. These barren exercises. I am like the old men who tomorrow will be sitting under the falling leaves in plac Pilsudskiego filling time with such questions as, What if Sikorski had suddenly appeared in Tehran? What if the English had acted, as promised, when the Germans stormed across our border? What if the Citadel sappers' bomb had detonated where Jerozolimskie Avenue meets Nowy Swiat just as Hitler's car passed over it as he made his entrance into Warsaw? I sit on this sofa lit by the light from the television screen and I think, What has she been doing all these years while I moved across the world running from the thought of her? Does she ever think of me? Sometimes I call out, Why did I not know you better? Where are you now? It startles me when I do it. A human voice in these rooms is rare.

I ask the questions, but I never think to answer them. I can see now that I have not asked them for the purposes of discovery. I have asked them because they confirm me in my private grief. Grief is an agony and then if it goes on long enough it is a consolation, for if we are in it we need look for nothing else. It is company, it is complete, it is certain. I have chased certainty as a child chases an escaping balloon. I chased it in dark churches as I stared at the crucifix looking for the communion with God that so transported the saints and made them willing to die in order to stay living in its light. I chased it in Berlin in debates and manifestos and righteous slogans. When Angelina went away I stopped all that because I had grief for my company and it was enough as I went about from place to place like dust being blown about in a wind. An unexamined life, all the while.

Am I in time to examine it now? Well, no one is asking anything else of me. No one is watching. I'm fit enough still, I suppose, to attempt the task.

I will imagine that after I left M. in the pre-dawn in Krakow his car would not start. I will imagine that when I walked out from Renata's the following evening to take a Zubrowka in the Stary Rynek I found him again at the corner table. I will imagine that he would have found it curious that an old Polish man sat before him for eleven hours, listening piously as his story fell like clotted blood from his mouth. I will imagine him asking the question, What was the source of your interest?

Then I would tell him all about Angelina. I would try to bring him to the sand at Miedzyzdroje, the light on the water, the feeling as she went into me, stitch by stitch. I would try to bring him to the room where it all happened. And just as he could not answer my polite question about the book by Werner Heisenberg he was reading in the Café Voltaire without telling me of the frail figure of his father or his dream in the lay-by or his search for a cure for his grief in the world of atoms, so I would answer him by taking him not only to the foot of the stairway in the lodging-house in Berlin where I first saw Angelina, but also along the road of Polish debris and bone and ash that led me to it. Maybe he would find some comfort there, were he to hear it. And if I follow him and his beautiful girl, if I mark each step, will I find a way out of this tiny world of memory and old age that has me turning as if on a spit over the past? What else have I to do?

I shop. I eat. I pray. And I ride the trains.

Since returning home from Krakow I have been restless and when I am restless I get on a train. I like to see the round, wide-eyed faces on the embankments swivelling as we pass, farmers at their labours, guards pushing barrows, that woman in sunglasses and a fur collar whose name or movements or secrets I will never know sitting motionless on the platform on a bench. The gentle drift of the coach, the click of the wheels on the track soothe me. Something is stirring. I can't settle. Faces rise up in my mind as though from graves and clamour. I feel Angelina moving through me like a poison.

I would not have gone to Berlin had I not first gone to Naklo, so it is to Naklo that I travel by train on this dank autumn morning.

In Naklo my grandfather tended the orchard of the family of Kazimierz Kuron, known to my grandfather as Jasny Pan, Illuminated Lord, and to the rest of us as Pan Kazimierz. That family had 740 hectares, a stableful of Arabian horses and a palace of forty-two bedrooms, but when my grandfather was about to be married this young nobleman arrived with his father and two brothers and a cartload of wheat and two small pigs as gifts and they set about building with their hands a house for my grandfather and his new wife. When my grandfather moved to take one end of a beam they were carrying they asked that he sit in the grass and enjoy the sun while they did their work. They gave him a bottle of beer and a hunter's sausage. They asked him to sing a song from Kotlina Biebrzanska. I knew Pan Kazimierz as an old man, and I can see him now just as though he is walking towards me across his wide lawn – tall and bony, a big grey moustache, hair sprouting on the top of his head like the leaves of a carrot and his one finger pointing to the sky while he explains something. He ran a school in the house and taught mathematics and the violin himself. He'd bring out an armful of violins from a room that had hundreds of them, it seemed, put on a black hat and teach wedding tunes to the children. I think he was without vanity or self-importance, though he especially liked to wear a long dramatic coat made of seal pelts. He wrote poems which he recited to the workers during harvest season. I don't remember how they were, but my friend Jerzy tells me now that the principal topics were religious tolerance and the psychology of the eagle.

It was here at Pan Kazimierz's that I met Jerzy. He was a pupil at the school. He had come from the east, from Lithuania, and I from near our western border. At that time wherever he walked he bounced a tennis ball out in front of him while dispensing his thoughts. He could rhyme without effort. I thought he was the most intelligent person known to me who was not an adult. When I first saw him he was throwing a discus on the lawn.

Later, Jerzy married a woman who could not speak. Something was happening to him in those years which he could not control. He had been the brightest student at the military academy in Moscow, but when he returned there to deliver a lecture he stood paralysed at the podium. They had to carry him away. No one knew the reason at the time, but I knew it was because his faith in the Party was breaking and he couldn't bear it. He had been and still is my guide through many of the turnings of my life, but when he was troubled and maybe needed me I was not there for him. I was in Berlin, thinking of myself.

Now that he is older he is more calm. You can see in his eyes that he has found peace in the licence granted to grandfathers. His mind sits easily and powerfully in him again. It's something fierce. You feel looking at him sometimes that it could ignite a pile of straw at the far end of the room. On Tuesdays a group of us meet for bridge. We take walks by the river.

It was because of Jerzy, and what he had seen, that I went to Berlin.

*   *   *

Always at Christmas and during the summer we travelled here to Naklo to be with my grandfather and grandmother. Then one August evening when I was ten my mother told me that I was to stay here and be a student in Pan Kazimierz's school and live with my grandparents. I didn't mind. I rode horses in the evening. I became a disciple of Jerzy. And each day my grandmother would sit me on a chair in the kitchen and clap her hands and cry and say that with my fine brow and noble fingers I was sure one day to be the saviour of our nation. If only she could live to see it.

At each Christmas in the house of my grandparents my grandfather's brother Zenon would recite the death scene of Prince Poniatowski as he battled against the Prussians and Russians at Leipzig. This could come at any time – when Aunt Zofia was tying a bow in the hair of her daughter, when a new baby was being examined, when the radio was delivering a message from the Cardinal in Warsaw. It always started with a low rumbling, like movement under the earth. Then it would build into a wild, high-pitched incantation. Huge tears would run from his dark eyes and down into his moustache as he recounted the heroic sufferings of Poniatowski and of our great nation, symbolised by the eagle, a nation so often erased from the map of the world but never forgotten by its people, the nation of Chopin, Copernicus, Mickiewicz and Curie-Sklodowska, that nation that against all the odds held our Holy Mother the Church closest to its bosom. 'Even Dostoevsky was part Polish!' he declared. 'And now we are a nation again, and no Prussian, no Austrian and no Russian will take it from us, for we are the friends of France and England, we are the heart of Europe, and defending us we have our own valiant warriors, the most valiant of all the world!'

We never failed to be stirred by Grand-Uncle Zenon's words.

We sang and we danced. And we lifted our glasses to him when he finished.

Then one Christmas when I was ten years old the door opened as it did every year to reveal Pan Kazimierz standing there with his violin and the gifts which he had brought to our family. Snow was circling in a little gust around his head and beside him was a man with a high silk hat and walking stick in his hand we had never seen before. We learned later that he was a French architect on his way to Moscow whom Pan Kazimierz had met in Paris, but just then he could not be introduced because Grand-Uncle Zenon was in the midst of his recitation. Tears flowed as ever and the Frenchman listened with his long fingers folded over the top of his walking stick. It was only after Grand-Uncle Zenon had spoken of the great luminaries of our country and we had all shaken the walls with our cries and our cheers for the motherland that we learned the identity of our guest. Not only not Polish, but from France! The room went silent. Heads turned away to look at the walls. Mother's hands moved over her lap as though she was knitting. Even at ten the shame hit me with a force I have not forgotten. I could see from the look on their faces that everyone in the room, even Grand-Uncle Zenon – even the Frenchman – could feel it. We were like schoolchildren caught boasting of adventures we had not experienced. We did not sing or dance that Christmas Eve night. And in all my years of wandering that followed, if just a single Pole at a gathering began to extol the glories of our nation, this painful sensation of shame that had been born in my grandparents' house would gather in me like a wave of nausea and I would have to leave the room.

The year of the Frenchman's visit was 1938.

At the border, the meanings of words change. Did M. feel that, I wonder? He and I can both understand 'teacup' and 'river'.

Such words do not change. But how are words like law or destiny or freedom carried over a border from one world to another? We have a history that has schooled us in defeat. We wait for deliverance and when it does not arrive we return to our homes. We do not ask questions. We do not complain. We refine our stoicism. I never looked for Angelina after she went away. I just tried to move faster than the picture of her that haunted me.

What has made us this way? You need only look at us on a map. We're like a virgin with a bouquet just off a bus from a village, standing between two convicts.

One bright August morning we stood together on the church steps in the sunshine – twenty-two boys in shorts and pressed shirts and with neatly combed hair, little satchels in our hands. A boy named Andrzej Przesmycki demonstrated tricks with a yo-yo sent him by an uncle in Atlantic City, New Jersey. The priests were taking the altar boys for a swimming outing in the lakes. The bus was waiting, the engine running. Father Boleslaw who was in charge of us was standing at the door talking to the driver. Father Boleslaw had a red face and round ears which stuck out from the sides of his head like poker chips. I guessed from his face that he was telling the driver a joke. Halina Makiela walked by with her mother on the pavement across from the church. I could barely see her. The sun was so bright that it took all the definition from people's faces. But I know that she smiled at me, with a particular sweetness. That embarrassed me a little, but also pleased me.

Just then the woman we all knew as Pani Ewa rushed from a side door of the church and spoke urgently to Father Boleslaw. When she stopped the two of them stood in silence, she looking into his face and him seeming to look at nothing at all. Then he placed his hands over his two eyes and leaned back against the bus. We all ran over to see what had happened. 'It's the Germans and the Russians,' said Pani Ewa. 'They've made an agreement not to fight one another.' After a long while Father Boleslaw dropped his hands. His skin was grey. He suddenly looked as though he had been suffering from a long illness. 'We're doomed,' he said then. I understood, soon enough, that we were once again to be the playthings of the monstrosities to either side of us. Maybe once again there would be no Poland. But for us then gathered around Father Boleslaw and Pani Ewa there was just that single unforeseeable word that settled over us like dust raised by passing horses – 'Doomed'.

Our skies filled with our enemy's planes and our roads with their vehicles. I could not understand how there could be so many of them or how they possessed so much machinery for war. I was alone, for Jerzy had not returned from Lithuania to our school. Then my mother and Renata came to Naklo to get me.

We moved out into the roads. There were little cars, wagons pulled by dogs, people dragging bundles. I saw an old woman in black who must have weighed more than the three of us put together being carried by boys my age, one at each corner of a chair. Trucks went by with people spilling off them, others trying to leap on. At night there were small fires and the sounds of praying and of sickness. No one knew where to go. Everyone seemed to be moving in different directions, following a different rumour. We were like a colony of ants that had lost the entrance to their home. It was only the Germans who seemed to know where to go and what to do.

We came to a town. We had been walking for twenty-two days but I don't think we were so far from Naklo. In my memory the fires are everywhere. They come up from the sewers, they surge from the windows of broken buildings, they rise like fountains from holes in the ground. Some are a deep red, with black smoke going up into the clouds. But mostly they are pale yellow. And very fast. They move like a beast in a mad, cold rage.

I am running with my mother and Renata through the streets. I don't think there were so many fires as I picture. But our fear is great and that is how the memory forms. The Germans are sending the fire down from their planes and the big guns they have set up on the bank of the river. Men tell us that this is the third time since the invasion that this town has been pounded by these weapons. People are running with bags strapped on their backs and photographs in their hands. The fires are making a roar like a terrible wind in a tunnel.

At every corner we do not know where to go. If we make a wrong choice a bomb will drop on us. With a wild look in her eyes my mother asks me to choose the street. For luck, she says. I never saw her like this before. We turn left at a bakery. A woman carrying only a handbag is standing still looking through the window at the empty shelves as though she is wondering what to buy. We run on. Up ahead of us two old men have had the idea of making a barricade. They are trying to push a mattress into place. What they are protecting only they can know. We have to slow down because of all the furniture they have piled in the road. To our left is a big hole where a building was. There are small fires among the bricks.

I see two dogs howling there. This street is quieter and I can hear them clearly. They are moving around among the bricks and the broken pipes. They make little charges forward and then run back. Someone is throwing stones at them but they won't go away. When they step forward another stone passes them. We begin to make our way around the barricade and I look back. I see Pan Kazimierz. He is standing against a wall with a piece of grey meat in his hand. His boots and his coat made of seal pelts are smeared with mud. It is some days since he shaved. He is trying to eat the meat and whenever the dogs try to advance on him he takes a stone from his pocket and throws it at them. He sees us and he turns. Mother and Renata do not notice him and continue on their way but I stand still and look at him. Our eyes meet. I remember so well his look in this moment. His wild ravaged expression fades away and his eyes narrow. He passes a hand over his head to smooth his hair and draws his lips into a tight, bitter smile, as if to say, What do you think of this, my boy? Do you remember how they danced when I played the violin? Would you like to hear a poem now about the psychology of the eagle?

Somewhere to the east of where I had found Pan Kazimierz and a little to the south we found a cellar with a Jewish clarinet player and his son hiding in it and we lived there with them nearly until Christmas. The man drew a piano keyboard in the dirt with a stick and taught us the scales and chords so that sometimes we made concerts by pressing our fingers on the keys and making the sounds of the music with our mouths.

One night I was climbing a stone wall. I had some trouble when my foot got snared in a vine but finally I got it loose. I was after eggs, I think. My mother had given me a silver-handled hairbrush to trade for them. Just before leaving the cellar I watched as Renata held our lamp in one hand while painting my mother's eyes with the other and I felt so much the man of the family with my father back at home operating the trams that I told them not to waste fuel on vanities such as that. 'You'll not be going to the opera tonight,' I told her. It was one of those things which it might have occurred to me to say but which normally I suppressed, only this time it slipped out whole. Renata aimed a kick at me and called me a hyena and I saw my mother turn away, ashamed of herself in front of the clarinet player.

Renata I did not see again until I arrived in Chicago in 1957. My mother I never saw again at all.

At last I got to the top of the wall. Above me was the domed sky, blue-black, a silver crescent moon among the starlight. I sat there and forgot about everything and watched it for a time with a feeling of being made of the air itself, as though if I let go of the wall I could drift up through the dark blue space into the white light of the stars. Never before, it seemed, had I seen so many.

After a while I thought of the eggs. I leapt from the wall and landed in the dust just at the feet of a German soldier patrolling for transgressors of the curfew they had imposed on us. I got a tap on the ear from the butt of his rifle. I stood and looked at him. The white light from the sky gleamed on his helmet, his face shadowed. I felt a little streak of blood run down my neck.

I cannot remember the next part so well. I was driven like a goat by the soldier along roads, down stairs into the cellar of a building, out on to more roads and down more steps and finally out again to a railway line where I was put into a wagon with sixty-eight men and boys. We didn't say much to one another. The train lurched, it ran for a while and then stopped. For hours we listened to the sounds of heavy pieces of metal crashing into one another. Then we moved again. We didn't know our fate. We had no means of asking. Sometimes we got soup. Almost everything was in darkness.

Then the way the memory forms for me now I awake from one kind of dream into another on a bright, cloudless summer day in a field of golden wheat. The land rolls away into hills. A river sparkles in the sunlight. There's a red house at the end of the lane where I have been put working for an old German couple. They have laid out straw and a blanket for me in a barn. They give me my meals in the kitchen. They turn on the radio at night and every Friday they dance around the carpet with one another for an hour. They smile at me all the time and say almost nothing. They treat me as if I am their cat.

I pass years this way, watching the wheatfields change colour. Later, I lived these years again in the memory of Jerzy.

In the darkness, in the train to Germany, we did not know one another. The only light came through small gaps between the boards of the door. Whether the light came from the moon or the sun, you could not always tell. You could see shapes inside the wagon, like small hills and trees, but no features of a face. Many stayed silent. Some spoke privately, like two cousins at a wedding. Then once when everyone was quiet and it was completely black outside the door of the wagon a man lying on his back on a high shelf announced himself as Roman from Bobrowniki, and began to tell a long story about an accordion player and an abandoned wife. I remember it all, but I won't say it just now. He let out a long sigh at the end and then fell into silence. I think maybe he was asleep.

Then after another while, maybe it was a day or even more later, he started without any introduction into another story. This one was about a carpenter who lost his teeth in a fight with his sister's husband and who then with all the care of his craft made a new set for himself out of a beautiful piece of pale blond wood. He lived with a small grey dog he called the Admiral and was always out in the lanes greeting people when he finished his work. Nobody in the village ever smiled so much as this carpenter with the new teeth. Even when someone was telling him something grave he leaned forward with his lips opened in a wide smile like a horse's.

It happened then that he was missing for some days. People didn't pay attention at first, but then they went to his door. They rapped and then shouted, but there was no answer. They looked through the window and saw nothing. Finally then his nephew was lowered down the chimney on a length of rope and was able to open the door from the inside. The crowd came in and searched through the house. They found the carpenter in a bed in the attic with the covers pulled up to his chin and his lips drawn tight over his mouth as if they had been sewn together. He looked nearly dead with the hunger. 'What happened to you?' they asked. 'Why didn't you answer?' He lay there under his blanket looking from one to the other, his jaws clamped shut. His sister pushed forward and knelt beside the bed, imploring him on the grave of his mother to tell them what was wrong with him. Slowly he opened his mouth, turning his head from side to side so they could all look into it. Everyone could see that the teeth were not there.

'Is it your teeth?' they asked. 'Do you want us to bring them to you?'

'It's no use,' he said in a weak voice.

He told them then that it had all happened because of the Admiral, that treacherous dog who had repaid him for rescuing him from starvation and nursing him and protecting him by reaching up to the table beside the bed while he was asleep and snatching away with his snout the wooden teeth it had taken him so many months to make. He'd looked everywhere for them, he said, but they were nowhere to be found.

'I'll never get another piece of wood like it,' the carpenter said. 'And what's worst of all is the self-satisfied expression on the Admiral's face!'

They were all crowded around his bed.

'But why didn't you come out?' they asked him.

He stared at them with watery eyes, his mouth a dark hole.

'The shame,' he said at last.

When this Roman from Bobrowniki began to speak, I thought, Please be quiet. Then because the rest of the wagon was silent and there was nothing else to do, I began to listen – but with low expectations. His voice got me. I felt as if I was gliding down a river on a raft. By the time he finished the story about the carpenter, I couldn't get enough of him. I thought, I could listen to you for a month.

When the train stopped in Germany and the door of the wagon was opened, I saw him for the first time. He surprised me. His voice was so smooth I thought he was a boy like myself, but when the light fell on him I could see that he must have been fifty or more. He made saddles, he told us. On one saddle which he made for the man who owned the village and the land around it, he spent two years. I imagined him sewing and polishing and working the silver with no thought at all of the time it was taking him. I envied him his stories. I pictured him telling them in Bobrowniki the way he made his saddles – the basic ingredients already known to everybody yet with him somehow able to make them his own, he with all the time in the world for the telling, and the people around him with all the patience to listen. There are stories told by wanderers who return and tell what they have seen and others by those who stay at home and gather what is already known. And then there is another different kind of story in which the teller can see through the pattern of others' movements and thoughts himself looking back at him the way a face appears in the veins of a stone or in a bank of cloud. I haven't stories like the first two kinds because I don't come from a single place in the world. The stories I know are of the last type. These are found, and told, alone, as I am doing now, in this room, imagining M. listening to me.

4

Mathilde and Ritso

Hanna's mother danced through trees because of something she saw in a single moment when she was seven years old. Her name was Mathilde and she lived on a farm outside the city of Rouen in France. On the day that her life changed direction her mother had taken her into the city to buy shoes. Just as she was coming out of the shop a man was nailing a poster into a tree advertising the arrival of a ballet from Paris. On it was a picture of a ballerina sailing through the air, arms, legs and neck fully extended, her face set and in profile. Already the trucks were unloading the scenery into the theatre. The dancers were in the cafés smoking cigarettes, long scarves around their necks. People stood on the pavements looking in at them.

Mathilde begged her mother to take her to the ballet. This was something that never would have occurred to her mother, but she agreed nevertheless.

Mathilde went on the first night, and then again on the two nights after. Her father went once and judged it ridiculous, her mother struggled in vain to find some meaning in it, her elder sister swung her foot against the tempo of the music and drew glasses and beards on the pictures in the programme, but Mathilde watched with her eyes wide and barely drawing breath as though it was her own life being presented on the stage. The leaps and shapes and all the little flicks of the feet, they seemed to tell her the story of who she was. She was a child. She hadn't any control over her life. But she knew that she wanted to perform the same movements, wear the same shoes and tie her hair up in the same way as she saw on the stage in Rouen. It was something simple and complete. It was her first truth.

Her mother found a Hungarian woman who offered ballet classes in an old foundry. From the first time she went, she was the way some people are with horses. They want to stay with them all the time. Even the smell of the stable is sweet to them. They would put their favourite horse into bed with them if they could. With Mathilde it was the satin shoes, the feeling of the wooden barre under her hand, that lofty, frozen look on the dancers' faces. But there was also something about it that frightened her. It was the wonder of the thing itself, and the fear that she would lose it. The more intense her feeling of excitement became, the greater was the fear that rose up with it. She did all her lessons at school. She did everything her parents asked of her. She never did anything she thought might upset people. She did not want to give anyone the chance of preventing her going to the foundry.

When Mathilde was eleven, something happened to her mother. She stopped getting dressed in the mornings. She spoke in a way that no one in the family could understand. She sat weeping under a tree holding a blanket in front of her face. She set fire to her husband's tractor. No one knew why. Finally she was taken from their farm to a hospital in another city and all the children were sent out to relatives. Mathilde and a younger sister went to an uncle who had a pig farm in Alsace-Lorraine. Her father thought it would be a healthy life for them. There was no ballet school there.

Mathilde tended the pigs. The Hungarian woman sent her letters from Rouen with dance exercises in them. She made lace and sold it. Finally when she was sixteen she took the money she had saved and went to Paris, where she found work in a millinery shop. She went to ballet school. She prepared herself to audition.

One day after finishing work she left the millinery shop and as she walked along the boulevard it began to rain. She ran from shopfront to kiosk to tree, the rainwater falling over her face and clothes. She laughed as she made the long leaps of the dancer from tree to tree.

She stopped suddenly when she noticed that the rain was no longer falling on her. She sensed someone standing behind her. She turned and saw a man. He was holding an umbrella over her head and smiling. Drops of water were falling from her face and his. He was standing well within the distance that normally separated her from people who spoke with her. She was out of breath, the laughter leaving her slowly. Her cotton dress clung to her body. The man had hand-made shoes and manicured nails. Everything was shining on him – his cufflinks, his skin, his teeth, his eyes. His hair was white as a dove and parted at one side as though with a ruler. He was wearing an English suit made of cashmere.

'A beautiful woman should be protected from the rain,' he said. He gave her the umbrella, bowed briefly, stepped into the back of a long black car and was driven away.

She stood in the rain and watched the car until it disappeared. No one had ever called her beautiful before. She couldn't even remember anyone ever speaking of her as a woman.

Two days later the man walked into the millinery shop. He stood in the centre of the room. Everyone stopped what they were doing. Again the smile with the gleaming teeth. Years later, Mathilde told her daughter Hanna, 'He looked like he owned the world and would give it all away in a tip to a waiter.' The long black car with the driver was waiting, the back door open.

There wasn't a sound. Then he asked her to dinner in front of everyone. She was just eighteen then. She tried to say no, but she couldn't.

He had a high rank in the Navy at the British embassy. He knew politicians. He went to casinos. He knew how to judge the value of horses. Mathilde hadn't the strength to resist him. Even the ballet went out of her life – if not out of her mind. What was it that drew her to him? 'He smoked these strong cigarettes,' she said later. It was as though she couldn't understand the force of this herself. 'It was the way he lit them.'

His job changed. He was to return to London. Mathilde already knew that he was married with four children in a big house in the country, but she went anyway. He got her a flat near his ministry. They lived there together during the week. He took her to Jamaica, Santiago, Hong Kong. Then when Mathilde was twenty Hanna was born.

By then his other children were grown. He divorced his wife and married Mathilde. He retired from the Navy and they moved to a house with a mill on the Isle of Wight. He had cancer of the stomach. When Hanna was five, he died.

'I can't remember him very well,' she told M. as they sat across from each other in the darkness of the bar. 'My idea of how he looked is from photographs. I remember his smell, which I got even through his cologne. And the rough feeling of his face against mine at the end of the day. I remember a moment in the sunshine when I was running towards him and he was waiting with his arms open. "Here she comes, a mile a minute," he said. I remember the blur of my feet on the pavement as I ran.

'I don't remember anything of his death or the funeral, but I remember that some time after that my mother was sitting in a bank vault and I was with her. She didn't even like him very much in the last few years and they slept in different rooms, but his death made her suffer. Maybe she was remembering, or maybe she was thinking of herself. But she was crying. It was the first time I ever saw an adult do this. It frightened me. I thought she was losing her mind. She was in the bank vault trying to get his papers in order. I thought then it would be up to me to do that. I thought I'd have to cook the dinner and look after her. I thought I'd have to drive us home from the bank in our car. I wondered if my feet would reach the pedals. I tried to remember how she drove it.

'She spoke well of him when I was growing up. She wanted me to have a good feeling about him. Later it was different. Maybe she counted all the dances she missed. She could be sitting at a table reading a magazine in silence and then suddenly take her glasses off and begin her analysis. "He was just like a glamorous, spoiled boy," she said, "everybody always gathered around him, looking at him, wanting him to think well of them, laughing with him, him laughing louder and longer than the others with even less heart." She said he could act shy in the face of compliments, and according to her he believed that this shyness too made him superior. "This is one of their typical affectations," she said. I suppose she meant English people of a high class. Anyway, once she started an attack she couldn't stop herself. "Above everything," she said to me, "he was cruel. Cruel words came easily to him. He impressed himself with them. Afterwards he would feel bad about it. He was drawn to cruelty because the guilt that followed it seemed to him magnificent. It was certainly more important than the hurt he caused. He thought he should be comforted in his distress over the things he had done. It all gave him a feeling of grandness. He had been around people with power for so long that he was incapable of believing anything or anyone could be authentic, except himself."

'That's how she would go on. It was as if she had been thinking

49

of these things through all the years since he died. And she had to tell me about it.

'I didn't believe her. This was my father. She could forget that. She could think instead that I was her friend. I would try to picture how he would be if he was still with me. I'd think of him and me walking along a road, his arm through mine. Maybe he'd have a stick. I'd tie his tie for him. I'd comb his hair. I'd think of us in a big room full of people, each of us going from person to person. We'd be having a good time. We'd be laughing. But we'd never forget about each other. I'd always know where in the room he was. I'd have to know if he was all right.

'It's not that I think of him so often. But that's how I do it.'

Hanna got down off her stool and lit a cigarette by the till. She walked out from behind the bar and over to the door. She looked up at the windows of the buildings across the street. She seemed to be thinking. Then she came back. M. looked at her closely. He felt shame at making her speak of these things.

But when she came back she went on with her story.

Mathilde, she said, stayed on in the house with the mill on the Isle of Wight. She had a pension from the Navy and some cash. She had Hanna. But she had nothing to do. She was twenty-six years old.

In summer she went for walks very early along the beach. One day she met a young man from Finland. At home in his country he was studying the construction of ships, but that summer he was cooking breakfasts in a hotel. He was just then on his way to work. They met later that day, then every afternoon in the house while Hanna was at school, then at night in the dance halls along the esplanade. Finally he came to live with them. When the time came for him to return to Finland, Mathilde sold the house and followed him there.

They lived in his small flat in the city of Turku. They married in the spring. Each day Mathilde took Hanna to school in the morning and then passed the day waiting for him to come home. He had become a kind of god to her. Sometimes they drank brandy. Sometimes they took Benzedrine. Sometimes he was not there.

One day she went to the bank. She had an account there where she kept all the money she'd got for the house with the mill. When she tried to take some of it out she found that nearly all of it was gone.

'How can this be?' she asked the man in the bank. 'I have not used this money.'

'You must ask your husband,' he told her.

She went around the town looking for him. She went to the university where he was studying, up and down the streets, into shops and bars. She found the man who sold them Benzedrine.

'Where did my money go?' she asked him.

'He has a mania for bingo,' said the man. 'Didn't you know?'

He got away before she could find him. Maybe someone at the bank warned him, or maybe the drug dealer. She heard he went to Denmark and was living with a woman who sang on boats.

She went into a kind of trance then. It seemed to go on for years. She moved like a ghost from room to room. She sat in a chair in front of the window while the light changed on her face. She did not seem to be seeing anything.

Then one day she was different. She went to the owner of a building that had some empty rooms. She rented the first floor. She put a sign out – BALLET LESSONS, FRENCH-TRAINED TEACHER. That became her life then. She started to teach young girls to dance. She does it still. Somehow she never forgot.

'It's a strange story, no?' said Hanna. Her eyes met M.'s and there seemed to be a flash of light in the dark bar. He thought he sensed in it an invitation. Then it closed. But he could not be sure.

She laughed, and pushed away from the bar.

'And you have no way of knowing whether any of it is true, do you?' she said.

Did M. tell me those last words? Did I add them myself?

Sometimes I think, and nothing appears before me. I go to the window and look out. I return to my chair. I get up and walk in straight lines up and down the length of the room. I get into bed and put a pillow over my head. Sometimes I let out a call like a crow. I will myself to see pictures. But nothing arrives.

At four o'clock in the afternoon M. drove along the main street of the little town where Hanna worked and lived. The shutters of the shops were closed. A dog lay at the entrance to a bar, one eye open. The cars in the showroom of the man M. found so monstrous in his pursuit of her seemed as strange and still to him as stones beneath the sea. Flies circled in the dusty air.

M. was very nervous. Two days before she had accepted his invitation to go with him up into the mountains and walk with him by the river. Would she be there?

The road bent a little as it neared her house and he saw her. She was standing in the sun. She wore blue jeans and what seemed a man's striped shirt buttoned to the neck. Everything starched and pressed, the two rounded sweeps of hair around her face like hands holding a globe. And lipstick. A deep red. She was squinting in the sun and looking in the wrong direction as she waited. He thought this made her look innocent.

When he stopped she took a skip towards the car and got in with a movement so fluid it seemed oiled. She was smiling, easy. She dropped a shoe on to the floor and hooked her foot under her knee on the seat. She leaned back against the door, facing him, and said, 'So, here we are,' which also seemed to ask, And what will you do about it?

He drove with her out past the warehouses and along the dry road towards the mountains. The air trembled over the hot earth, but it cleared and brightened as they rose. She put tapes into the machine, played one or two songs and then changed them.

They climbed higher, the turns growing tighter, the pines more dense. A single saxophone played on a tape. Light flared over the windscreen and M. put on his sunglasses. She was leaning back, her knees up on the dashboard, her bare foot turning to the slow movement of the music. As the sun lowered a little more the colours of the land seemed to him too rich for the shapes that were holding them. She could be mine, he thought, the way we are here and now – except that she isn't.

'What happened to your mother?' he asked her.

'When?' Her head fell towards him on the seat.

'After she started the ballet school.'

'She kept going. More girls started to come, and boys. She put on productions. She always has one at Christmas. One year a very big man in a red shirt came in and asked her for a part in her Christmas show. His name was Ritso, he said. He couldn't dance, but he knew something about acting. He had a big red face and he laughed all the time. She gave him a part. A little while later she began to live with him. She seems peaceful. I think he must be the kindest of the men in her life. He makes her laugh, he pays attention to her. At the beginning of every month he brings her a book in French.'

'Do you like him?'

She didn't answer right away. Her head rolled back on the seat and she looked out towards the mountains.

'He's always there. There's always the same ceremony when I come back – flowers, vodka and a cake with a strawberry on top.

53

He never changes. He doesn't ask questions. There aren't so many people like that.'

They drove through a village hung with banners for a festival, then out again into open land, the air cooling.

She bobbed her head lightly to the music on the tape. She tapped out its rhythm on her leg.

'He's very big,' she said. 'And round. Almost no hair on his head and a round red face. He has a kind of black beard, not very regular. He wears clothes that aren't connected – like striped trousers from a formal suit and then sandals with socks and a sweater with lots of colours like a child would wear. It's surprising how he looks because when he was younger he was beautiful. I've seen photographs. He looked proud, with big strong eyes and long black hair curling just over his shoulders and split in the middle. The lines in his suits were like knives. But something happened to him. He had an accident. He fell off a roof he'd climbed on to for a bet. He injured his legs. He didn't care so much about how he looked after that.'

A herd of goats ran up a slope, all their bells ringing together like chimes blown by a wind.

'Did you hear that?' M. asked her.

'What?'

'The goats.'

'Oh, yes,' she said. She looked over in their direction. She seemed preoccupied, as though she were working through an equation.

'Ritso was only a child when his father died,' she said after a while. 'Sometimes he reminds me of this, and then he says, "You see, we're alike, you and I." But Ritso had an uncle who was a diplomat and hadn't any children of his own. So he looked after Ritso and his brother. He sent them abroad to study. The last place they were in was Rome. His brother grew very religious there and eventually became a priest. But Ritso spent all the extra time he had going to the theatre. He got degrees – I think in mathematics and something about government. He also studied medicine for a while. But every chance he had to see a play, he took it. He wrote reports about each of them in notebooks. And he had theories about how plays should be presented. He said you could make discoveries if you looked at a play from different angles than just the one that people in the audience could see.

'When he came home to Finland he told his mother that he wanted to be a director of plays. But she wouldn't allow it. She said that would be ingratitude after all the help he got from his uncle. She said he was to go to him and ask him for advice and whatever his uncle said he was to do it. That would be the only way to show his appreciation. So he did that. His uncle never even knew about his interest in the theatre. He found a job for him in the government. It was in the department that dealt with currency.

'But he didn't forget. He came home in the evenings and made little models of stages with pieces of wood. For actors he put figures from a chess set. He used his notebooks from Rome. He tested his theories. He was like my mother with the ballet. He still does that. He pours himself glasses of wine with ice and moves chess pieces around his stage.'

M. stopped the car where the river cut between two high rock-faces before gathering in a pool where children were swimming. He walked with her upstream, the trees becoming more dense, small fragments of light running down her like rainwater on glass. She looked different by daylight. She seemed less a riddle, her skin pale and translucent.

At a bend in the river there was a gathering of large flat rocks in the shade of the trees. M. asked her if she would like to sit. It was cooler in the mountains. There was an edge in the air as the sun moved down towards the peaks that rose above them. She sat close to him, her arms folded over her knees. She seemed to be waiting.

M. knew that between a man and a woman there is a moment before which everything is possible and after which everything is lost. Was this such a moment? He knew too that there were those who would not fail to act. He felt fear pass through him as he sat on the rock. I know this fear – the fear of losing for ever what we do not yet and may never have.

He tried to find her in the way he spoke to her – the beauty of her lines, what hurt her, what moved within her. He wanted her to discover that he could know her, that he could walk with her through the world. He spoke of the fall of land there in the mountains, the light on the water, and that other beauty of the north where she came from of snow and night and stars. He moved through his memory for stories that would make a bridge between him and her. He spoke of those who had known loss as children, the emptiness they must carry, and he spoke of those forced to wander, who must leave their languages and landscapes and their beds behind them. His face was set in the evening light. His hands were moving in the air. His words were measured —

I am going to stop just now. I am going to listen to a music programme on the radio. It's old songs mostly, from when I was a boy. Very silly, I admit, but they give me comfort. It's just the sight of M. in this moment. I think even he would understand it, were he to know that I am doing this and could see the picture that I have made before me. If someone is concentrating very hard on a small, intricate task, or angry that a bus driver has ignored them or is trying to have a conversation with their dog, this can be funny, this can be pleasurable. But this most un-appealing spectacle of a man embarked on seduction – this just makes me miserable. How vainglorious they look, and how insincere. And how often I have been that way myself!

I take a small glass of beer, I listen to the songs. And then I return.

There was silence then – the only sound from the water moving over rocks, the stirring of leaves. Hanna was very still, her hands folded in front of her. M. wondered if her mind was in another place, if he had bored her.

'Sometimes I think about a room,' she said then. 'I don't know where it is. I don't know very well what's inside it. I know I've never been there. I've never had the feeling I know I could get if I was inside it. But still it seems very familiar to me. All around would be a forest. The room would be simple and clean. The walls and the floor would be made of wood. I can almost feel the peace I could get there. I don't know how to get it. I never truly felt it. Maybe I'll have to go a long way before I find this room. Maybe I won't be young any more. I don't know the way there or what the door looks like. But if I get there and I open it I'll know that's my room.'

She did not look at M. Perhaps she was embarrassed. Her eyes seemed to him still on the water, although he couldn't see them because of the fall of her hair. The water rushed past. It was like mercury where the sun hit it. Where it was clear he could see the stones as though under a microscope, their veinwork, the streaks of pink and green. Her breathing was faster, like a startled child's. He heard the ticking of the watch on her wrist. And then suddenly the words which would come to drive him alone along the roadways of Europe – 'Maybe you will be there,' she said. He took a breath, his heart pounding.

Two nuns drove by on bicycles, a large black bird called out from the sky and the sun dropped down behind the mountain. What remained of the day came flooding in. She looked at M.

She stood. She smiled a little, maybe with a trace of pity. He watched the picture of the room in the forest drain from her face.

What can an old man do? I think of the friends of my grand-father who lay on the floor of our kitchen and told each other stories on winter nights. They told them because the nights were long and they were skilled at the telling. Then there is a different kind of story that will grow like a tumour in the teller unless he releases it. I like to listen to stories, though it is not so easy to find those who will tell them. They stop the time. They take me out of myself. And I like to tell them, though it is not easy to find those who will listen. What is the reason for telling them? Because they are there to be told. Who are they for? For the stories themselves. I must take out the words, one by one.

I am in a café in this small Polish city unimportant to anyone except those of us living in it, my hands around a cup of coffee made from waxed paper. I am sitting in a green plastic chair. People are alone at tables eating thin grey hamburgers, and teenaged workers run around in striped uniforms, their names printed on badges. The lights are insufferably bright. I look out the window through the swirling snow at the shoemaker in the shop opposite hammering a nail into a heel, the bells ringing in the tower of a church and a girl with the voice of a child singing a song in English on the radio. I go along with M.'s story now like an elderly widower walking his dog. I feel well and warm and, strange to say, somehow guarded by its company. I feel different when I wake. I used to hear the dripping faucet. I could be irritated at something, usually a transgression. There might be just a trace of nausea and nearly always vacancy. What way to fill the day? Now I wake sharp, clear. I have the wish for food.

And there is the sense that I am carrying something, of the need to mind it well until I have the means of delivering it.

In my mind I go to places I've never been, pass time with people I would never meet. I don't say this is such a poor life here. It suffices, surely. But it is made richer by this. Pictures arrive unbidden. Just now this little café breaks up and I see the dance hall in Barcelona where M. told me that he took Hanna on the night that everything between them changed. Such elegance! – the soft warm candlelight, the waiters with their brilliantined hair and white jackets, the twenty-four-piece jazz band, a tall, slender woman in a long leather coat and with red lipstick lighting a cigarette as she waits for a table. How fine I could be there, I think, and how far I am from it now. I like the shine on the waiters' shoes, the smell of their cologne, the stories unfolding at each of the tables, the time stretching out like a tableful of food, ample and easy, the look of the drummer as he laughs to himself and shakes his head at some joke in the notes of the music, the rich, dark glow of the paintings in the candle-light, the look of eagerness on the face of a silver-haired man as he hands his coat in through the door of a cubicle, the single, merged voice of everyone rolling and gently breaking like waves against a shoreline.

M. had feared he wouldn't be given another chance after the day in the mountains by the side of the river. But then she asked him if he would drive her to Barcelona. She had to deliver a docu-ment to a government department, she said. He waited for her in a high vaulted entranceway with angels carved into the ceiling and guards still as hay bales at the door. Finally she appeared. 'Would you like coffee?' he had asked her. 'Yes,' she said. She assented too to dinner and then a slow walk through the dark streets. They came then to a glass door and he led her in.

* * *

M. sat with Hanna in a red velvet booth, the seat hooking in the shape of a scythe around the table. They had a bottle of wine. The walls were green and gold. It was dark, just the yellow and orange of the candles on the tables lighting the undersides of jaws and brows. A mirror ran the entire length of the bar, two gold columns to either side of it twisting like ship's cable up to the ceiling. The glass was imperfect, mottled black here and there.

M. sat close to her, looking just at her. He looked at the pattern of veins on the back of her hand and up her arm, the trace of pulse just visible on her neck, the way the lids dropped slowly over her green eyes, her fingers moving up the stem of her wine glass, the slow circling of her ankle acknowledging the music. He felt the aura of her beauty running over his skin. He leaned forward and poured wine into her glass, then into his.

In the first hour she looked twice at her watch, but another two had passed since and he ordered another bottle of wine without her objecting. Sometimes their shoulders touched and she did not move away. She was laughing more now, but very low and soft. When she spoke it was nearly in a whisper so that M. had to lean forward to hear her. Had anyone else there a sense of the power of these moments in his life? They did not, of course. They were in their own bitterness or gaiety. The booths were full and people were standing, smiling, talking. Dancers skipped from the floor, their faces reddened from the dance just ended. But the silver-haired man was collecting his coat and the woman with the red lipstick put out her last cigarette and drew on her gloves. How much time did he have? The music began again, slow and wondrous. She was looking down as she turned a matchbook around in her fingers. M. clenched his jaw and leaned forward and spoke to her. She leaned back and looked at him. She seemed amused by this little process of assessment of him and expected him to feel the same. He got to his feet. She looked at the hand he held out to her. What was she thinking? Maybe just the simple words, Why not? She took M.'s hand and followed him to the dancefloor. She moved towards him and settled as light as a mist against his chest. They began to dance. They danced more slowly than anyone else. She was in his arms for the first time and was going without demur wherever he led her. He looked down at the curve of her ear, the light moving through her hair. He felt her breathing, each foot taking her weight as she moved from foot to foot in the dance. Time, the waiters and barmen, the people in the booths and the world beyond left him. There was only him and her and the music. Currents moved like sheet lightning over his skin. He drew her closer, his leg moving against the inside of hers. She did not step away. She seemed suddenly lighter and a cloud of warm air rose from her neck. He drew back and her eyes rose to meet his. They held them. Where are we going now? he thought until the idea smeared and moved away. He saw her eyes close, her face lift to his, the lips moist, her mouth opening, and he moved down to meet it, the light going out as he lost himself within her. Of this place, he believed, there could be no end.

One hour later the band were packing away their instruments and the waiters were sweeping under the tables. M. and Hanna were still moving around the dancefloor, faces flushed, out of breath. A man in a tailcoat tapped M. on the shoulder and said he must lock the door.

He stepped with her out on to the pavement still wet from the roadsweepers and into his car. 'Come with me,' he said to her. She looked long into his eyes, and then away. 'I can't,' she said. He drove out then to the town where she lived, her head against his shoulder, her arm around his neck. He walked with her to the red door. 'This is everything to me now,' he told her. 'Yes,' she said. She touched his face and went in. He sat in his car and watched a light in an upstairs room turn on, then off.

M. sat in his home, all the windows open. He watched the light come in, a sea-blue early morning light. He could see everything, every particle.

Could it be that now she was his? He could not know. But he felt a rising power and glory such as he had never felt before, yet which he seemed to know intimately. Ahead of him, his life was opening. He would ready himself for it. He would not move too fast. He would say nothing that was false. He would take everything she offered him. He would love her with all that he had, all that he had known. It was to be a feast that would have no end.

M. stepped from his car with an armful of roses. The last of the day's light flowed orange and red over the stones of the buildings. On the air he seemed to catch her fragrance. The bead curtain at the entrance to the bar billowed, then stilled.

He walked through the curtains and stood where he had first seen her. He waited for his eyes to adjust to the darkness and wondered how she would look at him now. But even before he could see, he sensed a difference there. The air was vacant, the men were solitary over their drinks and anticipating nothing. As the light slowly came back into his eyes he saw that the distant moving shape behind the bar was not Hanna but rather a woman with long black hair hanging around her face like curtains in an abandoned house. She was wearing a blue velvet dress bulging with the rolls of her fat and was moving a cloth slowly over a beer tap, a lit cigarette in her other hand.

M. stepped further into the bar. The men who had so loathed him did not lift their heads. He watched the bar's owner come out from a back room in a white apron. He took a chair from beside one of the tables and stood on it, then began to push a bulb into a socket.

M. stood beneath him. He asked him was she coming in to work that day.

'What's that?' said the man.

'Hanna,' said M. 'Do you expect her?'

'She's left,' he said.

He looked down.

'Their visas ran out.'

'They?' said M.

'Her and that lame friend who came to visit her.'

M. stared at him.

'The one she pushed around the park every evening in his wheelchair,' said the man. 'You must have seen him. Round, badly cut hair, red-brimmed hat.'

The man squinted back into the socket to find a way to fix the bulb.

M. felt the smile he brought in with his roses still locked on his face. He walked back through the doorway into the evening light.

5

Something Cold and Undeniable

Years later, at Naklo, Jerzy told me what had happened to him during the time I was on the farm in Germany.

When the Russians came to his village he was sleeping in a field of potatoes. From far away the sounds of tanks and marching feet reached him through the ground. He lay flat among the leaves and the white flowers. As the first light broke he saw the columns arrive. Nothing so big as the tanks, nor so many men in uniform, had ever been seen in the streets of the village. 'Even if we had known about it for weeks, even if we had been shown film of exactly how it would look, still we would have been surprised,' he told me. He watched the lights go on in the houses. In one window he saw a woman place a photograph of Joseph Stalin and arrange around its edges a scarf of red silk. He moved forward a little. He was trying to arrive at a point where he could see his own house. That he did not see this, nor the round wooden table where he did his lessons, nor the painting of his mother in her long green dress, nor his father the village doctor ever again was because just at that moment two Russian soldiers moved to the edge of the field where he was hiding in order to urinate. Jerzy crawled back towards where he had been. He did not stop. He moved along the furrows past the leaves and the white tubers of the potatoes, over a low wall, into a field of long grass and finally into a forest.

When I heard the story I imagined us together in that forest, two men of legend, on the run, wild and free. During those years in Pan Kazimierz's school I had become a kind of secretary to Jerzy. On the lawn in front of the big house it was he who could lift the greatest weight, could run the fastest, had the most golden hair, knew words in French, dazzled the girls, could recite the periodic table and set the discus sailing furthest through the sky. And he did all of it naturally, easily, without a word of a boast.

One day a boy named Feliks who had teeth like a mule's put his foot out just as I was making a turn in a race. I went through the air and lost a tooth and blackened an eye when I went straight into a tree. All of us who were smaller were afraid of this Feliks. He'd make a fist with just the one middle finger protruding and hit us on the shoulder whenever he felt like it. He sent us on errands. He made us steal cigarettes for him. Even now when I think of him I cannot wish him well. What he didn't know was that just at the moment that he was putting his foot out to trip me Jerzy was parking his bicycle in the lane by the field where we were racing. As he stood laughing at me lying at the foot of the tree with blood running out of my mouth Jerzy tapped him on the shoulder. He turned, but before he could even draw breath Jerzy had him with one hand by the throat up against the trunk of the tree and with the other slapped him half a dozen times very hard across the face.

'Apologise,' he said.

'But you and I are friends,' said Feliks. Blood and mucus bubbled from his nose, and he was crying.

Jerzy hit him again, harder, with his open hand across the face.

'Beg the boy's forgiveness,' he said.

And Feliks did it, on his knees, in front of all of us. He had to. We stood smiling there on the grass like vagrants invited to a feast. From that moment I imagined myself in a pact with Jerzy, as though he had saved me from drowning. I stayed close to his side.

For six weeks after the arrival of the Russians in his Lithuanian village Jerzy lived on the fruits of the forest, what he could find in the fields and the graciousness of strangers. He walked mostly. Sometimes people took him in their cars. He got through much of Belarus in a train. In the middle of a road near Kobryn he saw a crowd of people fighting over a liver they had cut from a dead horse.

Finally he came to Lwow. In this city at this time Professor Rudolf Weigl was preparing his vaccine for typhus. The French Nobel Prizewinner Nivelle had discovered that typhus is caused by body lice, and Weigl was developing his vaccine from bacteria which he bred in the intestines of these small animals. There were more than one million and a half of them kept in small wooden boxes covered with gauze. The first time Jerzy entered the laboratory he saw over forty women standing still with expressions such as people have when waiting for buses, their stockings rolled down and their bare legs pressed to the boxes. The lice were drinking their blood through the tiny openings in the gauze. Some of the lice were healthy, others were infected with typhus.

Jerzy had been given a bed by a porter in the university buildings and he went to work for Professor Weigl. His job was to place mature lice under the lens of a microscope, press down on their heads while inserting a tiny glass tube into their anuses and then to discharge a drop of the typhus bacteria into them. There the culture grew while the lice fed on the blood of the volunteers who were immune to the virus. The lice then lived for just another five or six days. They grew pink, then red, and then finally were placed in a bath of carbolic acid. It was at this point that Jerzy performed the second part of his job – to insert a tiny hook into the dead lice and extract their intestines. These were then ground into a white pulp in a sterile glass mortar, suspended in distilled water and finally packed into ampoules before being sent to typhus-infected regions all over the world. While he worked, Jerzy asked questions of the laboratory staff, and sometimes of the professor himself, about biology. Weigl's vaccine halted epidemics in Chile and saved the lives of missionaries in China.

By this time Jerzy had learned to live with the cunning of the dogs made homeless by the slaughters and transportations. He began to move towards Warsaw.

What he did not know then was that on the night the Russians came to his village his father had been called to assist at the birth of a child. It was a boy. Afterwards he went home, and it was just as he was pouring himself a vodka before returning to bed that he heard the knock of the soldiers on the door. He and his wife and Jerzy's sisters were given one half-hour to take what they could carry and then go by cart to the railway line. A train was waiting there. A soldier for ever remembered by Jerzy's mother placed her sewing machine in the cart with them as they were moving away. 'This could help you,' he said. She didn't understand why. She thought they were only going as far as Wilno. The train carried two thousand Poles in thirty-five goods wagons with shelves to sleep on, an iron stove in the centre and a hole in the floor for use as a toilet for the journey across Russia to Siberia. It took them a month. When they got there Jerzy's father was sent eight hundred metres below the earth to mine for gold. He died before the spring. Jerzy's mother and sisters earned their money in the labour camp by making clothes with the machine the soldier had placed on their cart and were transferred to Palestine after the Germans went to war against the Russians. Jerzy escaped the fate of the others in his family because for the previous week he had been practising for the invasion by sleeping in the fields. The boy whose birth Jerzy's father assisted that night later became a military cadet and was already an officer in the Polish army when General Wojciech Jaruzelski seized power in September 1981 – an event I remember reading about on a bus on the way to a baseball game in Milwaukee, Wisconsin.

I telephone Jerzy.

'It's turned cold,' I say. 'Do you feel like a hot chocolate and cake at Krystyna's?'

We meet halfway, take a turn through the streets and sit together on a bench for a while before going in for our drinks.

'I've been thinking all week about the war,' I tell him.

One black eyebrow travels alone up his forehead and then settles down again. This is how he registers coincidence.

'So was I, just this morning,' he says. 'I had a letter from a former comrade in Philadelphia. In fact I was going to call you about it. Did you ever know a Zygmunt Szadkowski?'

I tell him the name is not familiar to me.

'This letter I have is about him. Very curious story. He was one of our most brilliant couriers. Absolutely fearless.'

'Why should I know him?' I ask.

'He was from your city, and the same age. Small, very pale complexion and hair as black as a raven. He wore round, extremely thick spectacles. He had the most terrible eyesight.'

I had him then. Trismegistus.

He was a pupil in the school I went to before moving to Naklo. One day a new priest came in to see us just before we made our First Communions. He was from Latvia. He wore a crimson cassock with little pearl buttons and his hair was pomaded. He took up a seat before us, folded his hands together on the desk and said he had a story to tell us about the

Communists. In Gulbene, not far from where he grew up, two Russian soldiers came into a church during Mass. When the time came for Holy Communion they went up to the rail along with everyone else and placed their tongues out to receive the host. The priest did not refuse them. When they had the Body of Our Lord in their mouths they stood up, fired their guns into the dome of the church, cursed the priest and laughed at all the people at prayer and went out into the street where they spat the hosts out on to the ground. What did we think happened then? he asked us. We were all holding our breath. No one moved so much as the smallest finger. I looked from the priest to the wide brown eyes of the statue of Jesus behind him, His thickened brows, His exposed heart ready to pour forth the sacred blood, then back to the priest again. 'Well, their laughter stopped soon enough,' he said, 'for just at that moment, from the doors and windows and up from the cracks in the pavement, the road all around them flooded with blood. They went mad there and then, and never spoke a word of sense after.'

The priest folded his hands again. He looked slowly around the room at all of us. It seemed that when he came to me his eyes went through my eyes and into my head. When he finished he said, 'You are God's children now. But soon you will be His warriors.'

Then he smiled broadly and addressed himself to the girls. Maybe he felt bad that we might have been frightened by the story. 'Now, how many of you girls feel the calling to be nuns?' he asked. As I picture it now I would say that just under half of them raised their hands. Some wanted to be schoolteachers, others nurses. There was one with the name Elzbieta Celmer who had the idea of being a pilot.

'Now the boys,' he said. 'How many of you would like to become priests?'

Every one of us, including myself, immediately raised their hands – with one exception. That was Trismegistus. He was a small boy with neatly combed black hair who rarely spoke and when he did you could barely hear him. His spectacles had the thickest lenses of any I had ever seen. We called him Trismegistus, but his real name was Zygmunt Szadkowski. Most of us had names then – the Brigadier, Tarzan, the Beluba. I was the Quaker. How these names came to be assigned, I cannot now say.

The priest inclined his head towards the master in order to get Trismegistus's name. Evidently the situation amused him greatly.

'Zygmunt,' he said. 'I note that you are the only boy in the class who does not wish to be a priest. That is your prerogative, of course. Not everyone is called. But I wonder if you could shed any light on the fact that you are alone in your disinclination?'

Trismegistus looked up at the crimson-robed figure before him. He swallowed once, and then he said,

'I'm Lutheran, Father.'

When I tell Jerzy this story he says, 'That's right. That was one of the things that made him valuable. He had protection because of his German blood. His mother was a German from Gdansk. That made Zygmunt a *Volksdeutscher.*'

'I lost track of him when I went to Naklo.'

'His father was given the directorship of the largest tobacco importers into Poland and they moved to Warsaw. They had a lot of money. They had a cook and a maid. The father drove a long black car from America, a Packard. Zygmunt was frail, but a brilliant student. He wanted to be a judge. It was something very specific and clear, like wanting to be a priest, or a jockey.

'Then one morning when he woke up he looked out of his bedroom window and saw the eyes of the cook looking back at him from the street. He told me about it. He said they seemed to be falling from their sockets. She was one of fifteen Jews hanged from lampposts in the night. He told me she used to sing to him when he was sick.

'He came to work with us. He began by forging identity papers for couriers. He was superb at that. Then he began running messages himself. He crossed the Slovak and Hungarian frontiers. He substituted for another courier who had become ill with dysentery for a nightmare journey to Stockholm, lying still on a pile of coal for three days in the hold of a boat being rained on by black water that fell from the ceiling. He even brought propaganda leaflets into the Reich itself. He really was astonishing. He was like a spore in the wind. No one seemed able to see him. He was very small and dignified-looking. Maybe that was it.

'Then he got caught. He was a law student by this time and was seeing a girl who was studying medicine at the same university. He had asked her to marry him and she had accepted. He called in one evening to see her and her family. Inside was the Gestapo. Zygmunt wasn't carrying anything and he had his *Volksdeutscher* documents, but they had information from somewhere. They went through the lining of his clothes and then they beat him. They beat the family too. No one spoke. One of the Germans broke Zygmunt's glasses and pushed the splintered pieces into his face. They took them all down to a cellar they used and brought Zygmunt's father in and beat him to death in front of him with bars. They left the corpse with him in his cell. They shot everyone in the family and dumped the bodies in the street. Then they pushed a live pigeon into Zygmunt's mouth and shocked him with electrodes. We knew all this from people we had in the building. The next day he was shipped to Mauthausen. We held a funeral service for him. He was awarded a medal.'

By now we are in Krystyna's with our hot chocolates in front of us. Each time we come here there is a ritual of flirtation between Jerzy and Krystyna which Krystyna always initiates and Jerzy endures.

'And how is your wife, Jerzy? Away in the south visiting her sister by any chance? Leaving you all on your own?'

'No, no, at home as always. And keeping very well, thank you.'

'My Tomas can't seem to keep his eyes open after eight o'clock at night. Always tired. I think he needs a tonic. I have so much time on my hands! I'm sure you're awake and keeping busy much later than that, aren't you, Jerzy?'

And so on. She is round, wide and ample-breasted and wears tight violet or red pullovers made from wool. Sometimes when she brings you your hot chocolate her breasts sit neatly on your shoulders like an oxen's yoke. Her hair is golden and turned up neatly at the ends and so lacquered it looks like a solid mass of sculpted wood. She has this kind of exchange with nearly any male more than fifteen years old, but she pays particular attention to Jerzy. She tells me it's because she worries that he's always so serious.

When she goes back behind her counter he turns again to me.

'But the thing is,' he says, 'that wasn't the end of the story of Zygmunt. That's what I wanted to call you about. I only heard this morning. The letter I received from Philadelphia was about him.

'Here is what happened. It seems there's a rooming-house with many Poles in the city of Paterson, New Jersey. In a room a young immigrant was listening to his radio. Something came on about the war in Poland. It happened that it was taken from a book written by the courier who had missed the journey to Sweden because of the attack of dysentery. The young man went to the door of an older man who lived alone. He thought he might like

73

to hear the radio programme. This old man was Zygmunt. He had not died in Mauthausen. He was transported from there because of his knowledge of German to work in a factory they had built under a pine forest for making planes. It was an incredible thing a kilometre long and five storeys high, completely underground. The Americans found him there.

'That night in Paterson, New Jersey, he listened to the man on the radio describe his experiences during the war, including how he had missed the boat to Sweden that time but how his place had been taken by one of the many unrecorded heroes of the underground named Zygmunt Szadkowski, who had long avoided the Gestapo but had then been captured and taken to Mauthausen, where he died. He had lived just long enough to see his father and his fiancée killed by the Germans.

'Zygmunt wrote a short letter to the radio station to tell them that he was not dead. The author of the book, who at that time was living in France, was informed and through him many veterans of the underground heard the story, including my friend in Philadelphia. It was him they sent to Paterson to find Zygmunt.'

'How was he?' I ask.

'As before, it seems. Quiet, serious. A little slower, of course.'

'What had he been doing all that time?'

'Well he never became a judge,' says Jerzy. 'He was cutting grass in parks.'

Something is happening to me which I don't understand. It's like having dreams while still awake. Something bubbles up as though from an underground spring and when it breaks to the surface there are words.

On a May evening in Warsaw, with the fortunes of war already turning, the trees blooming pink and white in the gardens and the setting sun shining red and gold on the buildings, Jerzy and a small group of his comrades were waiting in a second-floor apartment overlooking the spot where it had been announced that four people suspected of involvement in the underground were to be released due to lack of evidence. Three were men and one was a woman. Their names had not been given but Marek Koc and his sister Marysia had been arrested three days earlier and Jerzy hoped they would be among them. Marek had served in the army and gave instruction in the use of weapons and Marysia sang patriotic songs on the underground radio. Jerzy had met her when he went to a house in the outer suburbs of the city to collect a piece of a gun-sight scavenged from a disabled tank. He was struck by the sweeping curves of her short body, her blonde hair tied up by a black ribbon, her generous mouth and amused brown eyes. He had never thought of himself as being witty, but when he tried to be she laughed. It was a lovely sound, he said, like the tinkling of small bells. He tried to find ways of being around her. He brought her flowers he found among the ashes of Warsaw. One night after drinking vodka and waltzing around the floor to a tune on the radio she led him by the hand to her bed, only the second such time he had been with a woman, the first having been when he was traversing the land from Lwow and a farmer's wife whose husband was away smuggling pigs gave him shelter and then came into his bed in the night and took his virginity.

On the evening that Jerzy was waiting for Marysia, others were gathered on the pavement in the hope that it would be a member of their family who would be included among the released prisoners. The atmosphere, said Jerzy, was nervous, but light. They had seen the German army more than two years earlier sweeping eastwards in their gleaming vehicles like a herd of stallions. Now they were coming back, limping, bitter, bereft. You could see in their eyes the knowledge of their vanquishment.

When the Gestapo brought the prisoners out Jerzy could see that Marysia was among them. He stood up. He had the urge to call to her but repressed it. Two of the men were bleeding from the mouth, where, he later learned, their teeth had been torn from their gums with pliers. The Gestapo were holding all three of the men by the hair and when they arrived in the centre of the street they fired a bullet into each of their heads. The officer with Marysia called out in German that he had been fucking her for three days and he did not intend to waste a German bullet on a Polish whore. Then he cut her throat open with his knife and threw her in the road.

The three men died, but Marysia did not. This was the Marysia who had no voice and whom Jerzy later married after he passed his examinations at the military academy.

When this happened Jerzy no longer wanted to write messages insulting to the Germans on walls or to make careful observations of the movements of aeroplanes or to transmit patriotic songs on the radio. He had greater aspirations for destruction. But he was Polish, and the infinite ineffectualness of this condition was just as instantly apparent to him. He obtained a key from a sympathetic secretary and for three nights went into a chemistry laboratory in the university. He purchased paper and envelopes. Then he posted letters saturated with anthrax to Gestapo headquarters throughout Poland.

When I got to the capital after the war had ended people were down on their hands and knees in the ruins of buildings looking for photographs and rings and clocks. Some were pushing dirt and pieces of wood around to make homes for themselves. Their movements were slow, as though they were under water. Above them were buildings with the walls missing. You could see wallpaper and mirrors and pipes. They were like the drawings in textbooks of anatomy which showed muscles and organs. There was the smell of extinguished fire and of dead flesh. There were trucks and horses and people with loads tied to their backs moving around and above them a cloud of dust hanging over the whole of the city and turning in the beams of sunlight like tiny pieces of gold. I didn't know where to go. I didn't know who belonging to me was still alive. I walked around and looked at the people so gaunt and lost and speechless while I thought about it all. On the walls and railings were thousands of pieces of paper on which people looking for their relatives had written addresses. They stirred when the breeze blew. They were like the feathers left behind in a henhouse cleared of its birds.

I made my way to Naklo. I slept for two nights on the floor of the old ballroom where Pan Kazimierz's violins lay broken and scattered, and then I found Jerzy. He was wearing a soldier's tunic and a beret with a red star pinned to it. He'd found them in a camp left behind by the Russians, he said, and liked the look of them. We walked over the big lawn now clogged with weeds, down past my grandfather's cottage, among the trees of the forest and back through the ruined rooms without rooftops where orchestras played, knowledge was imparted and a life never to be known again was lived. This is our home now, said Jerzy. Where else had we to go? He told me about the death of my father and mother under the beams of our home and of my grandparents in their bed and of how Renata had survived it all and was living, he thought, in Plock, just along the river from Warsaw. He told me of how Pan Kazimierz had charged at a German officer with a drawn sword and a loud wail and how the soldiers had laughed as though at a circus clown as they fired bullets into him even as he lay dead on the ground. He told me about living on the fruits of the forest, about the lice in the wooden boxes in the laboratory at Lwow, about the letters drenched in anthrax and about the woman with no voice he had fallen in love with when the German drew the blade of his knife across her throat.

'After the Gestapo had shot Marek and the others and cut open Marysia's throat, they walked along the street. Their guns were still in their hands. They had the look of drunks searching for another drink. Soldiers were herding Jews who had been hiding in a cellar out into the street. The Gestapo ordered that they be tied to a lamppost and when that had been done they took grenades from the soldiers and blew them up. They poured petrol over the pieces of the bodies and down into the cellar of the building and set fire to it all. There were still families in the building. Then they got into a car and were driven away.

'We went down the stairs and out into the street. Just as we got there a woman with a scarf tied over her face ran out in front of us and took the shoes from Marek's feet. I looked at his face. He seemed to be staring at me. There was a wide hole in his forehead where the bullet had come out. He looked as if I'd asked him a question he didn't yet know the answer to. Two nurses took Marysia away and I was about to follow her when a priest tapped me on the shoulder. "I'd like you to assist me in the offering of a Mass," he said. I suppose I looked at him as though I had not heard. "A Mass for those who have died," he said then. People were jumping from the windows of the burning building, the bodies of the Jews were burning, Marek and his comrades were lying dead at our feet, Marysia's wound was leaving a trail of blood in the road and soon the scavengers would be out to take what they could from the corpses. "And to whom would we be praying?" I asked him.'

I studied Jerzy's face. He looked different – leaner, older, but more than that. His eyes could not settle on anything. When he walked he kept looking up or at what was behind him. He seemed to be trying to reach for something with the words he spoke, but he couldn't seem to get there.

'We need something new,' he said then. 'Something cold and undeniable.'

PART TWO

6

All Is Number

I like to find a seat at the long wooden table near the window on the upper floor of the library and let the light fall through the stained glass on to my back and hands. The room fills slowly, like a church during an afternoon in Lent. Here there are the old men who will read the newspapers before passing on to the square at the end of the street for the last games of chess under the elms before winter. There are students with their textbooks and religious zealots with pamphlets and citizens consulting manuals in the hope of repairing faults in their cars or the electrical systems in their homes. Each day I see an African reading books about radiography and a man with a pinched face who long ago ceded control over his hair and garments to the elements and who for twelve years has been studying the habits of eels. At eleven o'clock the African pauses in his work, polishes his glasses and eats an apple. These are my companions in the library in Mickiewicza Street in the hours between breakfast and lunch. Here is the place where in recent years I have read in the way one does when waiting to have a tooth repaired. Now each day there is a ration of knowledge which I must take. From the shelves I take two encyclopaedias, general and scientific, a biography of Pythagoras and a history of Western thought. I write my observations in the kind of blue notebook used by schoolchildren. Sometimes the whole morning will pass before I realise that I have not raised my eyes from these books. Has anyone ever before attempted to cure a broken heart with physics?

The man who began that part of philosophy which is physics was said to have been born of a virgin, gone to the desert for holy contemplation, never cut his hair or beard, performed miracles, spoken in parables and when he died ascended bodily into heaven. He had a group of disciples of whom he demanded that they forswear their previous lives and possessions and embark with him on a search for mergence with God. They were not to eat beans nor sit on a quart measure. He was the only man in Greece to wear trousers instead of robes. Schoolchildren know of him as the man who discovered that in a right-angled triangle the square of the hypotenuse is equal to the sum of the squares of the other two sides. This is one of the things said of him which is unlikely to be true.

Pythagoras of Samos studied the relations between numbers and the world. Because six, ten and fifteen dots could be arranged into equilateral triangles he called these numbers triangular. Four, nine and sixteen were for the same reason called square numbers. The idea that numbers are units of a language that can express form is the basis for all the equations of physics that have been developed since.

He applied numbers to time and to sound. Time he represented as a vast and complex system of cycles – minutes, years, the cycles of reincarnation lasting 216 or six cubed years – which could all be represented by a number. When he and his disciples experimented with the strings of a lyre they discovered that doubling a string's length produced the identical note one octave lower. Putting two strings into the length ratio three to four made the musical fifth, and four to three made the fourth. These discoveries made the world seem more sublime, more miraculous.

Through them the hand of God in creation was made more visible. He stated that harmony is the simple and beautiful expression of the relations between whole numbers. He did not think as did others of his time that the world was made up of four elements, or atoms, or some ectoplasmic substance secreted by a deity. He said, 'All is number.' That was his first principle. When souls were poised between lives awaiting reincarnation, said Pythagoras, they spent their time among the number gods listening to the music of the spheres.

Suddenly I hear the echo of my own laughter around the vaulted ceiling of the library. It shocks me, for I don't remember laughing. I look up. There are faces turned my way. The librarian looks like a nurse disappointed by a patient. I feel my own face reddening.

Then I turn to the African and see that he's laughing with me. Such a fine laugh he has – slow and deep in the chest and with rolling shoulders. Compared to him, I in my laughter sound like a nervous hen. He is called Jacob. Now when he shuts his radiography books and puts away his spectacles at one o'clock I go out with him and we walk around the plac Pilsudskiego together. Sometimes we take a sandwich in the Café Lara and once he came to my home where we watched football on the television and drank beer until the eyes rolled in our heads. He is a bus driver who has decided to come to Poland to learn how to make photographs of bones.

During one of our turns I ask him the reason for his studies.

'It was my father's tooth,' he says. 'He brought me an X-ray picture of it home from the dentist.' He turns his full round smiling face to me. 'I had never seen anything so beautiful!'

After we walk a little further he says, 'And you? Why are you reading about physics?'

'It passes the time, I suppose,' I say. 'I come upon subjects by chance and then take them up. There's curiosity, and then the obligation to serve what you're curious about. In this case there was a friend. Well, not really a friend. Someone I met just once. But he impressed me. He was suffering and he seemed to think he might find salvation in the study of physics. Something about the clarity and completeness of it. That's odd, I know, but it made me curious. And since then I've felt obliged to continue.'

But about what was I laughing when all the faces in the room turned to me?

I think for a time, then I have it.

It was about a mathematician named Agesilao from the island of Crete. He had been labouring over an algebraic proof through the whole of one winter and into the spring. Each day he would sit at a table thinking about it until his head ached and then lie down on his bed in a torment about his own worthlessness. One morning while eating an orange under a tree and thinking about the number of goats belonging to his cousin and how he had none because of his idiotic devotion to this infernal algebraic problem the solution came to him as though delivered by messenger from the heavens. He ran into his house and then through all of its corridors banging the doors and shouting out his own name until he collapsed on his bed laughing for a full hour as though being tickled by invisible hands. I couldn't help it when I read that.

Agatharcos developed the laws of perspective so that he could help paint the scenery for the plays of Aeschylus. When a god demanded through an oracle that the size of his statue be doubled the geometers at Plato's Academy began to work at finding the cube root of two. That is how I always supposed science moved. There was a need followed by an ingenious solution.

But that was only rarely the case with the Greeks. Above all else they loved theory, and because they hadn't instruments they based their theories on what they could imagine, rather than on what they could measure. They thought beauty equal to harmony, and asked questions of the world designed to give them answers they thought would be beautiful. They imagined that the world was composed of minute particles which they called atoms. When Aristarchus of Samos looked to the sky he could not have known the shape or patterns of movement of the heavenly bodies or have any idea how many of them there were. He would have seen flashes and trails of light, a glittering chaotic assembly, motion which he could not possibly decipher. But he was a follower of Pythagoras, and Pythagoras believed that the world was created according to principles of simplicity, harmony and beauty. To him the most beautiful shapes and movements were spherical and circular, and he based his thesis not on what he could observe, but rather on what appealed to him as an expression of mathematical beauty – that the planets, including the earth, were perfect spheres moving around the sun in circles. What happened to this idea? No one believed him, not Aristotle, certainly not the churchmen and scientists of the centuries that followed, until Nicolaus Copernicus, the world's most famous Pole, the wavy-haired astronomer-canon from Torun, vindicated him in 1543 with the publication of *On the Revolution of the Heavenly Spheres*.

A cold wind from the east has arrived loaded with snow. There are streaks of frost up the window pane, and outside people bent low into the wind. The dark sky seems lower each day. We pass from darkness to a half-light and then to darkness again. I want to get out of bed but I put it off. I think, That would be like falling through a hole in the ice over a pond. I lie under the covers in a tube of warm air with the scientists of ages past and Pan Kazimierz and Jerzy and M. and Hanna and Angelina and people I've never even met in here with me. They flit about. I can't get hold of the idea of where they are going. They are like birds trapped in a room. It's difficult to see them distinctly. I must put some order there.

The telephone rings. I run into the living room on my toes. It's my sister Renata. She says that the doctors have told her that they are not going to try to burn the cancer out of her with radiation because there is too much of it. She is just waiting, she says. What matter to anyone when it comes, least of all her. I think of her in her white gown in that white room in Krakow, her long white hair untied and flowing over her pillows. I think of the lines running over her brow, the little twitches at the corners of her mouth, her hands moving on the bedclothes as though trying to find the rhythm of a tune she has lost. That demon of hunger she had when she was young has turned to something else. Her eyes move from side to side. She looks like she's reading a letter that is making her angry. Really she is counting all the times she took a step one way when she should have gone the other. For each of these wrong turns she tries to find someone to blame, and when she fails and can see only herself her bitterness deepens. Can her son the manufacturer of paper clips see this when he looks into her face? If so, does it shock him?

I feel well, most of the time. I laugh at the jokes we tell during our games of cards on Tuesday evenings. I think of taking up ice-skating again, and I call Jerzy to propose it to him. I can get a good sleep, eat heartily. But then there are times when something breaks through. Something heavy, damp and all around me, something that makes me inconsolable. Am I alone in this?

* * *

As I cross the tramline to the library in the morning I see Jacob moving towards me through the snow. He has his eyes on the ground and is upon me before he realises I am there. He is wearing two coats, two pairs of gloves and a scarf pulled over the top of his head, around his ears and tied under his chin. Over it is a fur-lined hat. He has difficulty moving his arms. It's as if he's wrapped in bandages.

He sees my shoes and he looks up. His eyes open wide. He has the kind of smile already lost to most of us by the time we are ready to grow beards.

'It's unbelievable!' he says, a cloud of white steam like that from the engine of a train billowing out of his mouth. 'I never expected this.'

We turn together towards the library. He moves through the snow as if he's wearing buckets on his feet.

'Couldn't you have chosen somewhere warmer to learn about X-rays?' I ask him.

'It was my father,' he says. 'He sent me. He came here himself to study when I was a baby.'

A hard blast of wind hits us. Jacob's face grows taut, like someone's pulling on his ears. Finally we reach the doorway to the library and climb the stairs to the research room. At the long table where we sit he removes his scarf and gloves slowly, as if he does not trust the library's ability to protect us. He takes his books from the shelf and then returns to his place and removes the outer coat. He tests the air. He sits down and waits. Finally the second coat hangs over the back of the chair.

He sees me watching him.

'I can't help it,' he whispers across to me. 'The day I landed I nearly took the first plane back to Africa. And I still can't get used to it.'

'Let me take you tonight to eat bigos,' I say to him. 'It will warm you, at least for some hours.'

He nods, and we set ourselves to work.

There was a time when the philosophers of Greece looked out at the world like children who open drawers, lift the edges of carpets or try to remove the backs of clocks. This was the time of their great discoveries. Then their nation grew rich and powerful, and the philosophers turned their attention to good, civic behaviour. When Greece became weak again the philosophers developed superstitions and other systems of personal salvation. Then again after Greece was destroyed there were no philosophers for hundreds of years.

7

Three Photographs

To begin I order beetroot soup with dumplings for Jacob, the cabbage and meat stew with prunes we call bigos, and then go on to pancakes with cheese, accompanied by lemon tea. When he sips the tea the steam rises up from the cup and around his ears, leaving tiny beads of water like stars across his brow. We are in a small, quiet, dark place hung with curtains made from purple velvet. There is light, faint piano music being played by a man with poor teeth who has hair hanging down the back of his formal suit, the notes spread far from each other like farmhouses on a plain. His head is bent low over his keyboard, but I can see him scowling and talking to himself as he plays. I ask for one brandy for me, and another for Jacob. Young couples hold hands over their tables. We can hear nothing of what they are saying, just a low murmur and the tinkling of porcelain and glass. I am a little embarrassed to be in my blue suit and tie in this place contrived for romance, smiling at and ordering food for a man rather than a woman. But Jacob seems pleased with it all, even when the waitress looks at him as though he could take off the whole of her arm with a snap of his jaw. I envy him his ease.

He asks me how far along I am in my studies.

The sixteenth century, I tell him.

'You have a long way to go.'

'That's true,' I say. 'But I enjoy it. I like to read about the physicists. They are good company. They want so much for the world to be perfect and beautiful. They try to show with numbers how beautiful it can be. Their numbers are like prayers. They are innocents. At least that's how they seem to me. Maybe it's their white coats and instruments. Or the impossibility of lying successfully with numbers. I had not expected they would be like that.'

'They should come and drive my bus,' he says. 'They wouldn't stay innocent for long.'

I have found that he is never so guileless as when he is trying to be the cynic. Here we are the reverse.

'You remember I told you I was making this study because of someone I met,' I said. 'He told me a painful story one night when I was in Krakow. I found I kept thinking about him afterwards. His suffering was something terrible. It seemed to be breaking him up right in front of me, though he endured it well. That's something we put too high a value on here, I think. Anyway, he told me he had got the strange idea that physics could somehow cure him.'

'What's wrong with him?'

'What do you think? A woman.'

He raises his brow, shrugs.

'He'll get over it.'

'I don't know,' I say. 'That's possible, but so is the reverse. He says he put everything that he was before her. Nothing kept back. And it was worth it. He says he'd never in all of his life known anything like it, and maybe never would again. But then just in the middle of it all she disappeared.'

'Where did she go?'

'He doesn't know.'

He considers this.

92

'He should forget about her,' he says.

'She could be difficult to forget,' I say. 'She's very beautiful.'

'Did you see her?'

'No. But I have photographs. You can see for yourself. I tell you, Jacob, that if she were a dentist you would want for all of your teeth to ache.'

He laughs, and heads lift from tables in a single movement, as if pulled by a string.

'Have you ever – how shall I say? – had the misfortune . . . ?' I ask him.

'We've all had that misfortune, haven't we?'

'Who was yours?'

He looks at me, then away. His smile fades the way the fog of breath disappears from glass.

'She was a girl,' he said. 'I knew her when I was learning to drive buses. She worked in a banana grove outside the town.'

'And she went away?' I said. 'You lost her?'

'I went away,' he said.

'You went away?'

'My father stopped it. He found out that her mother was without her husband. He thought the daughter could go the same way. He said he couldn't extend to me the right to be with her.'

'Extend to you the right? That's how he put it?'

'Yes.'

'And you accepted that?'

'There wasn't the possibility of not accepting it.'

'I see. And did you tell her?'

'I didn't tell her anything. I didn't go to her. I tried to think of what to say to her, but I couldn't find a way. One day we were marking out on a map the place where we'd have our house, then I never saw her again. I didn't know how to face her.'

He turns, and the candlelight flows over the surface of his glasses.

'I'm sorry,' I say.

'It was a long time ago,' he says.

He lets out a short laugh which winds down and stops as though the current which powered it has been cut.

'Even so,' I say.

We look out over the room with its heavy colours of purple and pewter and deep brown. We watch the pianist turn slowly from his piano, a waiter turning off the illuminated sign in the window.

'This place is going to close,' says Jacob.

'Yes,' I say. 'Shall I get the coats?'

'All right,' he says.

We walk out into the street, the brittle snow crunching under our feet. I would dearly love to remake the last quarter of an hour, but of course I can't.

'Are you tired, Jacob?' I say. 'Would you like a beer?'

He smiles down at me.

'Good idea,' he says. 'Where shall we go?'

'I've got some at home,' I say.

'Fine,' he says. 'Let's go there.'

We turn down a street by Mrs Slowacki's shop, cross the empty square, and then pass through a narrow corridor between two buildings, Jacob just behind me.

'She must have had something very unusual,' he says as we emerge.

'Who?'

'The one who has your friend so crazy.'

'Oh her, yes.'

'Did he tell you what it was?'

'He talked about her all night. There was her beauty, certainly.

I'll show you the pictures when we get to my home. But she had something else going on too.'

'What?'

'She told stories.'

'True stories?'

'That's what he doesn't know.'

'That's dangerous for your friend.'

'Yes. He understands that now.'

I look around. The streetlamps and the buildings seem indistinct.

'In some ridiculous way I seem to be getting drawn in too. I find I'm thinking about her all the time. It's like I'm falling for her.'

He laughs.

'Let me see the pictures,' he says.

'All right,' I say.

When we get to my home I take out the photographs and place them on the table. We study them together in silence.

In the first, black and white, she is sitting on the deck of a boat, half in profile, her hair straighter and blonder than in the others. She is young here, around twenty, I think. Her lower jaw is pressed forward as though she's thinking, but self-consciously, for the camera. She is pretty, confident, accustomed to being looked at, I would say, and lacking in knowledge of herself. She is on the way, not yet fixed. There is a pale mist rising from the water and it floats around her so that that it seems we are seeing her through a fine gauze.

In the next it is winter. There is snow, a dazzling sun. She is standing on the street in a city wearing a turquoise jacket with a white scarf tied under the chin and is smiling and squinting into the sun. Behind her an old dark tower and a statue. The light has obliterated her features. She could be anyone. You cannot find her.

In the last we are brought closer to her. We can see each line of her face, the glow of her skin. The hair, a little darker than in the first of the photographs, falls in two crescents to her neck, a few loose strands trailing across her eye. The eyes are green the colour of stone rather than of something growing from the earth. They rise a little at the corners. Two wells that are without end. She is smiling faintly, a little crookedly, the whole of the face just a degree out of alignment, as though she is dazed, hypnotised, just awake. We see her bare shoulders, the shadows in the hollows between neck and shoulder. Just at the bottom of the photograph there is a blue line along the top of her breasts. Some piece of clothing, a sheet? What event has led to this moment? Who has held the camera? Was it M.?

'You were right what you said,' says Jacob.

'What?'

'About if she was a dentist.'

'Sorry?'

'And wanting for all your teeth to ache.'

'Oh yes,' I say.

He looks a little longer at the photographs, and then leans back in his chair. I reach to take them but he stops me so that he can look again at the one with her standing in the snow. He draws it close to his eye.

'There's something familiar here,' he says.

He holds the picture up then for better light, his finger moving across the dark buildings. There is a little pile of snow like a conical hat on top of the bronze head of the statue behind her.

'What is it?' I say.

'I'm not sure,' he says.

8

Certainty

The great astronomer-physicists were driven by their reverence for God. They wanted to explain the whole of His creation in numbers.

Copernicus put the sun at the centre of the planetary system because he thought the existing picture a kind of monster, and therefore offensive to God. Johannes Kepler, who thought geometry was God Himself, nearly drove himself insane over a period of eight years before discovering that the orbit of Mars was not a circle, as had been previously believed, but an ellipse. This amended the most significant flaw in Copernicus's work. When Isaac Newton built on what they and Galileo had done and discovered the equation for the universal law of gravity and put forward his three laws of motion, the physicists believed that all questions as to how and why things moved were finally answered. Now there were numbers where before there had been mystery.

As the discoveries of Newton became known to the world, the French mathematician Pierre Simon, Marquis de Laplace, wrote,

'An intellect which at a given instant knew all the forces acting in nature, and the position of all things of which the world consists – supposing the said intellect were vast enough to subject these data to analysis – would embrace in the same formula the motions of the greatest bodies in the universe and those of the slightest atoms, nothing would be uncertain for it, and the future, like the past, would be before its eyes.'

9

The New Man

I remember Jerzy and I standing still in a little street in Naklo. It was the second summer following the end of the war. I had just received my school certificate. We had jobs cleaning away what was left of Pan Kazimierz's house after it was broken into pieces by artillery shells. We worked with hammers and shovels. It was slow work, the dust rising around us all day, the rank smell of mould from the drenched, buried wood and the carpets. The scavengers had been over and back many times since the last soldiers passed through, probing and sifting and picking with their fingers, so there was little left but powder and stone. But sometimes the blade of the shovel pressed and lifted and I found a mangled spoon, the sleeve from a nightshirt, a tin of asparagus, a slide rule, the ear from a marble bust of one of Pan Kazimierz's forebears. I felt nothing there. I found lace made by my grandmother, one of my own shoes, but I didn't foresee anything, I didn't look back and I didn't think. We were clearing the site and when we finished the work a foundation was to be laid for a factory that would crush stones to be laid over the land to make a bed for railway tracks. Maybe that was to be the job I would do next. I didn't care. Jerzy looked into the future and thought. I was doing what was put in front of me to do.

We stood in the street on a Sunday in Naklo before a shopfront. The window was covered in dust, a long crack like a lightning bolt running over it. It must, I thought, have been years since anything happened here.

Jerzy pushed hard on the door with his foot. It gave.

'What are you doing?' I said. I whispered as people do in moments of transgression, though there was no one there.

'Don't worry. I've been here before.'

We walked through the silent grey room, our feet leaving prints in the dust. There was a table, some broken tools with sharp metal points, rugs stained brown. In the back was a kitchen with an empty tin of soup stood next to the sink and a black coat draped over the back of a chair. The remains of a stairway hung from the floor above.

'Do you know this place?' said Jerzy.

'I can't remember it,' I said.

'Reuben Zamenhof made cabinets and chairs here. He especially liked inlaying wood. The more complicated the pattern, the better. Pan Kazimierz said he'd seen better work, but no one so dedicated. He could get to the end and then dig it out and start all over if it wasn't right. Don't you remember him? Small, with round glasses, pink cheeks. He had to shave twice every day to keep from looking wild.'

'You know your memory is better than mine,' I said. 'And you got around more.'

'His voice was out of control like a boy's during puberty.'

'Oh yes!' I said. 'Prominent teeth. Always singing.'

'That's him.'

Jerzy leaned over to a wooden chest and lifted the rounded top. 'Look,' he said.

I moved around to the far side of the chest. There was something long and dark stretched out among old newspapers. I couldn't see it very well. I leaned over, and then jumped back. The thing that was lying in the chest was an artificial leg.

'Holy Mary!' I said. I started to make a sign of the Cross but something about this irritated Jerzy and he stopped me.

'It belonged to his brother Emmanuel,' he said. 'They lived together upstairs.'

'But where is this Emmanuel?'

'I don't know.'

'He wouldn't get very far without his leg.'

'Yes,' he said. 'That's the mystery. Maybe he didn't have time to get it. Or maybe somebody carried him away.'

He closed the chest.

'Reuben was very sensitive,' he said. 'There didn't seem to be anything controlling what he felt. If something good happened to you and you told him about it you could see tears in his eyes and he raised his hands in blessing. The same if you suffered. It seemed he felt it more than you did. He came from a little farm. He said he had to get away from there because his father and mother could understand nothing about him.'

'Do you know what happened to him?'

'He went out into the country when the war came. He hid in barns. People wanted money to keep him and he had to come back here to get things to sell so that he could pay them. Then it was too dangerous. For the last year he stayed in a graveyard.'

'How do you know this? Did he tell you?'

'He wasn't able to tell me. I heard it from others. He came back here after the Russians passed through. He thought he was safe. When he saw the people who were still alive he embraced them and kissed them and asked them how they managed. Then he told them about himself. Just then he saw his friend Stanislaw, the baker, whose shop was just two doors away from his own. You must remember him.'

'I do,' I said.

'Reuben ran up to greet him, weeping. He was so happy to

see him alive. What he didn't know was that Stanislaw had lost his seven-year-old son and his two daughters, nine and two. The only one to survive was his wife, and she had publicly betrayed him with a German engineer who was supervising the construction of a warehouse. "You!" shouted Stanislaw when he saw him. "You brought this on us. You and your brother and all the other Jews." He was out of his mind. He lifted a stone the size of a small pig and brought it down on the top of Reuben's head. A clear liquid came leaking out of it. The people could see his brains. His eyes blinked for a while and then they stopped.'

'Jerzy, why do you tell me this?'

'It's there to be told,' he said.

He stared at me. In silence, it seemed a long time. I could see the flecks of black and grey in his blue eyes.

'People spoke about how Reuben should be remembered. Well some didn't care, they said many had died, what was one more? But there were others who made suggestions. A collection of money to be sent on behalf of the village to his parents. A memorial with the Jewish star. It was said that a stone should be dropped on the head of Stanislaw, but nobody else was interested in that. A song should be written, flowers, prayers in the church. Something must be done, they said. It was wrong what happened.'

He turned then to stand directly in front of me, quite close.

'What would you have said? You would have had the right to vote. What would you say was the best way for Reuben to be remembered?'

Again the blue eyes. It seemed he did not blink at all as he looked at me.

Of what is Jerzy's power made? Why, even now, would I be extremely careful in my choice of words if I thought of making fun of him, lest he take offence? Why, were he to direct me, must I go where he tells me, and why am I always fearful when with him of letting him down somehow? These are questions which it would be fair to ask. Well, it would grieve me to lose him, were I ever to offend him. And then there is the way I felt about him from the moment he brought Feliks to his knees after he sent me flying into the tree in the field on Pan Kazimierz's land where we were racing. But that does not explain it.

It is the strength of his mind, so easy to see, and the severity of judgement which he imposes on himself. These make him a leader. And his courage, which has brought him to places and events and people I would never have known. This has made him for me a witness. And his suffering. It is not just all that happened to him, and that he endured it, that makes me think of him in this way. It is that I would not have been capable of feeling as strongly as he did.

Some time after he told me the story of Reuben Zamenhof and on a day when I was pounding and scraping and digging in the foundations of Pan Kazimierz's house beyond where the scavengers could reach, prayerbooks and a shawl and little silver bells bubbling up on to the surface of the rubble like things released from an underwater cave, Jerzy threw down his tools.

'We're wasting our time here,' he said.

'What?' I said.

'Just think for a minute. They're building roads and hospitals and houses and steelworks. New schools, theatres, gardens. A whole new life for everyone, and a part for everyone to play. It's like the beginning of time all over again. And what are we doing? Crawling around in the dust.'

'But they're going to make a new factory here.'

'There'll be machines for doing that work. And anyway for

us this place is different. There's a time for archaeology, and a time for building.'

We got on to a bus the next day and headed for Elblag. We went into an old stone building there and told a man sitting at a desk near the entrance that we were there to submit our applications to the Union of Polish Youth and that we were ready to assist in the building of socialism. He led us down a hall to a white room. Inside it was a woman maybe eight years older than me. She was wearing trousers like an American. Her voice sounded like she smoked cigarettes one after the other. I heard, or maybe would like to have heard, some kind of invitation in it. Her eyes were half closed and she seemed to find everything vaguely amusing. I was unable to stop looking at her.

She asked me questions and she got a picture of how I could best be used. I knew German. I had been away from Poland and Poles throughout the war. I had had some kind of recognition for my essays at school.

Then Jerzy. He had had experience with weapons. He had used codes, he knew something of logistical organisation. He was a Pole from a place soon to become part of the Soviet Union but nothing filled him with such contempt as did nationalism. He was strong, fit, intelligent. She said she felt she did not need to ask him if the taking of another's life for a good reason would trouble him.

We were ready to serve, we told her.

We left the white room and sat down together in a bar in Elblag to have a beer together. It was something we had never done before. We did not know it then, but the steps we took that day were to separate us yet again. Jerzy was to return to the East, beyond where he had come from, to the military academy in Moscow, and I was to attend university in Berlin. This would bring to him the only threat to the stability of his mind known to me, and it would lead me to Angelina. It would be thirty years before we saw each other again.

As we drank our beers Jerzy pointed across the square.

'Look at that man there,' he said. 'The one with the rag holding his shoe together. Is there a way of knowing whether he was a landlord, a criminal or a digger of potatoes? No. So you see? Everything has been flattened. The ground is prepared. Time is beginning to move.'

A photograph taken in the sunlight in Naklo, Jerzy and I by the side of the road before he went his way and I went mine. He has on a sensational suit the colour of milk, wide trousers flapping in the wind, one hand gripping my arm, the other in his pocket, the left foot forward like a boxer's, smiling at the wide open way before him. I have on a shirt and a badly knotted tie, the slender back part hanging below the wider one in front. Shoulders hunched up like a marionette with his strings being pulled. Hair carefully combed, trousers too high. I am squinting but Jerzy is not. Why is that? I am the boy from the farm landed down in the city, except that I am not. It's just that I am cursed with that look.

I don't know how much pondering I would need to do in order to enter just a few millimetres into the mind of the person that I was then. Maybe more than I have time left for. The posture, the way the head is inclined, the setting of bone in flesh, they all look wrong. Where are you, boy? Still being formed, grain by grain, though I suppose I did not know it at the time.

From the military academy in Moscow, Jerzy wrote me letters. He wrote about his studies, about his plans for marriage and gave his impressions of the world around him. But mostly he wrote about the creation of the New Man. The New Man, he said, puts clarity in the place of superstition, the common good in the place of personal comfort. He knows the nobility of work and sacrifice, and the purification inherent in conflict. He knows the rank smell of decadence and the light of historical truth. He can see further than has ever been seen before.

Jerzy told me that we must not be left behind. The world that was had turned to dust. All was there to be remade. We must seize the time. It was in our power to make a world with everyone equal and free, uninfected by the rancour of class or religion or ideas of race. If he needed to be reminded of what greed and corruption and nationalism could bring to us he had only to travel back to Poland to the home of Marysia, his future wife, and look at the red scar that swung from one ear to the other and at her mouth which opened and closed and yet could say no words. We had to be in the front line, he told me. We had to inhabit our places of learning just as long ago the monks inhabited their monasteries, but in the place of the murmuring of Latin syllables we had to put hard, clear thought, thought that could break up, penetrate and reveal. If we did not cease in this task, if we were vigilant and purposeful, surely we too would see it – the cold, beautiful truth, as clear as numbers. The burden would be heavy. The road would be hard. But what was the choice? he asked. The sleep of idiocy and superstition? Running after baubles? Permanent nausea?

In Berlin, meanwhile, I developed a love for analysis. Perhaps more the word than the process, which remained somewhat beyond my reach. I pictured analysis like a great maw devouring jungles and mountains and swamps and transforming them into a single radiant highway. I walked the streets, trying to think. On one side was me. On the other were Science, Truth, the Destiny of Mankind. In between was analysis.

That was how we were. We knew nothing of the catastrophes

to come. And just because, perhaps due to weariness and old age, I am unable to describe this phase of my life other than ironically, does not mean that Jerzy, or I, were stupid.

How did I look in Berlin, a year after taking the bus from Naklo? A little more recognisably myself, I suppose. But I ran more than walked. And the face was leaner than now, and the hair not a disappointment. Smiling. Fervid. Certain, or so I thought. I can see the others who were around me better than I can see myself, thrown together on a bench under copies of angry and righteous paintings smoking cigarettes and drinking beer and laughing at capitalists. I did it too. When we wanted to laugh loudest we thought of American capitalists. We had seen buildings filleted like fish by bombs. We saw men with whips herding people they'd never met on to trains. We saw schools turned into places of torture. We saw men who used to dress formally for dinner eating the flesh of dogs. We had seen necessity, like the exposed bone of a broken limb. How could we not laugh at a country where the most urgent questions concerned the activities of athletes, the apparel of movie stars or whether or not to buy a certain electrical machine capable of turning bread into toast? How had they arrived at such vacancy? How was it that their leaders could not think? There was not an idea from there that we had not discarded. In fact there were no ideas at all there, we declared. History had laid down the rails and we were on the train. Maybe they would come along in our wake. Or maybe we would devour them.

Where was the doubt that has accompanied me through nearly all the years since then, this doubt lodged somewhere within me like a polyp?

There was a light tap on the door of my student room in Berlin. When I opened it I found there a Soviet general of vast dimensions in full dress uniform, row upon row of medals and ribbons across his chest, jowls the colour of pork hanging over his collar and on to his shoulders, hat off and clutched in his little pale hands, a mirthful smile hidden away in the folds and gatherings of his fat. Was the delicate knock a joke, I wondered? He told me he was in Berlin for logistics meetings for a German–Soviet exercise and was calling on me at the request of Jerzy, whom he met after giving a lecture at the military academy in Moscow. I couldn't stop looking at him. If little children were to play on him they could drown in the quicksand of his stomach. How did he take a bath?

We went down the stairs and out into the street where a black car was waiting.

'Your friend Jerzy is a glory of the firmament,' he said to me, guiding me into the back seat. 'The brightest and most promising young man yet to come before me.'

Of course, I was proud.

At the restaurant I watched him. This, I thought, was how the lords of the continent ate long ago. Herrings with parsley and oil. Iced vodka. Salad. Plates of vegetables sending clouds of steam up to the ceiling. A whole fish bursting with mushrooms, its angry-looking mouth pointed at me. Then a slab of meat still clinging to the bone. This in itself looked like a piece of furniture. Two bottles of wine just for him. Crumbs and little bones and streams of oil coursing from the corners of his mouth and into the folds of fat gathered around his chin and neck. None of these things came out. I wondered what else was in there. A piece of chocolate cake buoyed up with ice-cream came next. Every now and again a long breezy belch. 'Eat! Eat!' he told me whenever he remembered that I was there.

He asked for a bottle of vodka to be brought to the table. He opened his uniform jacket, loosened his tie. Then he made that oddly feminine gesture I have often seen fat men make, arms pressed down on to the rests of the chair, the bulk lifting, bottom shifted one way and the torso the other, a few wriggles in this manner this way and that, then, rearranged, settled, lowering himself back down into his seat again, a little inclined towards the table, hands up around his chest like a squirrel's as he examined what remained before him. The candles were guttering, the cooks were removing their aprons in the kitchen, the waiters drawing back chairs to help people to their feet. The General made a long sigh, emptied a shot of vodka. He looked a little sad for a moment, the sadness of satiation perhaps, the monotony of it. But it passed. By now I was fond of him. It was his matronly gestures when asking me to eat, his affection for the food, his ease of manner when asking for and eating it, like a carpenter with his tools. He looked at me and smiled.

'You want to know about Jerzy?' he said. 'Of course you do. You are his oldest friend, he tells me. A good young man, as I can see myself.

'Well, I met him at a dinner. It was the kind of dinner I hate – thirty teachers and ten of the most promising cadets. They put me up at the top table with the senior professors. That was the worst of it. They won't let you eat. But you see they would have felt they had to keep me close to them. I go back to the Bolsheviks and all the way through Stalingrad. I was in the hunting party across Poland to Berlin. So you see? I am unquestionable. They fear me.

'After the meal they brought Jerzy up to sit next to me. I already knew about him. "None of the others can touch him," they said. They were right about that. Did you ever see Chinese cooks with their knives? They seem to have six hands. That's how it was when he spoke. Six brains. I've been around a little, but he shocked me, this boy. How old could he be? Twenty-three?

Twenty-four? How does he think so fast? Where does he get such confidence?

'The dinner ended. We all got up and walked out. I was still talking with Jerzy. You can see by now that everything in life except food is ridiculous to me. But I didn't want to go to bed that night. I wanted to hear more from Jerzy. He brought me back to some time, some feeling. We kept walking. We passed through the gymnasium. He said, "Would you like to swim?" "Yes," I said. We couldn't find the light for the pool. We undressed in the darkness. We had to go on our hands and knees just to find where the water started. He dived, I slipped in like an otter. I could have had the whole of the faculty on their way to the mines in the morning but somehow I was afraid of getting caught. Like I was a schoolboy again. We floated on our backs speaking of the decisions faced by Hannibal on the route into Rome. We went on like this for more than an hour.

'We got out and dried ourselves and went into a garden. I sat on a bench and he sat in the grass. We talked, we joked, we told each other stories. It wasn't light yet. It was still that time when all nature is silent. I thought, I am an old man. What am I doing here? But I couldn't draw away.

'At some point he became solemn. He spoke very softly. He was hesitating, he couldn't get all the words for what he wanted to say. But then they came to him. He talked about the soul of Man, how to ignite it, how to bring belief to it. He talked about building the tension in the world to such a pitch that all the forces of capitalism could do nothing to extinguish it and all the old structures would break and fall away. Then the true glory of Man could shine through. He was speaking of world revolution, of course. Well first of all that is not our policy. It's been debated at congresses and been rejected. No, forget that. That's not the important thing. My young friend, I don't know what you know and what you don't know. But I can tell you that everything is stupid. Everything is a mess. There will never be anything done about it. This is what your friend Jerzy will face in his life. But somehow, there in the garden, the way it was, the quiet, the darkness, and you know, the way he was speaking, I believed him. No, that's not right. I couldn't do that. But I believed *in* him. He was making such beautiful sentences. He was excited and I was watching him, his hands moving in front of him, his wonderful shining eyes and I was . . . What am I saying?'

The General looked around the room. His hands opened and closed in the air. He took a shot of vodka.

'Well, yes. I will say it. I was falling in love with him. That's what was happening. I mean, it's ridiculous. That's clear. And where did it come from? All these years in the army with boys and men and never thinking these things. Married thirty-five years, three sons all in the military. A grandfather. So fat I nearly have to be helped out of a chair. But it wasn't a sexual kind of love. I didn't think of that. It was that he brought me something that I hadn't felt since I was young. It was his eyes. They were so magnificent, so beautiful. The excitement he felt, the words that came out of him, his eyes, so pure, so committed, so honest . . .'

He looked around my face and then sighed. His chin dropped down on his chest.

I think suddenly of a hot summer evening in Chicago. I was walking through a park by the lake. It was August 1969, the shadows long, the dusk slowly falling. The Appalachians were dousing the charcoal in the barbecue pits and packing up their baskets. The baseball diamonds were silent. Out on the lake, boats glided on the serene blue water. At a stand selling hot dogs and drinks I sat in the shade and drank lemonade. I was not thinking about much. I had been standing all day in a blue and gold uniform with hat at a turnstile taking entrance tickets to a furniture exhibition. I walked on past the transistor radios and the lovers under the trees.

Ahead of me, in a clearing, was a fire. Yellow flames in a wild dance, an orator with a weak chin and black hair like a heap of wool on his head to one side of the blaze and on the other a gathering of young men and women. Some of them had motorcycle helmets on their heads. Some were carrying spears. I didn't get it at first, but then I came to understand that they were getting ready to move, to sweep down with others into the city in order to destroy everything that was in their path. The orator was working their anger like a man lifting a car with a jack, notch by notch. The jailers, the murderers in uniform, the thieves in suits, he reminded them. They will send you off to die in a foreign war just to make themselves rich. I had seen this malignancy and the men who engendered it too, I thought. And then I thought, Why not? How many opportunities for rage had I let pass unmarked? I had lived in a time and a place where nothing else was apt. Yet I kept it to myself. I slipped in among the young people, and then we ran out together into the streets. We moved like a plague.

That night I broke twelve panes of glass and set fire to three cars and a bus.

I come now to that moment in the hotel room in Erfurt of which I spoke earlier, that moment when I became myself. I was working there during the summer in advance of my final year at the university. It was the idea of my professor of history. 'An education should include the knowledge of what it is to be a worker,' he said.

The morning when it happened was bright and hot. I was

wearing, as ever, my polished shoes and the bow tie I'd had to forgo two days of lunches for. I had orders to go to the room of a Russian apparatchik to clear away his breakfast plates. I remember, just before, the black eyebrow of the chef travelling up his forehead as he cut the head from a fish in the kitchen. I remember the whorls in the dark grain of the wood on the stairs as I ascended and the thickened air of the room as I opened the door, the smell of human sleep there, of melon and leather and privilege, with a light sweet smell of perfume drifting through it as though to a tune played on an accordion. On a round table with little wheels, amid the plates and cups and debris of food, was a cigarette case made of silver, dark chocolate pressed into the shape of a fan, the trace of lipstick on a cup. I could see all the tiny creases of the woman's lip where it had met the surface of the porcelain. The smell of cognac was gathered like a low fog within the confines of the cup. A blackberry bled its juices into the fibres of the white cloth that covered the table.

The bright morning light fell through the window and on to the bed and I went over to sit on it. How demure the apparatchik and his woman had been. I could see the impress of two bodies and ripples like water makes in sand, but otherwise the sheets were crisp. Of the man there remained his leather bags and newspapers and cigarette ends, but of the woman I got only the perfume, hanging like a phantom over the sheets.

I saw then at my feet, half hidden by the bedclothes, a book face down on the floor. I remember the book's faded green cover and the delicacy of the hand that had inscribed a name inside – Lena Nowak, 1946. The book was written in Polish and it was on the side of the bed where the woman had lain through the night. Now she was gone with her lipstick and her roubles. I had not seen this man of the Kremlin, but I pictured him fat, flatulent and without joy. And she with lips like a little red bow, delicate white shoulders and a voice that never rose above a whisper. So many pretty girls in rooms such as these from towns like mine – so well presented, so polite, so helpless. Why was she not walking with me on that morning along the lake shores of Pomerania?

I often felt when I entered rooms such as this so filled with the lives of strangers a feeling of exaltation – the exaltation of invisibility, perhaps. I sat on the bed in a little cloud of perfume and began to read. The sun warmed my hands and face. I have tried in the years that have passed since to remember the title of the green book and the name of the man who wrote it, but I cannot. And I remember nothing of what he said. I remember only that he was a monk and that these were his prayers and meditations and that I badly wanted to know what Lena Nowak was reading as she lay beside the sleeping Russian she had been summoned to entertain. I tried to catch the rhythm and the meaning of his words, but it was difficult. I would read five sentences, maybe eight, and then stop. The words seemed out of order. I could not grasp them. They were like a thicket. I looked at the little clock at the side of the bed. 10.14 it said. How long before they came looking for me? I closed my eyes and lifted my face and let the sun fall over it. The silence of the room seemed like a kind of music. Inside I felt movement, very sweet and sure, like the whirring of a hundred dials. It seemed to cool me. I looked down and began again to read and when I did the words of the monk went in through my eyes and mouth and the pores of my skin, they were in my lungs and were carried along in my blood, each of them like a living thing, and when they came into my head they opened like a rose and let out a sheet of flame, a brilliant light that had whiteness and gold and carried no heat. It burned with its cool light the things that stood before it – things that had blocked my sight, the frustration I had felt as I struggled to make a picture of the world as ornate and perfect as a cathedral through the power of analysis. It lifted me, and I let myself be lifted. It was fast, and I had no fear. Then it stopped and there was silence and stillness and peace. The clock said 10.21. I looked around and so many things – the trace of the Russian's body on the sheets, the wallpaper, the little pile of dust on the window ledge – they all seemed so funny to me then. Something amazing and irreversible had happened. All that I had struggled to understand with logic and categories was now flowing and churning around me. I was in the world as if for the first time, thrown into it somehow by the words of the monk. I no longer had to arrange or comprehend it. I could just be in it. I was free. It was so simple and obvious. How was it I had never felt like that before? What had stopped me? I lifted Lena Nowak's pillow to my face and took in the last traces of her presence. I thought, My girl, how fine I could be with you now!

After my time at the university I was put to work in an office concerned with the distribution of eggs. Our area was Thüringen. We were in a room high up in a building looking down on to a square, the trees heavy with leaves. We kept the windows open from spring to autumn, the breezes blowing in. The square was like the mouth of a child losing his teeth, gaps in the terraces where bombs had removed the buildings. To one side of me was Pawel, a tall dark Pole with spectacles, caustic in a way that was sometimes too familiar to me, too exhausting. At other times I turned to him for this same quality when I wanted the comfort of the familiar. On the other side was Dieter, the son of German communists driven to Manchester in England, where he grew up. He came back alone. He did not want to miss it, he said, this great adventure. He had red hair and freckles. He was so short that his face had always to be inclined upwards when he spoke, even to women. At night he helped make scenery for a youth theatre and worked in a literacy programme for factory workers. And no one took more seriously his responsibility for the efficient movement of eggs. Sometimes it was too much for him and his head dropped down on his desk. When this happened Pawel tied him to his chair with a complex system of knots and tickled him behind his ear with a feather. 'Where did you get those knots?' we asked him. 'In the Scouts,' he said. 'I know more knots than a sailor.'

We were watched over by our head, Gottfried, camp veteran, conspirator. He liked us to call him 'Onkel', or uncle. He was never without his pipe. He moved around our rooms like the basketball coaches I saw years later on the school playgrounds in Chicago, enthusing, cajoling, clapping us on the back, poking at the air with his pipe. 'Talk! Think! Stimulate! Debate!' he called out. 'This is not just about eggs. It's a way of looking at the world!'

Once a month we got on a bus for meetings in village halls to try to persuade farmers to form collectives. They listened politely. They applauded the speeches. Then they stood up one by one to make their declarations. 'Martin Furster is taking too much water from the river.' 'Karl Winter put poison out for my dog.' 'The son of Kurt Vorchert goes out in the night stealing turkeys.' Once Dieter was beside me on the bus back to Berlin. He was long in thought, and then he spoke. 'You cannot stop believing, even for a moment,' he said. He had the look of surprise and fear that can come with a malign revelation. 'Otherwise everything falls in. Isn't that right?' He blinked rapidly, as though a wind was throwing dust at his eyes. 'But how is such a belief possible?'

When I think of Angelina, it is usually at that moment when she turned the corner of the lodging-house in Berlin, her hand on the railing, her grey dress falling and folding as she moved down the steps. It was there that I first saw her. Just as then I can let it pass, turn the other way. But I don't.

When she reached the foot of the stairs she lifted a coat from a hook on the wall and placed it on her shoulders. She did not put her arms in the sleeves. She did not fasten the buttons. It was the kind of coat an old man from the times before the war would wear to his law office, a belt across the back, velvet on the lapels. She took a step and her grey dress moved up her leg. The man in the blue metallic suit had gone through a door, the parrot had called out and the caretaker was carrying a basinful of wet steaming clothes into her room. I was sitting on a bench by the door under a round bronze clock waiting for Pawel and when Angelina passed by I stood up as though she was a general. She looked at me. I remember her eyelids lifting very slowly, like the wings of a huge bird. She smiled deeply and then moved on. Her eyes were deep and brown, in a minor key. It was not the electricity of expectation that I felt, but rather a sense of completion. I did not know how this could be at the time, nor ever after.

When she passed she left behind the trace of her perfume. She did not look back. There was a shake of her black hair over the back of her coat, then the turn of her ankle at the door.

Even after forty years I cannot make peace with my memory of her. With her I had rapture.

PART THREE

10

White Horses

As I entered the bar and heard to my left the clinking of glasses and scurrying speech and laughter, I already knew that here were Pawel and his colony of Poles. At the counter were two building workers reading the same newspaper and opposite them the barman with his enormous head propped up by his hand. I did not look at any of these people because ahead of me, in a corner, was Angelina. She was alone. There was a small lamp beside her, she was smoking a cigarette and she was reading a book. The long black coat was over her shoulders. A glass of crème de menthe was on the table before her. She was smiling as she read, an eerily polite, accommodating smile, like that of a school-girl being introduced to a new teacher. The entire time she was in this bar reading this book she had on her face this identical smile. Nothing she read caused her to change expression. I tried to see the title of the book, but couldn't. The light from the lamp fell on her hands. Her fingernails were short and ragged. There was something white and congealed like plaster on the backs of her hands, a hatching of little cuts on the top of her thumb.

I had seen her on the streets since that night in the hallway of Pawel's lodging-house, carrying a bottle of milk, waiting for a bus. She never seemed to see me. You are a distributor of eggs, I told myself. And she is a woman a war could be fought over. I never approached her, but I knew from Pawel that when people tried to know her it seemed she turned to smoke. In the lodging-house over cups of coffee in someone's room they passed whole nights like theologians at a seminar debating the origins and the direction and the meaning of her life. It was a time and place of small pleasures. I was occasionally there too, but I did not speak about her. I thought it would be an intrusion. I thought it might break the spell that I imagined had existed since our eyes met in the hall under the bronze clock. She had come by foot over the Carpathians, they said. She had been mistress to a Hungarian prince. She had worked for the British. She was a gypsy who in answer to the slaughter of her family at the end of the war had led seventeen Germans to her bed and castrated each of them. She could play the cello like a master but would not do so because of her sorrow.

I sat down at the edge of the group of Pawel's Poles. I watched Angelina. I paid no attention to them even when they taunted me. Finally Angelina closed her book and walked out, her head down, the same smile still on her face.

I turned to Pawel.

'Why don't you have a party?' I said.

'I'm always having parties. What's new?'

'Well, have another one. Except make this one slightly bigger.'

'Why?'

'So I can meet her.'

He rolled his eyes.

'Have you heard him?' he said to the others.

'Please,' I said.

He considered this, then he said, 'You buy the vodka.'

'All right.'

'But I have to tell you, no one can be sure that she'll come. She's been living with us for more than a month and I've only ever heard her speak twice. And that was in a whisper.'

*   *   *

I did not hear this voice until just after two o'clock on the night of Pawel's party. Cigarettes spilled from the ashtrays into pools of beer on the tables. A girl from Poznan had fallen asleep on the lap of a young man who had once been a candidate for the priesthood in Katowice. Two students of electrical engineering leapt from chair to floor to bed fencing with umbrellas. There was a couple on the balcony, the boy singing to the girl. I passed the night walking out to the landing, looking at myself in the mirror and talking without listening.

Finally she came in. She was wearing a long green velvet dress such as might have been worn to a ball. Her hair was swept back, her red lipsticked lips sparkled in the light. She was barefoot. Her nails were polished, but there was a streak of white plaster running up her forearm. What was that?

'Sorry,' she said to Pawel, meaning the hour.

He asked her what she wanted to drink.

'Red wine, if you have it,' she said. She held up her hands, looked down at the dress, laughed. 'It was all I could find. But not the shoes.'

She walked around the room, looked at the oleographs of old Polish patriots, a view of Gdansk taken from a plane, the titles of books. She nodded sweetly to those she recognised and took her glass of wine from Pawel. He put a record from France on the turntable of his gramophone and then made an elaborate gesture to me behind Angelina's back as if to say that the stage was now mine. The voice on the record was that of a woman, mournful and plaintive. Angelina stood before the bookshelf and swayed to the rhythm in her long dress.

I was sitting on the floor in a corner. She looked at the leaping dancers, the sleeping girl, the kitchen air billowing with cigarette smoke and talk and then sat down on the floor with her back to the wall just adjacent to me. Our knees were almost touching.

What was I to do with this stroke of fortune? On her face was the same smile she wore in the bar while reading, this smile of virtuousness and agreeability I would come to know well which she used while walking in the street, stepping along the aisle of a tram, sitting at the edge of a group of people who would like to have known her, a smile like the veil of a dress hat. She leaned her head back against the wall and listened to the music. Her forefinger traced a circle around her thumb. I wondered how much time I had. Her nail caught the edge of one of the dried cuts on her thumb. A bead of blood appeared on the surface of her skin. She didn't notice this. It was a tiny cut, growing into a red globe, catching the light, like a ruby mounted on a ring. Then the blood's frail viscosity could hold this shape no longer and it ran in a track down her thumb and on to her wrist. I took a handkerchief from my pocket and pressed it to the wound. She turned, but slowly. I got the idea that she used no speed faster than this.

'Your thumb,' I said.

'Oh,' she said. She looked down and then back up at me. The grand, grave notes of her eyes. She let me press the wound a little longer, then lifted the handkerchief to take a look.

'You look like you've been building walls,' I said.

Her brows rose, a question.

'There,' I said, and pointed to the streak of plaster on her forearm.

She picked it off, dusted herself.

'I didn't see that,' she said.

We began to speak. It was simple, like moving through a door into another room. It was about nothing other than what could be heard and seen there at Pawel's party. I would be lying if I said I could remember. Her voice was light, caressive. I can hear this voice now as clearly as if she were speaking into my ear. It was the voice of a person accustomed to speaking seldom. She moved back as though surprised when she said something she was uncertain of. I begged her pardon, leaned forward to hear and then she spoke again just beside me, chin upstretched, the pulse beating in her neck, her hand on my arm. She laughed often, knowingly and without mirth. Her laughter was collusive, meant to be directed at men. Everything seemed so alive and unknowable. The room began to disappear. There was no time other than what we were making. Nothing was hidden. This was an illusion, I knew, just as I thought it – Nothing was hidden. Yet that was the feeling, eye to eye, a question and then an answer.

When he thought of it Pawel returned the needle of the gramophone to the beginning of the record of songs by the Frenchwoman. She was singing, I think, about walking alone under the light of the moon. It was an hour when no one in the room was aware of what anyone else was doing. I asked her to dance.

She laughed.

'But no one else is dancing,' she said.

'That does not mean that it's forbidden.'

'It's more than four years since I danced.'

'Look at yourself,' I said. 'You are wearing a dress for dancing.'

She looked down at the dress.

'I found it in a trunk. There was a photograph with it. It was of a woman in a straw hat with a dog, laughing. There is a boathouse behind her. I imagine she could dance well.'

'There you are then,' I said. 'Come. No one is watching.'

She considered a moment, looked at me, then stood. When we began she kept herself a little further apart from me than was usual for dancing. I saw her looking soullessly at the wall. In this I refused to believe. There was too much to lose. I tried to

remember how long this song about walking under the moonlight lasted. I drew her a little closer. I felt the long muscles of
her back tighten as she stepped one way, then another. Some
dialogue of the body began, of which we were the spectators.
Then the song came to an end.

She stopped and drew away. She seemed embarrassed. Pawel
turned on a light and with the others was down on his knees
looking for a lost ring. The couple on the balcony had gone, the
girl from Poznan was standing up and rubbing her eyes, one of
the duellists was gathering glasses and bottles. At any moment I
could lose her.

I touched her on the arm.

'Would you like to walk?' I asked her.

'Walk? Where?'

'Anywhere. Just to see the first light.'

She looked down, pointed to her bare feet.

'I can't walk without shoes.'

'I'll wait,' I said.

She went out and started up the stairs to her room, holding
the front of her dress up out of her way. Pawel watched her, then
called the attention of the duellist with the handful of bottles.

'Do you see that woman there?' he said. 'Since she came here
to live in the rooms at the top of the building we have all
worshipped her. Us and our guests. We have sat together like
schoolboys discussing one of the stars of Hollywood. We have
lain awake planning our tactics and dreaming of how it would
be to be with her. She comes, she goes, she smiles a little, she
says "Good morning" or "Good evening". But no one gets to
know a thing about her. Certainly no one gets to *dance* with
her. And what happens? My comrade here presumes on my
good nature to get me to host a party so that he can meet her.
All right, I think, he will have the same disappointment as the

126

rest of us. I think this will be a good experience for him. Consider him, please. He works in an office that decides where to send eggs. He is neither short nor tall, fat nor thin. There is nothing about his aspect or his experience that would set him apart from the rest of us. Yet within a couple of hours of meeting her he has held her in his arms and now he is leaving with her! How has he managed it? He has *listened* to her. That is his secret.'

'In order to listen,' I said, 'you must be able to be fascinated by something other than yourself.'

'Listen to the philosopher. And at such an hour. Is that a slogan from a Party meeting? But no. We in the Party don't recognise such a thing as self. That would be too banal.'

I thought, Pawel, be careful.

Pawel came to have troubles, bad troubles, and not only because of his loud, caustic mouth. But in time he prevailed. I followed his progress. I had reason to do so. He married a very pretty doctor's daughter from a small town called Zywiec in the south of Poland. She bore him four children and never lost interest in sitting in her chair with her hands folded before her on her lap looking at him with delight.

Angelina came down the stairs and stood at the door. She was holding her coat and wearing flat shoes and a sober brown dress meant to mark a frontier. Yet her fingers touched mine when I held up her coat to lay it over her shoulders. On the way down, the bulb on the stairwell did not ignite and she let me guide her, hand in hand, past the ticking clock and the red parrot racing back and forth on his perch. As I closed the door the caretaker put her head out from her room, her hair in a net.

We walked slowly through the streets. There were paper streamers lying in the road, and an upturned carnival mask. Dark clouds moved past the moon like a procession of carriages. High up in an attic window there was a light and we could hear the slow playing of an insomniac violinist. We moved down a hill through the rubble of a broken building, the moon throwing long shadows like mountain peaks on to a far wall. We seemed to be entering a world of blue and white and black that was being made for us as we walked.

Her foot turned on a piece of masonry. She lifted her leg, rubbed her ankle and then sat, looking out. Ahead of us there was not a thing that was whole. There were just the peaks and troughs of a long rolling field of brick and timber, like a sea in storm, a single wall standing, the moonlight flowing through the holes where once there were windows.

'It's beautiful, no?' she said.

'The moon?'

'Everything just lying there. Given up. The moonlight shining on it.'

'Were you here when any of this happened?'

'No.'

'Where were you?'

'South. Another city.'

'Did you get hurt?'

She laughed.

'Did you?' she said.

'I was lying on my back on a bale of hay most of the time.'

'At first I was in Belgrade. That's where we lived. I was in an academy learning to draw. My father had a factory. My mother had already gone to her sister's house in the country because we all knew that we were going to be overrun. When the invasion came there was more noise than I had ever heard – bombs, artillery shells, everybody running around. There was something exciting about it. I suppose not everybody felt that way, but many did, I think. There was a feeling that all the laws had been revoked. But then people were getting hurt, too. Hundreds, thousands. I thought I would like to help. Maybe I should say I wanted to get closer to it. I volunteered. One of the people organising the services had the mad idea that I should do nursing because it was supposed I knew something of anatomy from studying art. There were places in shops and cellars and tents and I went from one to another doing what I was told by people who were supposed to know. Most of the time I was useless. Often I was worse than useless because I got in the way. I ran and got things. I lifted people. I cleaned wounds with soap and water or bottles of raki and bound them up with bedsheets. A child could have done most of it. Sometimes children did do it. I watched a lot. It was best to keep clear when something serious was happening. I used to long for something serious to happen. That's a confession here in the dark. You could get bored fast. At least I could. You could sit for hours and hours, maybe even for days, and suddenly there was bone and blood and screaming. It didn't seem to be connected to anything. Not to people, not even to pain. A man arrived who had lost a piece of his skull. I could see the brain. It was like a wet snake. He came in carrying the piece of bone and a nurse fitted it back into the hole. Nobody there knew anything about what to do. The injured man opened his eyes and looked at each of us in turn. Then he died. Usually that's the way it was, we hadn't any effect on anyone's fate. But sometimes I could do things. A shell hit a tram and the driver came in with a wound the size of a dinner plate at the top of his leg. Blood was pouring out because the artery had been cut. I was told to take off my blouse and stuff it down into the wound and press. This was meant to close the artery until a doctor could come and sew it shut. And it happened as it was supposed to. The man was all right. Then you would go on to the next thing. Or at least you hoped to.

There were so many surprises, things you would never imagine, things you couldn't take your eyes from. Then it would change again. There was a blast in a house that drove nails out of a door and into a woman's head. We had to find a hammer to take them out.'

I watched the glow of her cigarette as she drew on it, the lines of her face. I seemed to be falling, as though into a river, willing to be carried somewhere.

'There was something different about wounds to the legs,' she said. 'Especially if they came from explosions from below – if a shell hit the lower floor of a house, or the ground blew up when a person was walking. Everything gets pushed up. The bones in the legs splinter around the pelvis. The feet appear under the hips. The legs are there, or what remains of them, but you can't see them any more. After I saw this I looked differently at people walking around in the streets. It looks so improbable, don't you think? Walking, I mean. The head, the torso, the area around the pelvis. The size of all those things and the weight, all that happens in them. For it all to be held up on two long thin legs and then balanced on the feet. They don't seem very secure. It hardly seems possible. You wouldn't think that the mathematics would work. And then for the whole system to be able to move, back and forth, side to side, slow, fast. Well . . .' She laughed. 'This doesn't seem sane, I suppose.'

'No,' I said. 'I understand you. But I hadn't thought of it before.'

She launched her cigarette out into the rubble and then folded her arms around her knees. I looked at the hand nearest me, the serrated nails, the dried blood on her thumb, the fingertips with their network of tiny cuts like shattered glass.

'Is your father still there?' I said.

'I don't know. I lost him. One day he left me to go to my

mother, but he never arrived there. I looked for him. But nothing.'

'I'm sorry,' I said.

'It's not unique,' she said.

'Your mother . . . ?'

'She's all right. She's in England, with my brother. He's very clever. Already he owns part of a newspaper in Portsmouth. He looks after himself very well. That's the first thing he does with his brain. I get letters from them. They're very careful what they say, but I get the idea they don't approve of what's happening here.'

'They will,' I said. 'It will become obvious.'

Or did I say that? This was forty-six years ago. It is like trying to see something in a forest, the wind blowing, the light moving through the trees. The mind completes what the eye of memory does not entirely see. But that is what I then believed – that we would triumph.

We were silent for a while, looking out. Then I said, 'What are you doing here?'

'Here? With you?' She laughed.

'No, no. I mean your work.'

She turned to me, still smiling. She looked all around my face, very slowly. I heard the machinery of a clock. Her eyes settled on mine and did not move, her face close, soft, open, even as she made her judgement.

'Why do you want to know?' she said.

Well, everyone wants to know, I thought. Hadn't you realised? 'There's just the two of us here,' I said instead. 'And I think your story is likely to be more interesting than mine.'

She laughed and then stood. We began to walk over the broken stone and timber. She faltered and I caught her hand. On higher ground I could see a band of pale blue along the line of the horizon, silhouettes of gargoyles, stone horses, statues with raised swords. We reached the street and I let her hand go slowly. We went back the way we came, the lamplight fading on the walls and the cobblestones seeming to ooze a kind of oil, early morning workers stepping from their doorways. We turned into Pawel's and her street. A brief wind rose and the carnival mask clattered like a tap dancer over the stones. Above, the violinist's light was out. I thought in a sequence of maybe twenty things that could be ahead of me as the night passed to morning, but I settled on none of them. I walked along next to her in silence. She put her key in the street door, turned it. The minute hand on the brass clock jumped forward, the parrot's head was buried in his feathers. Our footsteps sounded across the hallway, up the marble stairs. We passed Pawel's door and wound higher upwards, the whole house still and deep in its sleep, her movements slow as she reached again for her keys, her eyes flashing across to mine, a nerveless smile, the pressures building within me, the key fitting in the lock, turning.

Inside, all was dark. I heard her moving, then the lights came on. We were in a hallway, a single small lamp and a trunk spilling clothes on to the floor. Her green dress was there. There were two doors. She passed through one and I followed her into a large room with a gas ring and sink at one end and a camp bed pushed against the wall of the other. She took off her coat and laid it across the bed, then thought again and hung it on the back of the door. It was difficult to see what was there because there was no pattern to anything. Stacks of books, clothes, coffee cups, shoes, pots of paint, a bottle of ink, coiled brass tubing, all spread in heaps and drifts across the floor as if blown there by a random wind. On the wall colour plates cut out of books, deep reds and blues, and drawings in ink on paper, hanging by nails.

'No one ever comes here,' she said.

She went back into the hallway and held open the other door. She gestured for me to enter. I stepped into a large emptiness, the ceiling high, the wooden floorboards sending out an echo. There were some bulked shapes, but I couldn't see them. She moved past me to the far wall and opened the curtains. A weak blue morning light leaked in. She stood still by the window looking down at the shapes that I could see then were sculpted white horses, four of them, smaller than life but the size at least of large hounds, set in a crescent in the centre of the room. They were all perfectly formed, muscles tensed, eyes brown and imploring, veins raised in the flesh, teeth bared, a streak of grey across the flank of one, a blond forelock on another, all of them caught unposed in the midst of a moment of life or death. I stood in the doorway looking at them.

The first was on its side, head thrown back, mouth fully open in what would be a cry if I could have heard it, the forelegs limp and broken, the hind legs two bloody stumps, raw bone pushing through the flanks. In the gut was a wide wound. Through the hole, sagging downwards, were the grey-brown and purple organs of the horse. Soon this horse would die.

The second horse was pictured in the moment of crashing to the ground, its four legs snared in a coil of barbed wire. Its neck was flattened along the wooden floorboards of the room. Its ears were down, its eyes partly closed from the force of the fall. Its hindquarters were raised because the back legs were nearly straight from the way they were hobbled by the barbed wire. There were drops of blood from where the pointed shards of wire entered the flesh of the horse. This horse seemed unaware as yet of what had happened to it.

The next horse was emerging from sand. The sand was heaped in a dome on the floor, the horse coming up out of it, only its front visible as it struggled upwards from where it had been buried, the right foreleg free and crocked, the head inclined to the side, the eyes half closed and the mane flying as it shook the sand from itself.

The fourth horse, a colt, was standing, its legs splayed. It seemed uncertain of how it got to this position and unwilling to test its ability to walk forward. It looked amazed at the strange piece of luck of being able finally to get to its feet. Its head was bowed but it was looking upward, towards the door, where I was standing.

I looked over to Angelina.

'You did that?' I said.

She nodded.

'Well, you asked,' she said.

In the days that followed I went to my office like a sleepwalker. I attended to my papers. When I could no longer resist it I wrote Angelina a note. I went from the office to her. We cooked meals on her gas ring, we walked under the trees and then we found each other again on the mattress we put on the floor as though it was something new each time. I went back to my desk the next morning, often without sleep. There is something that carries you at times like this. I have seen it shining through the eyes.

Gottfried seemed to see it. Whenever he passed me he bounced back as though he'd walked into a spring. He laid his hands down gently on my desk, he tilted his head, he smiled a little coquettishly. He told me jokes, he asked me if I'd heard what the English had done in Africa, or if the shipment of eggs had gone to Lübben. One day he called me into his office and told me he believed that he was to be given new responsibilities in military transport. He did not know when but he thought it could be soon. He took a bottle of vodka from a drawer in his desk. He would have some influence over how his position would be filled, he said. He poured us each a glass, smiled.

We drank the vodka and then had two more. The meaning of the order sheets, the eggs, the Party and Gottfried seemed far away. It was as if we were speaking to each other from hilltop to hilltop, wind scattering the words. All that was real was Angelina. We moved on to a bar and drank more, our jackets off, our ties loosened. I thought it was as well to be passing the time that way as any other, for Angelina had gone to the library to look at pictures of horses. We spoke about Wilhelm the bookkeeper who was making his way steadily through his club's chess championship, Ernst the driver, who took back roads all the way to Bad Freinwalde at the Polish border and when he arrived and opened the back door of the truck was nearly drowned in a flood of broken eggshells and yolk. Gottfried bent over helpless with laughter, his fat little hands beating on his knees. He turned then to our office, his 'little team of immigrants', as he called us. How were we managing, how were we settling in? Well, very well, I told him. We have a laugh among ourselves, I said, it's not just eggs and eggs only, and I told him about Pawel's parties and his pranks, the use he made of the knots he learned in the Boy Scouts. Gottfried nodded, laughing again, that soft, tolerant, fatherly laugh we heard every day.

'And Dieter,' he said. 'I worry about him. He seems so frail and solemn.'

I told him it was true that Dieter put himself under great strain. His commitment was so fierce, yet he lacked strength. 'I worry about him too,' I said, and I told him about that day we sat together in the bus coming back to Berlin from the farms, how he turned to me with those pale blue eyes and asked how it was possible to never stop believing, even for a moment, to carry such a weight.

'Yes,' he said. 'Those pale blue eyes.'

*　　*　　*

From a rooftop high above the street I watched the white and gold clouds roll and churn, the sky blue and bright all around them. They moved as though in huge vats boiling, white columns of froth thrown up into the air. It was evening, the richness of the light deepening into a yellow-orange as the sun descended. I looked down. Tremendous shafts of concentrated light poured through gaps in the clouds and hit trams, steeples, walls, windows, faces. I saw everything magnified – creases in iron, the tiny pits in the bricks. This glory of love.

I looked down into the street. A rectangle of light with some rose in it hit the pavement as Angelina rounded the corner in a yellow dress. She walked directly into the light. There was never to be a time when I would be ready for this, the shock I got at the way she was made, the way she moved. A small round man in a long coat and with a walking stick scuttled past her with steps so short it seemed he was on wheels and then turned to watch her until she reached the door, his hand on his stick. She shook her head, her black hair flew and then settled. I heard just her last steps as she reached the landing, her key in the door. I watched her through the open window from the rooftop as she entered the room where we lived. She was wearing canvas shoes for playing tennis in and white socks made for a man. She took them off, her fingers working the laces. She stood, her back to me. I saw her hands move down along the front of her as she unbuttoned her yellow dress. She lifted it from her shoulders and it fell. She turned, just herself, her arms opening to draw me to her.

I returned to my room after eleven consecutive days with Angelina. I needed shirts, and a book I would like her to read.

I found a letter with a postmark from the Crimea. It was from the General, the one who went swimming with Jerzy in the middle of the night and then talked with him until dawn and later sat in front of me in a restaurant in Berlin eating enough for ten.

He wrote,

'I greet you from the Crimea, where we are on manoeuvres with the Poles. What I have to say concerns our mutual friend. I have not been in contact with him since the time I was teaching at the academy, but one of the Polish officers has given me news of him. This news has disturbed me.

'As you no doubt know he left the academy with the highest distinctions. He returned to Poland and has been ascending through the ranks of the army there. I am told that there is no more brilliant young officer in that country. Of that, my source tells me, no one is in doubt. Great things are expected of him.

'Recently the academy invited him back to give a series of political lectures. This is a considerable honour for so young an officer. He arrived one month early and spent all the time that was available to him in the library. He read there, at meals and back in his room at night. Then he would think. He was putting a great strain on himself. The impression I have been given is that he was attempting to arrive at a complete understanding of the workings of power in the world. Comrades began to note that his behaviour was becoming strange. He rarely slept. He could be seen down in the courtyard of the academy standing absolutely still with his back against a tree through the whole of the night. He did not speak with others.

'The first lectures went badly. His voice was weak, he made all manner of mistakes with dates, places and names. Occasionally he would lose his train of thought and could not recover unless he returned to the beginning. This you will find surprising, I am sure.

'On the fourth day he entered the lecture hall, took up his

position at the lectern and looked down at his notes. The students waited, but Jerzy said nothing. He looked up at them and they could see in his eyes that he was trying to say something, but he could not speak. They went to him then and found him frozen there by the lectern. My young friend, something seemed to have broken inside him. They had to carry him out. He was nine weeks in a military hospital in Moscow.

'Now he is in Poznan. His wife is with him. I am told he speaks more or less normally, but he reads nothing at all. He is also eating a great deal. This is to do with a theory he has about the restoration of his strength. There is every wish to accommodate him there in Poznan. Much is still expected of him. But they are anxious. His weight has increased from 79 kilograms to 102.

'Forgive me for writing to you with this news, young comrade. You should be assured that your friend is in good hands. His wife is there, there is a psychiatrist in attendance and his fellow officers wish him well and are ready to assist him in every way. But his problems are not yet over. I felt helpless when I heard this story. Perhaps you can imagine. I did not know where to turn. I thought of you because his family are all dead or far away and to my knowledge you are his closest friend.'

I stood at the foot of the bed where I no longer slept. I felt the spreading of a stain, the sense of something vague shaming me. I did not look for the root of it. I took the letter, my shirts, the book for Angelina, and I went out into the street towards her, everything I was flowing towards her. I heard my footsteps sound against the walls, nervous footsteps here in Berlin. I thought, and as I did the shame came back. I tried to concentrate on Jerzy. I saw him with his shoulders down nearly to the ground, hinged on one leg, the line of his back pointed up to the sky like a heron bending to water, his calm eyes following the flight of the discus across Pan Kazimierz's lawn. I saw him before our class explaining the workings of the internal combustion engine. I saw him in his white suit, a shaft of sunlight hitting him as he said goodbye. Did the story about what happened at the academy become corrupted by the time it reached the General? Was the General playing a trick? Was Jerzy? What force could there be in him that he could not control?

I told Angelina the story of Jerzy as written by the General. We ate fish on the floor with candles spread around us and drank a bottle of wine given me by Gottfried. Later the last of the candle was flickering, beads of wax slithering to the floor. Angelina's head was on my shoulder, her breath slow and regular, her long leg wrapped in a single stitch around mine. I was awake trying to think of what to do about Jerzy. I thought of going to him in Poznan. But there was the money, the explanation I would have to give to Gottfried. Of Angelina alone in Berlin while I was in Poland I did not wish to think at all. I thought then of writing to him. The General had given me his address at the bottom of his letter. I thought of how I should approach such a letter, what he might best be able to receive. A few phrases formed, and then there was sleep. I carried the thought of it around with me in the days that followed, trying to get it right and clear, imagining the moment when I would write it. Sometimes I forgot about it for a few days, then the idea came back.

But I did not go to him. I did not write to him. This man who as a boy held the bully Feliks with the mule's teeth by the throat against a tree and told him to apologise to me. One year after his bad time at the academy he was sent to Africa to run a mine. I did not see him again until long after he returned.

I felt something small and sharp strike me on the side of the head, just over the ear. I had to think for a moment of where I was. A political meeting, I could see, from which my attention had strayed. I saw a small ball of paper in a fold in my grey trousers. I turned to my left and saw Pawel. He was pulling at his moustache and grinning and about to throw another small ball of paper at my head. He was trying to get me to look at something, but I did not look, I turned instead to face the front of this room in which there were maybe forty others in their office suits facing a long table occupied by Gottfried, two local Party officials and the Russian named Odiniktsev I then clearly remembered we had been assembled to hear. He was slender, pale, fair, good-looking, I would say. A kind of speed and sinewiness about the arms. His jacket was off, his tie had been loosened, the sleeves of his white shirt had been rolled up. A small, blond goatee. Difficult to imagine him drunk, or at least drunk and having a good time. He did not try to draw us in through his manner of speaking. He did not try to charm us. He spoke instead with the steadiness of winter rain of Russia and the Red Army and the German advance towards Stalingrad: '. . . and when their vehicles could not make progress through the mud they shot our prisoners and laid out their bodies like planks to make a road. They took our food, demolished our homes for firewood. They rained bombs down on us, they slaughtered orphans, they rounded up tens of thousands of our citizens telling them it was for relocation and then shot them and threw them into pits. They sought to end our culture, our nation, the bright flame of liberation which we held up to the rest of humanity. Those of us they did not kill they tried to turn into slaves. This is the naked sadism and egomania of the mystical Fascist. But . . .' I had heard this before, but though I did not find it displeasing I turned back to Pawel. When he saw me looking at him he held up a square of paper. I had to lean over to see it well. It was a drawing made with a pencil. It depicted a hyena standing up on its hind legs

140

on the back of a saddled donkey. In the manner of the posters of the time, the chin of the hyena was held high, his chest was out, wind was blowing through his hair and he carried in his front paw a large spanner. There was a drawing of the sun in the corner with the rays coming out as if they were pouring over the face of the hyena. Pawel had drawn a goatee on him in case I did not understand that this was a picture of Odiniktsev. And with the donkey he was equally clear. The moustache, the broken front tooth, the two thick eyebrows angling upwards towards the middle like regimental pistols were those of Gottfried. He had even placed a smouldering pipe in the donkey's front hoof. It was not the funniest joke ever made by Pawel. But there was something about the smug displeasure of the hyena as he rode towards the setting sun and the eagerness to please of the donkey that were exactly right. And that pipe, the smoke rising up around its ears. I held myself taut but I felt a fit of unstoppable laughter forming within me such as afflicts schoolboys during particularly solemn moments in the classroom or in church. I knew that the more I tried to escape it the worse it would become. Pawel caught it, as always happens in cases such as this. He was even worse than me because he felt it was the glory of his wit which had made me so helpless. We tried to hold our breath and look straight ahead at the Russian, but it was no use. We knew that if our eyes met we were finished. We ducked down behind the backs of those in the row in front of us, our torsos convulsed, our hands beating at the sides of our legs, tears streaming from our eyes. Just when it seemed we had stopped and we made to rise to our former positions, it hit us again and we dived down.

Odiniktsev's oration continued.

'And now we in the socialist world are struggling to implement our various national plans. We are striving to liberate the peasantry from ignorance and poverty with a new way forward in agriculture. We are rebuilding industry from the wreckage and bringing security, health and education to the masses. We are forming a new culture. Great progress has already been made and yet we are only taking our first steps along this road.

'I ask you to look to the example of the Red Army in the face of the Nazi advance. What sustained them? What was the source of their heroism? Patriotism, yes. Hatred of Fascism. Belief. Acceptance of sacrifice. These things, yes. But there was also vigilance. For all that they faced from the brutality and firepower of the Fascists they faced also the enemy within – cowards, deserters, turncoats, paid agents. Our intelligence services had ceaselessly to comb through the ranks to rid our army of this infestation. Justice in these cases was swift and exacting. It had to be. We were fighting for the survival of freedom, for the future of civilisation itself.

'I ask you now to look at two further examples. They are in every way different from the soldiers of the victorious Red Army. I choose them not only because of who they are and what they have done, but also for what they represent.

'In the first case we have a man with a past. This past was not revealed voluntarily, but rather through actions and words let slip in an unguarded moment. The meaning of vigilance is not to react to something that has already happened. It is to anticipate. It is to look all around a person – his tastes, his past, his family and his associates. I present you with the case of Pawel Gorny.'

Pawel and I looked at each other. I felt the blood drain from my face. What had he done? The drawing? Our laughter? Maybe that his parties had been making too much noise? We listened to Odiniktsev.

'A Pole, as most of you will know. But what is he doing here, in Berlin, capital of the new German Democratic Republic, first line of defence, I need not remind you, of invasion from the

West? This we do not yet know. Perhaps we never will. But the question should cause us to look a little further. And what do we find? Father a professor of economics at the University of Warsaw before the war. Mother from a land-owning family. Both capitalists. Both class enemies. Of this there can be no doubt. When a child he joins the deceivingly named Boy Scouts, a proto-Fascist youth movement founded in England and exported around the world for the purpose of spreading its reactionary philosophy. And what happens when his country is invaded? Does he join the partisans? No, I am afraid he does not. Instead he joins the Home Army with its oath of allegiance to the reactionary government-in-exile in London. Well, you may say, a person can see the light, can they not? They can change. I remind you that we are at war. A war fought not with artillery and bayonets and bullets, but with ideas. We face a corrupt but for some seductive ideology, heavily financed and dispatched to us with cunning and treachery through its agents. They have the idea in the West that if they wait long enough and work hard enough we will rot from within, and fall into their hands. Can we look the other way in cases like that of Pawel Gorny? I think we must all agree. We cannot afford to.'

I turned again to Pawel. He was looking down at his hands and feet as if they did not belong to him.

'I have spoken of the qualities that sustained the Red Army during the Nazi onslaught. Think of them among the fires and broken buildings of Stalingrad, fighting with shovels and knives. And even with their hands. Victory came to them because of their belief in its necessity. No other result could be contemplated. Even in the face of the most terrifying assaults, unbroken during all hours of the day and night, month after month, their supplies all but gone, bodies piling up around them, they did not doubt. Think of those men, and then think of the second example I bring before you. Dieter Kroll. Another who has come to Berlin from elsewhere, in his case England. This Berlin so saturated with spies. Welcomed into the Party. Given a home, a job, access to our industrial workers and cultural groups. Yet it seems that Dieter Kroll is suffering from a crisis in belief. What is it that has brought him to this? Torture? A bribe? Intellectual anguish? No. It was an argument among farmers in a village hall. That was enough to undermine Dieter Kroll's belief in our socialism. We must ask ourselves, comrades, is this the kind of man we need in the Party?

'What has brought this to light? We return again to vigilance. In these cases the vigilance of Comrade Gottfried here and a young man working in his department. It is them that we have to thank. Vigilance and belief. Each has no use without the other.

'I have only a single motion to put before you, comrades. The expulsion of Dieter Kroll and Pawel Gorny from the Party. Our courts will attend to the rest. Who is in favour?'

The engineer in charge of the boilers in our building raised his hand first. The others knew what they were to do. I kept my hands in my lap and looked over at Pawel. He was stuffing his cartoon into his briefcase. I stood and walked towards him. He sensed me there and looked up at me.

'Fuck you,' he said. 'Fuck you and fuck your Party. What's the prize for your vigilance? Are they going to make you chief egg distributor? Don't come anywhere near me again. And if you need a pimp, look somewhere else.'

He stood and walked to the door. There was the sound of chairs scraping across the floor and briefcases snapping shut. Odiniktsev, Gottfried and the two officials were leaning into each other, conferring. Office workers stood up in their suits and stretched their arms as though they had just risen from sleep. I watched Pawel, and then saw Dieter. He was backing out of the room, his hand raised toward me, his mouth opening and closing as if he was looking for air, his blue gaze going into me like a blade.

Dieter and Pawel did not return to the office for distributing eggs. I did not see them again. Two Germans not far from the age of retirement took their places within a few weeks. Gottfried stayed on, but told me he was soon to take up his new position with military transport. He was not alone, he told me, in noting my abilities. I asked him nothing about Dieter and Pawel. There was a form of silence we assumed about individuals when those individuals entered into an unfortunate conflict with the progress of History. It was the boiler engineer in the building who told me what had happened. Pawel was cutting trees in a gulag and Dieter was undergoing psychiatric treatment in the hospital wing of a prison outside the city of Chemnitz.

I tell the stories of Dieter, Pawel and Jerzy because they happened. Those were the times we lived in and that is the way that we were. I offer them in good faith and with the hope that it will be understood that they are not told here for entertainment or to lift the weight of my guilt or, least of all, to offer vindication to those who later triumphed when the whole edifice came falling down around us. What did we do by not keeping our movement whole? We let ourselves be washed over by greed and vapidity and the virus of loneliness. How did it happen? We became paranoid. Was that to do with the guns and the words that were aimed at us from the West or the spies that came to us from there and moved beneath us in places we could not see? Did I hear somewhere that it is only the paranoids who are in full possession of the facts? What about us was so offensive? Well, who knows or cares now. I tell the stories to describe a sadness.

A dream was broken. It was a beautiful dream to have when Jerzy first showed it to me as we looked out over all that had been ruined by war. A dream in which to believe. It was company for me. It transported me from one part of my life to another. For Jerzy it was more than that. It was, for a time, all that he was.

Jerzy, as ever, was a spectator with a better view. He saw revolutionaries with their own beautiful dreams come together and harden into a caste. He saw the Party bear down on the people, the Central Committee bear down on the Party and the Dictator bear down on them all. He saw the whole ugly apparatus of gulags and spies and bullets put into people's heads in the night profaning his belief and his labour. He had already seen it by the time he was to deliver his lectures at the military academy. There is not much thought spared any of it now. But for Jerzy then it was an anguish. His mind could not hold together all that he knew and saw and felt. He ate until he nearly exploded. He took his family to Africa. They waited with him until he was ready to return.

The dream I had was light. It pleased me to look at it and to think of it. I struggled for a time to give it more substance. I thought it right to do that. I was responsible to it and guided by it, but I never gave myself to it. Not wholly. I hadn't the means. When it went it was a sadness, nevertheless. It happened inside me before I knew about it in my mind. Some kind of internal alignment had shifted. I could no longer receive what I had received in the past. I went on looking for it, I yearned for it at times, but it was gone. It wasn't because of Jerzy and what I imagined he had seen. It wasn't Angelina, at least not altogether. Nor was it Gottfried or Odiniktsev and what they did to Pawel and Dieter. I did not see them as bad men. They were men of faith. They bore the marks that had earned them this faith. For me, it was more to do with Pan Kazimierz and his spectacular coat made of seal pelts, his ungainly hair, his poems and his frenzied dancing, the melancholy sound he could get from his violin when he went into his orchard in the evening, the day he broke down in the corridor of his school when a small boy looked up into his eyes and handed him a pear. I remember him running out of his house in a snowstorm with a bottle of vodka and then sailing off the roof of a barn astride a barrel. He landed in a snow bank buried up to his neck and then he got up and did it again. He couldn't stop laughing. I studied him. I followed him. I loved him. I tried to be like him. He stayed with me through my years in Berlin. It was he who caused that movement inside me, it was he who would not continue to receive the dream, it was he who would not tolerate everlasting method, the controlled and scrutinised life, History as science, charts and programmes and manifestos and Five Year Plans and posters of blonde-haired women driving tractors, their blue eyes alight and their jaws set as they rumbled on into the future. It could not be. Yet it was a sadness, this passing, for when it went there was vacancy.

What was Angelina like? She had dark hair to the shoulders. Brown eyes. She wore plain dresses without sleeves cut just above the knee, a long scarf around her neck. She moved silently. You couldn't think she was much in the world, the way her eyes were. They so rarely seemed to be looking at anything directly. She liked to walk at night. Always she seemed a little out of focus. You couldn't entirely see her. She looked as if she was listening to music only she could hear.

She could not abide the company of women. She liked schnapps, and she liked red wine. She particularly liked the red wine that came to us in those days from Hungary. No matter how much of it she drank, her step would be no less certain. Her step was slow and smooth. She could look amused sometimes, her lips turned up at just one corner. You wouldn't know the thought that brought this about, and you would not ask her. But if you told her something that really got to her – something grotesque, some story of human helplessness – she could lose all control. Her laughter would threaten her breath and she made sounds that were without grace, her arms moving like a drowning person's.

You could not say that truly she had warmth, or sympathy, or honour. She could be vain, in her quiet way. I would think that if a person passed out of her life, a picture would remain of that person, and a story, but no feeling. She lived in what was around her, with the past far away. It was as if anything that had happened to her up to any one time was all in another country. She was without fear. She never complained. She could follow each turn of your mind, see where the light fell and where was the shade. She could take you by surprise in a hallway or in a park. She would look down at your lips and then up into your eyes and you would feel yourself falling down into her as though from the top of a cliff. She felt her beauty deeply. You could see it in the way she looked at a painting or a waterfall. In an instant she could make the world around you go away and there would be only you and her. I was awed by the way she arranged her long slender arms, the movement of her eyes when she looked to the side, the way she folded her things before placing them in drawers, the splay of her fingers when she ate an apple. I go around and around and always I come back to this. I cannot make it stop. I cannot break it.

You could never feel you had the whole of her. But all the same, I gave myself to her piece by piece.

Last night when sleep would not come I watched the end of a movie on the television. It seemed to be about a family living in

148

a small town in America. I watched the husband leaving home for work, his wife at the front door waving goodbye to him. It was a sunny morning, the light falling through the trees on to her face. She had a towel in her hand, a little apron around her waist. Her hair was tied up with a ribbon. She was pretty and slender. Her eyes sparkled in the sunlight. She was loyal and honest and devoted and bore life's iniquities with steadiness and without complaint. The music rose as she watched her husband. She was full of love for him. His weaknesses could not lessen it. How fine to have a woman like that at our side, we think, or are meant to think. But it is not this kind of woman, for some reason, that I have been drawn to, nor M. either, it would seem. It is not this kind of woman that enters into our beings like an opiate and has us running out into the night.

I am alone here and will be. I hit the wall with my small bony fist in a sudden and useless fury for all the years I do not and did not have Angelina with me.

I did not tell Angelina what I heard from the boiler engineer about Pawel and Dieter for nearly a week. I came and went heavy with the thought of them and of Jerzy. 'Why are you staring at walls?' she asked me. 'Am I?' I said. 'I hadn't realised.' And I hadn't. I heard about them on a Monday and on Sunday I made her a stew of pork and olives I bought from a colleague who had been to Yugoslavia. We had it with some beer. Afterwards I lost the track of something she was saying. She reached up and turned my face towards her with her hand. 'What it is?' she said. I told her where Pawel and Dieter were, and about my part in putting them there. She took a short breath. She drew me in towards her. I lay with my head on her chest, her hand running through my hair. She shook her head as if she heard slow music. I listened to her heartbeat. She held me close to her. We lay like this in the silence, the sky darkening, the light in the room just a faint pale grey. I felt her warmth, the roundness of her breasts. I kissed her neck, her ear. I moved up and kissed her mouth. She shifted until I was above her, her hands holding my face. She drew me down and we kissed again. She began to move beneath me. I felt a vapour, warm and thick, rising from her skin. I breathed it in. It seemed to concentrate. She reached for me, her legs falling open around me, and then I was inside her. Her back was like a drawn bow, the veins high in her neck, the skin flushed a pale rose, her hands behind to pull me to her, a flame scurrying over the ends of my nerves, the thick humidified cloud rising from her body and circling my head, and this was all there was, no thought, no pictures, no past or future or any other being, just this here and now holding all pain and sadness and power and wonder, just this brimming over of life one into the other until we reached the end, she and I, in a moment somewhat different from what we had known, the note of it high and sustained until it faded, slowly, waveringly, like a falling leaf. We lay beside each other in the darkness, our breathing slow. After a long while she moved on to her side to face me.

'There's nothing for us here,' she said.

'No?'

'You know it. It's impossible. We must leave.'

'But how?'

'Just leave.'

'Where do we go?'

'Somewhere else.'

'Yes?'

'To the forest, to the sea. I don't know. We'll find a way.'

I looked into her eyes. I could see nothing else.

'All right,' I said.

II

Jerzy

I did not see Jerzy until 1983.

Before that I was in Chicago digging ditches for water pipes. It was good work with good money, transistor radios sitting up on the lawns beside us playing the baseball games while we worked, cold beer afterwards in the summer nights in the taverns with the Mexicans, the college boys and the Mississippi blacks in our little team. There were a couple of young brothers from Nowy Targ there too. The housewives would go by in their little skirts looking at us out of the corners of their eyes. But the knees were troubling me. I suppose it was the damp down under the ground. And I was wearing a brace for my back. I took a soft job in a uniform reading electricity meters, going along the alleys with a Commonwealth Edison notebook from basement to basement. They smelt of damp, trapped air, washing powder and stored tins of chemicals. How is it they all smelt the same? I felt a fool in the uniform. It was the kind of work we laughed at when we were riveting girders or laying pipes. I'd feel bad about it when I woke in the morning.

After I trained they put me on a route up in Roger's Park, a quiet, leafy place with little apartment buildings and houses made of brick, tidy lawns in the front. Everyone moved slowly through the dappled, humid air under the trees. I'd talk with the mailmen. We men in uniform. One day I called at a house with green shutters around the windows and roses running up the walls. No one answered and I made to move away, but then I saw a face looking up at me from the basement, a very pretty face full of sharp angles as if made from cut glass, neat black hair around it. She had a hammer in her hand, gold braided earrings in her ears. She was laughing at me. I was listening through earphones to a tape player I kept in my pocket and hadn't heard her calling. Just as I saw her I caught myself singing along to a line in the song 'That's Amore' by Dean Martin. I followed her in through the basement door and read the meter. She was trying to fix a light to a wall down there and was having a bad time with it, so I helped her. She gave me coffee then and we talked for so long through the afternoon in her kitchen that I had to sprint from building to building through the final hour of the working day to get through all the meters that had been assigned me. That was Maggie Collins. I found her number in the telephone book and called her and we went out for an ice-cream and a long drive along the lake shore. We kept on then through the summer, strolls around her neighbourhood, barbecues in her back yard. She took me to the opera. One weekend when her two teenaged boys were visiting their father who now lived in Columbus, Ohio, we rented a small house among trees beside a lake in Wisconsin. I cooked the breakfasts, she cooked the dinners and we put our lunch in a straw basket and took it out with us in a boat that came with the house. I couldn't imagine her having a malign thought about anybody. How would the run of my life have been had we met at another time? I don't know. I was very well with her. But whenever I came to see her I'd have to step around her sons' baseball gloves and bicycles in the hall. Out ahead of me were more jobs in uniform or sweeping somewhere. I could do the jobs but when I looked at all the rest of it I didn't see where I could fit. I didn't say anything but she felt a turning away, I think. I regret that still. I'd see her looking out through the screen door of her kitchen as it blew in the wind, wishing she were on the other side of it for a while when the silence went on too long. We went out walking one evening to a park that had a pond and tennis courts and a little zoo with ostriches, a llama and a big black bear. We sat on a bench. It had been so easy with her that summer, the way her hand slipped into mine, the way the talk flowed, but on this evening even before they formed in my mind the words had a sour taste. They were weak, they didn't go anywhere. They were false. I couldn't find the way to improve them. I listened to the hisses and squawks and complaints of the animals, the ringing sound of the tennis balls being struck. I told her I'd been thinking a lot about Poland. I couldn't get it out of my mind. I missed it. It had been twenty-seven years. I owed debts to people there. There was my sister. The taste of the words grew more rancid as I spoke them. She had been looking up at me through sunglasses and now she took them off. Her green eyes were vivid and direct. I felt an ache there in the silence and in the presence of those eyes. 'Would you like to come?' I said. I hadn't planned that. It just came out because I lost my nerve. It was ridiculous. She searched my face for some kind of explanation. She looked for a moment as she might have looked as a teenaged girl when faced with something her years had not prepared her for. Then her features reassembled and cleared. She smiled. She pressed my hand between hers. 'Write to me,' she said. 'Will you?'

I flew into Warsaw with a single suitcase. I took a train to Krakow and called on Renata. She gave me herrings and vodka and told me that since I'd last seen her in Chicago she'd already passed through her second marriage.

'That was something you didn't write about in your Christmas cards,' I said.

'It all happened between Christmases,' she said. 'From start to finish.'

'That was fast.'

'I give thanks for that.'

'Who was he?'

'A little round man you wouldn't notice. Wojtek Barski. Spoiled from birth.'

'Where is he now?'

'Back where he came from, with his mother. He couldn't bear to be without his mother. He was always telling me that I *failed* to cook in the manner of his mother. Can you imagine? That's just the way he put it.'

'That's bad luck.'

'Bad luck has nothing to do with it. It's the way it is. If men are anywhere over forty at all and they're alone, they're simply *ruined.*'

'Me too?' I said.

She laughed. She poured out more vodka and we had a long night of it together, but whatever debt I had to Renata I didn't manage to pay, not then anyway. I never gave it the time. I had more debts in the north, and I headed out by bus the next morning to Szczecin. They let us out every now and again in the little towns on the way. I had a hat on with the name of a Chicago baseball team and a walk set apart from those around me by its quickness. They have a habit of staring at you in these towns, I thought. That was something I hadn't remembered. There were times in my years in America, slow times usually, when I'd think of the sombre colours here in Poland, the sting in the jokes, the farmhouses set among trees. These pictures would quicken into life. I'd had them on the plane all the way from Chicago. But as I moved north through land I knew well enough once I couldn't find those things I had pictured, or at least not the way I had felt about them when I was only imagining. Things faded as I looked at them. The ground didn't seem wholly solid. It was as if a liquid was running along underneath it. My place on it felt uncertain. You will get over this, I told myself, though it may be said that I haven't, not even now, not altogether.

The debt I had in Szczecin was to a man named Piotr. The nature of the debt I will describe later. But I couldn't find Piotr, not in Szczecin, nor in Miedzyzdroje either. No one knew anything of him in those places.

From Szczecin I went east to this place here, this small city from which I am now speaking, for of all the debts I carried through the years since I left the one that troubled me most was the one to Jerzy. There'd been letters both from and about him. I'd had one from his wife Marysia after they came back from Africa telling me that she didn't think he'd quite recovered from whatever had troubled him in Moscow. She was worried. She didn't know where to turn, she said. I'd heard this before, of course, from the General, and I had failed. I sat paralysed with a pen in my hand over a blank sheet of paper and with Marysia's letter beside me for the whole of a Saturday afternoon in the room I had then in Chicago. I couldn't write a word. Finally I got something down the next morning and it was useless. 'Be patient,' I wrote. 'He's a strong man.' Well he was a strong man, the strongest I've known, but not strong enough to prevent his grand and noble mind from veering out of control like a plane whose pilot has lost consciousness. Why could I not do better than that? How many times must I fail to repay something of what I owed him? I walked around the block where his apartment was three times thinking of what I would say to him before climbing the concrete stairs. How would he be? He'd sounded clear, steady, cogent when I'd spoken to him on the telephone. But what if he wasn't?

As I stood on the landing the picture of Jerzy in Naklo with the wind rippling through his white suit before he set out for Moscow entered my mind and when he appeared it seemed he stepped directly into the frame of his younger self. For this first silent instant it was as though I was looking at a double exposure, his hair a muted white now like eggshell, the girth thicker, the clothes more sombre and practical, but his aspect still authoritative and his eyes alight with intelligence. I raised an arm to embrace him but he did not seem to see this or accept it maybe and he directed me inside with a traffic policeman's wave. 'Very well, very well,' he said. 'Come in. We've been expecting you.'

A small woman appeared behind him and he backed up to be at her side. She had grey and blonde in her hair, smooth, slender hands with rings on each finger, and a pale silk scarf tied under her chin, two faint jagged scars rising up from it to the tips of her ears like licks of flame.

'This is Marysia,' said Jerzy. 'You've been hearing about her for nearly forty years and now finally she is before you.'

She extended her hand. She had a smile both warm and ironical. I thought again of the mediocrity of the letter I sent from Chicago and wondered was this the source of her irony.

She and Jerzy went into the kitchen to fill a tray with small cakes and cups of coffee. I heard doors opening and closing and water bubbling and saw them talking animatedly to each other, he with speech, she with hand signals. I moved slowly around the living room as if in a museum, looking at the patterns on the sofa, the titles of books on the shelf, photographs, wooden boxes, the way the carpet was worn before the chair I imagined he sat in, his reading spectacles on the table in front of it, a smudged thumbprint on one of the lenses, trying to see how his life was as he lived it then and wondering if I would find the right words to ask for his forgiveness. I didn't have them yet.

Jerzy and Marysia came in then and placed the things around the table and we sat beside it for this ceremony of welcome. I saw their ease with each other, a physical thing of nods and gestures and indecipherable movements in the face, her rush of hand signals followed by his sudden explosion of laughter – a joke, it seemed, that would remain untranslated – and I saw too his reserve with me. He was too great a figure to me for me to begrudge him any of this. I asked him questions and he answered each with careful thought and economy and no more. Was this how it was to be, I wondered?

After the cups and the plates had been emptied Marysia took them away and then seemed to ask me to excuse her for absenting herself to a chair in an alcove in front of the television. She turned it on, the volume low, the blue and white light from the screen passing over her face through the afternoon shadows. Then she took up a pair of knitting needles and began to work.

'For our granddaughter,' said Jerzy. 'Our third.'

'Yes, I know,' I said. 'I saw her picture.'

We were alone. It was not yet time for me to speak of what I wished finally to rid myself of, yet nothing else arrived. There was a silence then but for the rolling murmur from the television and the clicking of knitting needles during which he studied my face and I felt the seconds sound within me like drumbeats in a slow march. I looked at his farm labourer's hands, the thick fingers laced together, his legs planted before him, his great still head which looked as if it was carved from stone. I needn't have worried about him. He was who he was, neither more nor less. It was my own insubstantiality which I could feel flaring visible as a rash over my skin.

And then maybe out of pity or curiosity he questioned me

about America – the quality of the buildings, the wages of the workers, how the transport worked, the percentage of land given over to agriculture and of the citizens who voted, what way the newspapers were, what I would do on a day when I was not working – until he stopped, cocked his head, and called over to Marysia.

'Where did that happen?' he said.

She moved her hands, her eyes still on the television.

'Radom,' he translated for me, watching her. 'A strike . . . state confiscation of wages . . . a demonstration charged by police . . .' He turned to me. 'Do they speak of these things in America?' he asked.

'The Poles do,' I said. 'Other than that, not very much. You have to look for it in the lower corners of the papers.'

'I would have expected so,' he said.

'What do you think of them?' I asked.

'Who?'

'The people demonstrating.'

'I like them,' he said. 'It's alive, it's interesting. We haven't had much of either, liveliness or interest, as you perhaps know. If that demonstration had been in Warsaw rather than Radom my youngest daughter would have been at it. She's on a Solidarity committee at her university. I might have been there myself. In fact I have been, twice. It's something incontrovertible, and necessary.'

'Are you still in the Party?'

'No. Not for more than twenty years.' He looked at me. 'It's sludge. It has to be swept away. You would know this if you were here. We gave ourselves to something based on a dynamic prin- ciple which lost its capacity to renew itself. That is nothing other than fact.'

He stood up, smiled.

'Let's take a walk along the river,' he said.

He led me out then through this town as yet unknown to me, past the chess players under the trees in the square, out behind the library and then along the tramline, leaves clattering along the cobblestones and around our feet. When we reached the river-bank he took my arm and reminded me of the night we got up from our beds and moved through Pan Kazimierz's ballroom after one of the great parties there, drinking from all the glasses left behind by the guests.

'We got drunk,' I said.

'*You* got drunk,' he said. 'You stood waving back and forth in front of the big mirror in the ballroom. You pointed at my reflection and you said, "That person should be called Adam." Then you pointed at yourself and said, "And he should be called Staszek." Then you fell down. I had to put you over my shoulder to get you to bed.'

We sat down on a bench then and looked at the river. He pointed out the steeples of churches and told me their names, a factory where beet is turned into sugar, a street where a saint is said to have halted a man's fall from the top of a building by pointing his finger at him, potato fields, the beginnings of a forest that spread away to the north and west.

'I fish here sometimes,' he said. 'I didn't think I'd like to do that, but I do.'

Was there an invitation in what he had said? Probably not. He was too self-sufficient to issue invitations of this nature. But I felt I could be well in that place, as well there anyway as some other place. To live and to work there, to feel it growing familiar, to take a walk now and again along this riverbank with him.

'Jerzy?' I said.

His eyes turned towards me, but his face remained set out towards the river.

159

'There is something I must say to you.'

He smiled.

'Say it,' he said.

'It is an apology.'

'For?'

'For not helping you when you were having trouble.'

'And when do you suppose that I was having trouble?'

'When you went back to Moscow to give the lectures.'

'I don't understand,' he said.

'I heard that you had a bad time there, that you suffered very much.'

'From whom did you hear this?'

'From that general you sent to see me in Berlin.'

His eyes returned to the water.

'There was a time when I lost faith. There was another later time when I accepted this. In between these times I struggled to prove my loss of faith to be incorrect. Suffering is too large a word for that. It was more like frustration. It is kind of you to have thought that I needed help, and to have wished to provide it, but the moment was not exceptional.'

He continued to look at the water. This, of course, was meant to bring the subject to an end. Yet I went on.

'But Jerzy, you lost your speech. You were sick. They kept you in hospital.'

'The General was no longer there when I gave the lectures in Moscow.'

'I know. He was in the Crimea. He heard about you there. He was worried.'

He turned around on the bench to face me.

'He must have been misinformed,' he said.

He was looking directly into my eyes. He was very grave. I felt the full weight of his being pressing down on me.

'I see,' I said to him finally. 'I'm relieved to hear it.'

He turned slowly back towards the water.

It is rare that we get our day in court, or at least the one we feared, or wished for. I did not get mine there by the river with Jerzy.

12

I Go Dancing

I have neglected to visit Renata on the anniversary of her husband's death. He was a war hero named Wladyslaw Kovic she'd married in a cellar in Warsaw and then emigrated with to Chicago. There he sliced cured meat in a delicatessen. He was never right in Chicago, Renata said. He couldn't settle. He wouldn't learn the language. They had a little boy whom Renata called Bobby and Wladyslaw called Ryszard, but that didn't help. He began to fear everything in that city – buses, banks, shopkeepers. He'd seen something during the war through the floorboards of an attic he was hiding in. He couldn't be made to talk about it, but it had marked him somehow. When you looked at him you couldn't quite see him. He was like a photograph that had been smeared while being developed. In the end he kept a vigil by the window watching for the parking attendants who patrolled the streets in their uniforms. He couldn't understand their schedules. He thought they'd leave a paper on the window of his car which would cause him problems from which he would never escape. One day he stepped out of the window of their apartment, his pipe still in his hand. 'The coward,' Renata said to me. 'And he had to wait until I was no longer pretty enough to find someone else.'

Still, the day was to be honoured. There are certain days when my absence cannot pass without explanation – her birthday and saints' day, Christmas, this day on which Wladyslaw went sailing like a diving penguin from the window of their apartment in Chicago. I did not even think to lift the telephone. 'Why didn't you come?' she says to me when she calls. 'You know how nervous I get.'

I have nothing to offer in the way of an answer. It's just that I couldn't help it. On that day and the days before and since I have been overcome by a feeling of laziness as irresistible as a tide. I get up and then lie back down on the bed when I have finished my breakfast. I read a book and the words fall like pieces of melting snow from the page. I play cards with myself. By the third day I try to set a limit of just eight hands before lunch, but then I cannot stop myself and I go on until I win or until it gives me a headache. I get a bright idea to polish shoes. I think of going for a walk, put on coat, scarf, hat, gloves, then take them off and sit down again. From the chair I watch the light fade. When I feel the time must have arrived for concentration, I heat soup. I can't get a picture of M. It's as if I'm trying to look at him through smoke. I can't even bring back before me the pictures I have already made, or find the wish to make more.

Why do I feel that I am about to enter into a darkness? Why do I feel that all effort is just dust thrown in the wind?

I think more than usual about praying and there are times when I actually do it. Mostly I advance and turn about like a fish in an aquarium in a vacant, colourless state that seems primarily an absence of everything else – sadness, happiness, curiosity, hunger. I know nothing at all then but after a time I find I can concentrate for a moment. Then I feel bad about Renata or about M., or about the books in the library which have not been consulted, or about the condition of my mind which in these days has resembled an unmade bed. There are moments when I look nervously to the future for what may already be drained from it, or when shame races like a lizard up the length of my spine. I had not known such things before, being pushed here and there into parts of myself I never visited. It began with M. in Krakow. But why all this commotion? It's only thinking and remembering. And making pictures. It is a companion of a kind, yes, I will say that, but an unruly, quarrelsome one that never seems to go out of the door. Or if it does I mourn it and sit in my chair like now waiting for its return. I am too old for this, no?

Here in the room just now the shutters are closed. I can't know if the morning has arrived, or if it's still the night. M. is in the room like currents of air. I feel them moving around me, all his different possible selves. Which is the true one? The physicist Erwin Schrödinger said that a thing unobserved will propagate endless possibilities about what will become of it, but once this collection of possibilities is observed – say by a measuring device in an experiment – all the possibilities except one disappear and only that one thing remains.

I see now how the process works. I think of M. and in their time the words themselves make a single selection. Maybe the words do not concur with the true nature of a thing that has happened, or is felt – if there can be a true nature of something that has happened or is felt – but if they have the right arrangement they carry a truth of their own, or a semblance of one. They give me a way to understand, and to move on.

I walk out. I have the intention of buying bread and paying the bill for my consumption of electricity, but I pass Mrs Slowacki's shop without entering and when I arrive at the turning for the post office I go the other way. I feel the cold tauten the skin on my face. There are fine points of blue reflected light sparkling like stars in the snow. I have brought the photographs of Hanna with me for I fear thieves. It wasn't so long ago that we didn't have thieves. I stop at the entrance to an arcade to look at them and then move on again. It is the hour of school and of work. I am among a sparse crowd of salesmen and the old and infants with their mothers, all of us labouring along the cold pavements behind the white columns of steam which rise from our mouths. As I walk I have in my mind the photograph of her with her dishevelled hair and skewed look. I have looked at this picture every day since bringing it back with me from Krakow, yet it looked odd to me there just a moment ago, unfamiliar, as though I knew nothing about her. Who is this woman anyway, not as M. saw her, or I, but in herself? What matter any of it, for it is just words thrown out like cards in a hand of solitaire, for M. cannot hear them fall, he or anyone else. But why does it seem as if she has stepped wholly made out of a bank of cloud? Why do her stories have the feeling of something composed rather than lived? Why is she without a man, or even a story of one from the past? What is the cause of her opaqueness? She is not part of our great community of the wounded and stumbling and myopic. But of what community is she? What of that ring she said she borrowed from the woman upstairs from the bar? Those papers in Barcelona? And of course the man in the wheelchair? They suggest something tangible, yet out of the range of M.'s knowledge. And mine. Something is moving there.

I look up now and find that I am walking along a road without pavements and no one around me, the last of the town's buildings behind me and ahead of me huge silent fields stretching away to a distant forest, all of them covered with unbroken snow.

* * *

After my days of behaving like a mote of dust in the air I hear a rap on the door, very light. The sound is so strange and surprising that I let out a call like a dog whose tail has been stepped on. I get up from the sofa and go to the door. I put my eye to the little hole and see that it is Jacob. He looks very grave. I begin to laugh. I try to bring this laughter to an end, but I cannot. So I let him in then just as I am, stubble sprouting like weeds on my chin and the hair standing up on my head, a little embarrassed about being barefoot and in my pyjamas at 7 p.m. but still laughing. I am very happy to see him. He seems too big for the door. He narrows his shoulders, ducks his head. He looks at me and says in a whisper, 'Are you all right?'

I tell him I am fine and bring him into the room. He can't see very well because his glasses are fogged from the cold. He rubs them clean and then takes from inside his coat a bottle of whiskey and hands it to me. I take away the plates and cups which have been spreading like a mould around the room. I shave and pass a comb through my hair. I put on clean clothes and then come out and sit across from him, a glass for each of us. I feel as though I've awoken wholly remade after a long coma, that I am part of a vast army experiencing this same thing.

He tells me he's had a day off.

'I needed it,' he says. 'I've been reading too much. Nothing more would go into my head.'

Like me! I think. Then I say to him, 'What did you do?'

'I made an excursion,' he says. He rose very early, took a train to Krakow and then went by bus to the salt mine at Wieliczka. He'd been wanting to see it ever since his father first described it to him in his village in Africa.

'Do you know it?' he asks me.

I tell him that I do not.

'You would love it,' he says. 'Copernicus went there and one of the chambers is named after him. The salt in it is pure green!'

Green salt! I have to turn away and walk over to the table and think of something else, for laughter threatens to overtake me again. What is happening to me?

I suggest that we watch a football match on the television in the hope that it will calm me. I go into the kitchen and collect two large bottles of beer. That is the correct drink for football, I tell myself. We'll have the whiskey later. I find a game being broadcast from Germany between a team from Frankfurt and another from Thessaloniki. The game is tied at one all with only minutes remaining. The Germans look so disdainful that Jacob and I immediately align ourselves with the Greeks, and in partic- ular with one very short Greek player with long hair arranged into a ponytail on the top of his head as though his brains are bubbling up in a black fountain and who is racing frantically around the pitch like an insect trapped in a box. The minutes tick on and the Greeks seem unable to hold on to the ball. I look over at Jacob. His fists are clenched on his knees. I feel as if a trigger has been pressed inside me and that laughter or tears or even some wild expression of love will come flying out of me like bullets.

As the game enters the final two minutes both teams accel- erate the pace. The Germans press forward like a thunderstorm and the Greeks move among them with a rhythmical grace we had not seen before. The tackling is vigorous. No one can hold the ball for a sustained period. Then with seconds to go on the clock the Germans move in very fast on the Greek goal, there is a great chaos of leaping and flailing bodies, a German foot connects with the ball and sends it crashing into the post, from which it returns directly on to the same player's forehead, rebounding powerfully towards the corner of the net and it seems all over as the goalie stretches desperately and Jacob lets out a long bird-like cry, but then a red-headed German with a long moustache and a melancholy look running across the mouth of the goal and not having seen what has happened receives the ball flush on the side of his face, leaving it to dribble quietly over the touchline while he collapses face-down on the pitch.

Now we are in injury time. Jacob is gripping his bottle of beer so tightly that I wonder will it splinter in his hand. The ball seems for minutes to be moving back and forth within just a few metres of the midfield line with occasional long kicks by the goalies. Jacob and I are speaking only in grunts and sighs. The Germans make a break for the goal, which results in a corner, but nothing comes of it. The referee has by now looked twice at his watch.

Then a long clearance by a Greek defender finds one of his own players well into German territory by the right touchline. The whole of both teams charge downfield. The player with the ball on the wing is moving down into the corner and looks as if he will be trapped until he feints right with such violent force that the German defender falls to the turf. The Greek steps forward and now with a clear view and plenty of time sends the ball into the centre, where it is taken on the chest of the Greek with the ponytail sprouting on the top of his head. He drops the ball lightly on to the toe of his right foot. The camera moves in on his face. He is smiling and his wide brown eyes have a dreamy look as if he's just finished lunch. Around him the German players are diving and lungeing and kicking, their faces grimacing like souls in hell. The Greek is tapping the ball up and down on his foot as though he is alone on the field. When a player moves in on him he directs the ball through their legs or over their shoul-ders and picks it up on the other side. His own players look incredulous, their hands on their hips. Tap-tap he goes on. It's as if the others are swimming in mud while he laughs at this hypnotic spectacle of the ball going up and down on his foot. Then with his back to the goal he sends the ball high up into the air, waits for its descent, and then flips backwards, his arms and feet extended and his body spinning like a pinwheel until his right foot connects with tremendous force with the ball at the apex of his leap. Jacob and I are seeing this from behind the movement of the action, towards the German goal. We see the surging entanglement of defenders rising to meet the ball. We see the German fans all in orange looking as if they are watching an impending train crash. Some are covering their eyes. In the second row, just behind the goal, two Greeks in tall blue hats are raising their arms and screaming. The ball thuds into the bottom of the net. Two German players scramble for the ball to put it back into play while the goalie stays locked in his crouch in front of the goal as if this has not yet happened to him. The whistle blows. The Germans fall down on to the pitch and don't move. The Greek with the ponytail looks at them with what seems like concern before trotting off to the tunnel leading to the dressing rooms.

I am more giddy than ever and Jacob seems to have ascended into this part of the atmosphere with me. Everything makes us laugh – the song the barber Stankowski is singing in the flat next door, the solemn faces of the Polish footballers with their moustaches and long hair looking down from the poster on the wall, the drained bottles of beer. We get straight back to the whiskey. We declare our wish to drink lakes of it and then run up the side of a mountain. We drink toasts to the Greeks. We drink toasts to our respective nations and to extraordinary feats of athleticism we have witnessed in our time. We hail the Germans and wish them better fortune in their next match. We get through the bottle of whiskey and head out into the night in search of more. Jacob pays no attention to the cold. I ask him the day and he tells me 'Thursday'. I cannot immediately understand the meaning of this word. I walk on, trying to find the way back into my own skin. We pass a policeman looking at a gold chandelier in the window of a shop, a group of boys sliding around the ice on their bicycles. There is not a thing that does not make me laugh. I take a few steps and then I have to stop. Tears are running down my face. Jacob is laughing too. We are holding on to each other in case we might fall. I look around and recognise some windows and corners but cannot place myself very well. I seem a bit dizzy. I wonder is it the lack of food. A white light flashes before me. I reel back. I don't know whether the light is in my head or outside. I see then that we are standing before an underground bar, fast electronic music surging up to us with clouds of hot air smelling of sweat and perfume. This seems just the thing for us, and we head down the stairs. The lights flash brighter. Young people are waving their arms. On a big television screen above the dancefloor is a black man dressed in leather coat and hat with his fingers full of rings bobbing and pointing and crossing his arms in time to the music. I follow Jacob through the people, my fingers in the grip of a drowning man on the sleeve of his coat. We get to the bar and I order whiskey. I look down at my tapping foot and then move to the edge of the dancefloor. I look around for a while, bobbing up and down on my knees. I can't seem to get that to stop. I set down the drink and slide like an ice skater into the rhythm of the music. I get a spot and stick there. My hands flick out like I'm trying to rid them of water, my whole torso jerks forward and back. Where did I get that? I throw my coat and hat on to a chair and move deeper among the dancers. They look at me as if I'm a pigeon that's just landed in their soup. But I can see from the eyes of a few of the girls that they like to see me there.

I don't miss anything of the music. Its secret pulse courses along my nerves and into my muscles. I look up at the black man and follow his gyrations and spins and strange coded language of the hands. They clear a space around me. I am getting the warm open looks such as I never got at dances when I was their age. I go down on to the floor and kick my legs up supported by one hand. Soon they all stop dancing and make a ring with me in the centre. They begin to clap to the music. I take my jacket off, then my shirt, and I am down to my vest. It's a little grey and sorrowful-looking so I take that off too. I stand still among them for a moment, feet together, straight-backed, bare-torsoed. I do not give myself a moment to think or to form a picture of myself in my mind. I crouch low and stalk the edge of the ring and then begin to spin. I see Jacob clapping with the rest of them. I wonder will I fall. But I am held together in a kind of infallibility of the body. I move out through the crowd, pick up a chair and bring it back into the ring. I have the delirious idea of standing on my head on it and then do so, my quivering body held up by my forearms pressed against the chair's back. I flip back down to the floor, pick up the chair with my teeth and prowl the perimeter of the ring, my hands clapping in front of me like a seal's.

I see the people who had been facing me suddenly turn and look behind them. The crowd parts to form an aisle. Advancing towards me then is a solidly built woman in early middle age. She wears a woollen dress cut to the knee, a thick cardigan and a heap of blonde and silver hair piled up on her head. Her glasses sweep up to points at the corners. I haven't seen any like them in a long while. They are like the tailfins of an American car from the 1960s. She looks very grave. I remember seeing her when we first came in, sitting with a woman of a similar age, the two of them maybe teachers at a vocational college in a nearby town. She begins to dance. She is moving along the ring of people, her grey, opaque eyes never off me. I move with her at the far end, the two of us endpoints of the circle's diameter. The disc jockey turns the music higher, there is a great shout from the crowd and I break into a flurry of finger pointing and head rolling, my feet planted like a weightlifter's. She pays no attention. She takes off her glasses. She takes the pins from her hair and it falls like a cascade of water down around her shoulders. The cardigan drops to the floor. She kicks the chair out of the way as she walks across the centre of the ring towards me. I take a few steps in her direction and stop. We move around in a tighter circle now like two wrestlers about to grapple, eye to eye, me moving my arms in big loops and hopping about as though the floor is in flames. She rolls her eyes and wags her finger as if to say, 'Is that all you've got, boy?' She bobs down and shakes her shoulders, her huge breasts heaving from one side to the other. Then she leans way back and throws her hips forward, her dress sliding up her thighs to the tops of her stockings. When she's up again she looks me in the eye and strides towards me. I back away and try to find a lateral move. But she cuts me off. My angle of escape gets narrower as I am backed in against the crowd. She presses on. She is as implacable as a tractor. A lane opens in the crowd behind me and she continues on, bobbing from foot to foot. I try to save myself with leaps and pirouettes and furious movements of the hands. But soon my back is to the wall. She presses in against me. I feel the air go out of my lungs. She leans over. Then she whispers in my ear in what sounds like an accent from the Ukraine, 'Now let's see how you can move.' Around us the whole of our audience are standing on tables and chairs whistling and clapping and cheering these two people they are astonished to find here in this underground bar instead of at home in their beds with hot water bottles and rheumatism tablets. She turns away from me and slides slowly with her hips and back down my front all the way to the floor, swaying back and forth. What will she do now? Will the music stop? She turns to face me again and climbs slowly upwards along my body, led by her hands and followed by her breasts and thighs. Little gusts of warm air from her skin waft around me. When she reaches her full height she rests her brow on my shoulder. Before it seemed she had the weight of a loading dock but just now she feels very light. I have to say that I do not find this unpleasant. But what am I to do? I cannot get away. I look around at the crowd and fan my face with my hand as though I am beside a furnace. But she pays no attention. She is not in the mood for jokes, at least not jokes which involve laughter. She places her hands against the wall just above my shoulders and gyrates up and down, her whole body pressed against me. The air is getting scarcer. I am like a little rowboat facing the whole of a fleet. I look around for Jacob but I can't see him. I feel her skin and sweat and breasts and the bones of her pelvis. Everything is flesh and movement and whirling lights. For one sweet moment that extends like the howl of a dog into this night I let myself go with her, shoulder to shoulder, hip to hip, the two of us like a single body as we clutch each other and the music builds to its final frenzy before crashing in a furious pounding of drums to silence. I hear the crowd roar as if from far away. Sweat has drenched the waist of my trousers. I can barely breathe. I reach then into my pocket, take from it my handkerchief and wave it at the woman in surrender.

She pushes slowly away from me, her face averted. She too is breathing heavily. The young people move into the circle where we were dancing and I can see her only intermittently. She is walking back in the direction from which she came. There is a primness to her movements, little dainty steps, her hands clasped in front of her. I would like to speak with her but a boy with blond hair and cheeks the colour of apples steps forward and hands me a full glass of vodka with ice. A girl arrives with my vest, jacket, shirt and a towel to dry myself with. She keeps her soft, liquid eyes on mine as she presses them into my hand, an act of charity for a man drawing a pension. I keep looking around for the woman. Finally I see her walking towards me, settling her fan-tailed glasses back on to the bridge of her nose. She stops, nods briefly and says, 'Thank you.' Then she shakes my hand like a priest at a church door and disappears back into the crowd. I watch her pass through the tables towards the door. She is big, the biggest woman I have yet been so close to. I stand with my glass and think of the comfort I found with her on the dance-floor. Jacob comes up with my coat and hat.

'Where are we going?' I say.

'We'll go somewhere to cool off.'

'All right,' I say.

I drink the vodka, and then rise like a vapour up the stairs and back into the night.

In the library I read of how an uneducated Englishman's construction of the first dynamo ended one hundred and fifty years of tranquil certainty in the world of physics. Up to then it had been thought that Newton had found the mathematics for all the workings of the visible world. There remained only the work of refining them and building on them and closing some gaps in what they addressed. But the dynamo demonstrated the existence of wave radiation and there was nothing in Newton which could make sense of that. Shortly afterwards it was demonstrated that light moved at a constant speed irrespective of its source or what was around it. It was the only thing in all of the world to behave in such a way, but it was enough to break the most fundamental of Newton's laws, the laws of motion. Einstein found the solution in his special theory of relativity. Then he in turn was upended by quantum mechanics. And so physics has moved through time, a beautiful, harmonious and nearly complete picture of all that is elaborated by one physicist undermined in turn by a single troublesome discovery made by another.

There is a sound here now of books closing and of shuffling feet. I look up. The stained-glass window is black, the light inside harsh and white. Jacob clicks closed his pen and places it in his pocket. I am a small man, all around me now the records and the written labours of others with whom it is fruitless to compare myself. When I go I will leave no mark. Yet in this history of the scientists is a kind of dream of my life. That feeling of reaching for the final piece, then it all falling away. There is something in the thinking of this that pleases me. Those prayers at the foot of the altar. Dialectics. Love. Are they all illusions? Or is it that I expected of them the wrong thing? I don't know yet. Maybe it's that I can't know. Still, I would like to go on thinking of it. But here and now there are only the librarian and Jacob, waiting for me to leave.

13

Eleanor

I get up. I put on a cardigan and then my bathrobe and go out to the kitchen. I make tea and a boiled egg and bring them with a banana and a slice of bread back into the bedroom. Light spills like a halo around the curtain and I think to look out. The day is cold and bright. There must have been rain, for there's a fine skin of gleaming ice on the pavements and window ledges and frozen drops like crystal earrings on the trees. I look out for a long while until the cold drives me back into the bed. I eat my breakfast there sitting up. I get some strength. I begin to feel ready for M., and for her. I want to hasten to that part of the story where more of her may be revealed, but the hell of this kind of thing is that you must be patient, you must go step by step, for each of the steps can change what follows. You cannot afford to miss even a single one. So first of all M.'s sad interlude, and the story of Eleanor.

The day after M.'s father's funeral M. got into his car and drove to the home of his aunt. He was to bring something. I can't remember well what it was. Let's say it was a photograph of his grandmother in a silver frame. He had it beside him on the seat, face up, as though she too had been laid out for burial. On the night before his death M.'s father had got up from his bed in his pyjamas and walked around the house with his hair on end touching walls and photographs and books, smiling and nodding and whispering. The nurse who was minding him followed him. She got him back into his bed and played tunes on a whistle for him and then he went to sleep. The next day she got him up to bathe him. He stood beside the bed, his knees shaking. 'I can't get there,' he said. He lay back down then, closed his eyes, and she watched the life go out of him.

There were six messages for M. when he got home that night in Barcelona. They had to hold back the funeral for a day to give him time to get there.

The air inside the car pressed in like a solid wall over the entire surface of his body as he drove. When he arrived at the driveway of the house of his aunt he did not enter. Instead, he kept driving. He was in a fine, smooth-running car the colour of lemon which his father had bought from a German whose fish farm had failed. He moved out of his aunt's village on to the open road. The tyres hissed, the cool air flowed around him. It was a winter morning that had begun with rain but then the clouds rolled away and now the air seemed unable to contain the late morning light which flooded the valley around him. The trees were black and twisted and the grass shone with rainwater. Steam rose from the mouths of a gang of men cutting trees by a lake. He did not know where he was going. He did not turn the radio on. For a long while he looked at nothing save the road and the sky flaring out above it. He did not wish to see anything familiar. He did not wish to know where he was. He was alone, and free. Who was there to report to? He thought, What if I don't stop? He imagined himself far away, the wheels endlessly turning, just him under the sky gliding along as though through space, on and on through the villages and forests and fields of Europe to some place out beyond the limits of his knowledge.

Autumn had passed into winter and on into a new year since

he entered that bar with his armful of roses. Did he think of her still? Not so much. He would like to have known where she was, why she went. He would like to have known about the man in the wheelchair. But the feeling was vague now. It embarrassed him to place so much drama into something so lacking in form. He did not labour at the memory any more. She was passing, it seemed. When she went away he filled the time. He took up hill-walking. He went into churches and attempted to pray. He applied for jobs in distant places. There were diversions. They preoccupied him, but they did not please him. A Hungarian. A girl in his office. There was time and he filled it. He went on, alone, prowling, vacant.

Before the light faded he arrived at a town by the sea he knew well. He stood for half an hour like someone hypnotised and watched a boy with enormous teeth screaming ballads in a square. He thought his veins would burst. He had a pocketful of his father's money. He bought a newspaper and sat down on a bench but found he could not read it. He took a drink and watched the people come and go, their bags of shopping, their loud hailings and imprecations and eruptions of laughter. He had the idea as he sat there that he hadn't the ability to look normal. He had lobster and wine in a restaurant and then drove out of town. He would find a hotel somewhere, then another the next night. He felt for a moment the great unending freedom in this idea and drove on into the darkness. I remember those roads. They are full of twists and pastel-coloured villages, dogs attacking your wheels and children eating chocolates. They are dark and empty for a time and then they are full of intimacy. You cannot be lost or unseen. You cannot get that feeling he was looking for when he had the idea of driving without a destination. He pulled over to the side of the road by an entrance to a field and sat there for a while before turning around and driving all the way back to his father's house. He turned on all the lights and opened the windows. He played music very loud. He lay down on a bed somewhere. He knew that he would not sleep.

M. is with me now. Well, let us say the M. that I have found somewhere between him and me. I have the feeling that he will stay with me now until the end. Perhaps that is presumptuous. But there is not far to go and I know the way. How is it that in one phase of our lives everything is impossible and in another everything is clear, open, possessable? Why did M. leave me one day and come back another? It is noticeable in athletes. The great have days of mediocrity, others briefly rise. But they train laboriously and learn all manner of tricks to minimise the effects of inevitable lapses of strength or rhythm. And the rest of us? Does it happen too to plumbers and hairdressers? If it were so wouldn't a portion of our buildings be erupting with water and certain unfortunate people bear scars on their faces where a razor slipped from its path? How does this work? Why do I feel so well just now? I wake sharp, clear. I have the wish for food. And there is the sense that I am carrying something, of the need to mind it well until I have delivered it. I never had that before. I had something very like it with Angelina, but accompanying it, unseen, unacknowledged, was a feeling of dread, as though just as I was living that glorious time another force was labouring at destroying it, as termites gnaw at posts supporting an edifice, so that whatever the effort, whatever the care, I was to lose it anyway. But this is something, at least now, that I feel I can keep close to me. Well, I must make the most of the hands as they are dealt in this unfathomable game.

He went through the rooms of the house of his father taking pictures from walls, making lists of furniture, placing objects in boxes. Some things for his aunt, some for the fire, some for the nuns. Every hour he got so tired of this that he went out and walked around this house which now looked as cold and inert to him as a corpse. Someone had come around and cut the grass after his father died, the cuttings still in lank heaps. The green paint on an outbuilding door was flaking, one hinge rusted through. Why does a corpse seem less than stone or a plank of wood? There was nothing out there for him, just a dark landscape, a house losing its meaning. He went back in and continued with his work. He telephoned his father's banker and lawyer. M. hadn't thought the bicycle valves he made would bring in so much. Or was it that he spent so little? He called an auctioneer about selling the house. He called the local refuse collection department. He found one of his school essays trapped beneath a desk drawer. Photographs, funeral cards, letters, a silver spoon sent on the occasion of M.'s birth from an uncle in Massachusetts. There was a cloth shoe bag containing his mother's bracelets and rings. 'For your wife,' his father used to say to him. 'When you get one.' The past assembled and disintegrated. He went into the room where his father died. He sat at his desk. There was a pile of unopened letters going back three months. 'He feared the post,' the nurse had told M. Bank statements, promotions, bills, news from the church. This tired M. too and he got up and began to open drawers. Vests, socks, a kind of corset for his father's bad back. He found a leather box he vaguely remembered. Inside were tie pins, a nail file, pens, all neatly arranged in the compartments of a tray. He lifted this off and put it aside. Below were religious medals, his mother's wedding ring, an old photograph of Vienna and another of M. at his First Communion, a comb, a few silver strands of his father's hair still caught between the teeth. There was a poem about a father's love for his son cut out from a newspaper, yellow at the edges, the border jagged where his hands couldn't control the scissors. He walked through the rooms, out the door and along the road into the hills until all this played itself out there in what was around him. He looked out to the hills, then to the house, then back again. It did not gather itself into a meaning for him. He found no love for it, nor did it give him comfort. It has only familiarity, a little tired, not altogether welcome, like a school door, or the sound of the footsteps of a disagreeable neighbour as he passed through his gate. Yet to rid himself of it all, to make a cut so harsh, to have no way back . . . ?

M. walked back along the lane to the house. He called the auctioneer. He told him he was withdrawing the house from sale. 'Maybe later in the year,' he said.

That night he drank with his cousins in muted yellow light in the corner of the pub, rain lashing the windows. Men from the village tipped the peaks of their caps at him as they passed. A girl came in not long before closing time, red-cheeked, rain sparkling on her face and in her hair, a little out of breath. 'I thought I might be too late,' she said to one of M.'s cousins. 'Eleanor,' the man said, nodding, then bought her a tall glass of beer. She sat down across from M. She called him by name, expressed condolences. He tried to find her in his memory, but couldn't. 'I'd have gone to the funeral, but I'm only back,' she said.

'That's all right,' said M.

She had blonde curls, clear mahogany eyes and a laugh that surprised him. It was raw, guttural, like something you might hear from an old man selling wares in a port, someone who maybe once was a criminal but no longer had the strength. She didn't hide her mouth with her hand in that feminine way whenever she did it. After another round of drinks M. understood who she was, the daughter of a doctor who came to the village two years before he had left for university. Her older brother, a spectacular athlete, was in his class. Where had she just come from? he asked. From the Andes, she said, helping to plant maize. She and M. spoke Spanish together then for the amusement of his cousins. By the time the bell rang to close the bar he had nearly forgotten that they were there. They stepped out together into the rain.

'Have you a bicycle?' she said.

'Yes,' he said. 'There's one in the shed.'

'If it's fine tomorrow will we go out the coast road together?'

'All right,' said M.

The day broke well, the high clouds blown inland by the sea wind and the sky clearing as if the earth beneath it had been shifted by a lever. She called for M. on her bicycle and they drove out along the coast. She knew about everything there – saints' wells, ambushes, the way the stone was formed, the place where some warrior was said to have seduced a beautiful girl with black hair. She had a poem about it. She took him off the road into a valley where there was a small lake rimmed in orange earth. She had fruit in a saddlebag and they ate it by the shore. They pedalled on then through the rain-cleansed air, her legs pumping rhythmically in front of him, high cliffs leading down to the sea silver in the sunlight, blue mountains beyond. A man went by on a tractor and saluted. Dogs lying on stone walls watched them pass. Water flowed around and below them, rocks tinkling like ice cubes in a glass. The land swept down from the mountains in clefts and wide green valleys, white houses set against the rises in groves of trees. She turned off the main road again on to a neck of land thick with pines and oaks and ferns. It turned to grassland and dunes on one side and rock frothing with waves on the other and at the end there was a small cove and harbour with a pub beside it. They went in and ordered lunch. She told M. stories about her wild aunt who lived up on the top of a hill with her hens. When the food arrived M. went to the bar for more drinks. His hands were full as he sat and she took a shrimp from her plate and placed it with her fingers in his mouth. A softer, slower version of that laugh, the mahogany eyes closing a little. He wished she'd go on doing that.

Eleanor did not make him think what man was, or woman. She did not make him think of miracles and wondrous things. He did not go down into the marrow for her, and of course I need not speak of whether he kept anything back from her, for he offered her almost nothing at all. What she got were the forms he had learned, not the thing itself. Yet it was not as it had been with those other women whose paths he crossed in the months after Hanna had vanished – the farmer's daughter, the Hungarian, and that other woman, somebody's wife he told me, who drove him around on the back of her motorbike. I forgot to mention her before. They all made him feel alone, futureless, they awakened a distaste because that was what was inside him. He liked to think of Eleanor. At least in moments, and then he moved on to another thing in case the thought turned bad. He liked the spring in her hair, the way she knew about trees, her lack of elegance. He found he could be easy with her. She came out of his world, or at least a world he had known well and not entirely forgotten. He understood her gestures and jokes. Nothing had to be guessed at. The days went by one by one like time passed in a stadium waiting for a spectacle to begin. But what he was waiting for he did not know. He unpacked boxes. He signed documents. He brought mementoes around to neighbours and members of the family and clothes to nuns. He looked at a pair of his father's shoes as he placed them in a bag and wondered who next would be wearing them. In the afternoons he went out with Eleanor on the bicycles and found her in the pub in the evenings.

The days began to pass easier than before. Finally then she walked back with him along the dark road to his house with her arm around his waist and in the morning he found himself climbing the stairs to deliver a boiled egg and tea to her in his bed. He stood in the doorway for a moment and looked at her. Her head was propped up with one hand and she was facing the window. He looked at the sunlight running through her hair, at her narrowing back, at how easy she looked there. Open, curious, lacking in malice. Quick to laugh. A deep appetite. The idea came to him that she knew that chaos and helplessness were never far away from anyone, that they just took you as a strong wind does a tree, and that their victims are to be commiserated with rather than scorned. That's a feeling he had not come across in a while. It relaxed him. He felt well moving in beside her again with her breakfast, the way she turned towards him. Her breasts were against his chest, heat rose. 'The tea can cool,' she said, and he closed his eyes.

Somewhere, Hanna was folding her clothes and placing them in her bag. She made her last calls. She looked in her mirror, adjusted her hat. She ran a finger over her eyelashes and painted her lips. She closed her bag then, drew in the shutters and stepped out into the street. It was dark, iron streetlamps throwing down pools of yellow-white light. I picture her walking as though with an acceptance of fate. M. of course knew nothing of this. He had by then returned to his job at the trade delegation in Barcelona. She was in his past, troubling him a little from there. By day he translated documents and by night he moved around hoping for deliverance to come to him from behind some as yet unopened

185

door. It never did, but he maintained the expectancy neverthe-less. He telephoned Eleanor at the weekends. A whale had appeared on the beach, she told him. She put roses in around the doorway to his house to make it look more lived in. She was to go back to the Andes before the summer. 'Will I pay you a visit first?' she asked. 'I'd like that,' he said. If she caught the helplessness in his voice she did not speak of it. What curse, he wondered, had been put upon him that he could not yet fully begin to live? Somehow Hanna was still in him like a virus. Had he heard her footsteps, hard leather heels on dark stone, had he turned and seen her moving from pool of light to pool of light, had he even been able to look into her bag and see the ticket she carried, still he would not presume it was him she was moving towards.

This girl. I seem to get a glimpse of her at times, the way car lights catch something indistinct, a rock or an animal. I close my eyes and concentrate. I press the sides of my head. Nothing. Yet I have the feeling that if I wait long enough, I will see.

Eleanor arrived in Barcelona with a bottle of whiskey, a bagful of music she wanted M. to hear and a framed map of the head-land and bay where he grew up. The days were growing longer, brightening. The city filled with people walking slowly in the evenings in the late sun after the winter, stopping to talk, sitting out on the terraces. When the weekend came M. drove with her out into the mountains. This was a season he had not seen there before. Water tumbled down the rockfaces and surged through the crevices, wild flowers blooming, the red-orange earth wet and loose and with an aroma of ferment rising from it before the summer sun scorched it to dust.

At night she cooked for him and they carried the food up on to the roof with candles and wine and a little machine for music.

Afterwards he went back down for the bottle of whiskey and then leaned back against the tiles and they looked at the sky together, a clamour of car horns and laughter and the shouting of names rising from the street. She told jokes. She planned expeditions. She slid over to be nearer him. He looked at her there, her head on his chest, the light of the city glowing on her brow. Is it in any way possible, he wondered?

One morning M. rose earlier than usual. In two days Eleanor was due to leave. I can see from here two lives moving towards each other from far away and soon to intersect. He knew nothing of this. He went out into the street for bread and fruit. He came back and laid the things out on a tray. While he waited for the water to boil he picked up a local newspaper lying folded over on the table. It was open at a page advertising jobs. He noticed that Eleanor had placed small marks next to two of them.

That day he took her to lunch. She'd put a ribbon in her hair and was wearing a white dress. She smiled at him across the table. She held his hand. There would come a time, he knew, maybe here, maybe later, some time anyway before she left, when she would speak to him about the future. He wished he could halt it, for already as he looked at her there a little nervous and expectant he was wondering when and how and why it must end.

After lunch they went back home and he got into bed with her. She was naked, pressed against his back. After a time he heard her rhythmical breathing, felt her thigh slip from his. Why, he thought, must he refuse this gift? This moved around in his mind until the leaking of consciousness transformed itself into a fleeting dream, and it evaporated then and finally he too was asleep.

The telephone rang and he woke. Eleanor murmured and rolled over on to her side. He went to answer it.

'Hello?' he said.

There was a pause. He felt a presence on the other end of the line, something he knew well in the drawing in of breath.

'Hello,' she said.

'Is it you?'

She laughed.

'Yes.'

'Where are you?'

'I'm back,' she said.

He looked into the bedroom. Eleanor was turned away from him, her hair on the pillow, her shoulders reddened a little from the sun. Then he looked at the telephone. A force rose within him, there was a slipping away of something and out ahead of him a growing brightness. He lifted the telephone and began to speak.

PART FOUR

14

Sand

I come now to the sands at Miedzyzdroje. Those were my days, the days of my life.

I am at my table, the light shining down on my head. The night is still, just the sound of snow receiving snow. My radio is here, the sound off, the aerial like a long arthritic finger. A newspaper folded over, a teacup and a bowl with a puddle of ice-cream in it. I can hear just now the sound of water coursing through pipes as the barber Stankowski drains his bath. I seem to be waiting for something. I feel well – calm, alert. I am not going anywhere tonight. I have no wish to be in any other place. I sit still in my chair, arms outstretched before me, eyes on the wall. I wait, I watch the hand sweep across the face of the clock. Then I go into the story, just at the point when Angelina said that we should go to the forest or the sea, this time of ripeness and loss. The sands at Miedzyzdroje. A picture of us walking together under the dunes rises like an object dredged from the sea. Well, let it come. There is no hiding from the fact that it can hurt me still, but just now I am thinking more about the words, about whether the words can catch this picture and the others around it. There are more words, I think, for longing than for rapture. Or at least they are more easily found. Can I find them, can I make my way to those glorious days? I take my eyes from the wall and look down. My hands are the colour of a ceiling stained by smokers, darker liver spots spread over them like splattered ink, the nails thick and yellow. A pale green shirt, a cardigan unravelling at the sleeve, a bathrobe for extra warmth. Two blue flannel slippers, a spot of dried gravy on the right one, two thin bald legs going down into them like dead stalks, skin white and smooth as marble. Some kind of blood running through the pale blue veins, some kind of comical version of life. But I don't mind. Truly I don't. I can even laugh, if I catch the words.

These are the feet that walked through the sand. These are the hands that moved over her skin. But how can that be?

The forest, the sea. That was where she said we should go. What was I to do? In our new world we had created a population of watchers. Each kept his watch and did little else, except to report what he had seen. How to become invisible in a place such as this?

I went to Gottfried. He puffed on his pipe, the two heavy black eyebrows like caterpillars walking towards each other as he frowned. 'Travel permits and a week's holiday in Poland for you and your girl?' he said. 'Hmmm.' Then he grabbed my shoulders each in one hand and tilted his head, his eyelashes fluttering like a coquette's. 'Why of course you shall have them. You deserve it.' Our days in Miedzyzdroje were paid for by each shovelful Pawel dug in his gulag.

On the morning we were to leave Berlin I watched Angelina move through the room and had the idea that we were just what I told Gottfried we were, a couple like any other, flowing along in a stream with all the other couples of the world, setting off for a holiday in my homeland. She put clothes and some drawing materials in a small suitcase. She put out an envelope with the rent. She opened the door to the room where her horses were, looked slowly from left to right, and then closed it. We will be back to see them again, I said to myself. She tied a pale blue scarf around her neck. I looked at the ballgown she wore the night of Pawel's party spilling from the chest in the hall, at the bones in her ankle as we went down the stairs. If I had nothing else I had this being, I thought, this body, or at least pieces of them. I heard a radio play in the room where Pawel lived. A gymnastics instructor was living there now. Then we moved out past the big brass clock, the red bird sleeping on its perch, the bench where I watched her turn the corner of the stairs. The caretaker put her head out from her door, her hair in a net, then drew it in again, like a tortoise.

Out in the sunlight Angelina took my hand, kissed me. Then she looked out ahead of her as we walked, as though she expected to see something she liked.

'What about the horses?' I asked her.

'What about them?'

'What are you going to do about them?'

'I'm not going to do anything. They're finished.'

'But what will happen to them?'

She looked at me as if she hadn't understood the question.

'I don't know,' she said.

'And the drawings?'

'They're *finished*,' she said, smiling. She said it as though I needed to be convinced. I stayed quiet for a time, embarrassed by being less than her. I watched her striding along out of the corner of my eye. How many homes, I wondered, had she left without looking back? Had I thought more then I would have seen in this a warning. But I couldn't.

We got on a train to Szczecin. I was against the window and Angelina was leaning against me, her head on my shoulder, her foot hooked around mine. I saw her eyes close, I took in the aroma of her hair. Where are they learned, these tiny, significant gestures, this arrangement of limbs? On whom had she practised? I turned away from this thought in time and looked out the window. The dense weight of the city broke up and we moved out into flat open land, back along the way I came so solitary and hesitant after saying goodbye to Jerzy and before any of this had happened. I saw the backs of the men in the fields rising and falling as though driven by pumps, the black trees with their new leaves like a child's scrawl against the sky. The land was heavy with water, the light pale as though it had arrived through steamed glass. We rolled on in a steady rhythm, the carriage swaying easily, the clicks of the wheels on the track. We crossed the new border into Poland. Already those transplanted from the East at the end of the war had made it their own. Everything slowed, the gestures, the way people walked or rode bicycles. The air was more solid than on the other side of the border, the smoke rising from the chimneys black and nearly inert, the fields and buildings screaming their defiance against being understood. I knew that place, those gestures. It was the feeling of putting on an old coat again when the weather turned cold after the summer. My mind too slowed, moved down among the roots and the basements. I knew that place, it was familiar. What I had lost was the intimacy. I had only Angelina. The train rolled slowly eastwards. Across from us an elderly man sliced a gherkin. He offered us shots from his flask of vodka. We were going to Gdansk to elope, we told him.

We got out at Szczecin and walked along the riverbank past the bridges and cranes and masts of boats. There was wreckage everywhere, single walls still standing pocked with shell holes, all that had been of the buildings now heaps of rubble below. We stopped and looked downriver towards the docks. Angelina read the names of the boats, repeated a Scandinavian one in a whisper to herself, trying the alien sounds. Above us the castle lay flat-tened by bombs, a little like our pasts, I thought, memory seeping out through the cracks and from the broken masonry. This made me laugh loud enough for her to hear me. The sweetness of melancholy, the minor note – gifts from Angelina. She looked at me as if with a question. 'The castle,' I said. 'It's like us.' She took this in, looked at me, smiled. We went back up then through the town to the station and the train which would take us north to the sea.

In Miedzyzdroje we walked along the promenade to the band-stand and looked out at the sea, grey and rolling beneath the last pale yellow light coming from the west. Wind whipped the hair around Angelina's face and she shivered. We turned then and walked into the hotel behind us. There was a man at the desk, slow of gesture, face a little brown from the spring sun or maybe the wind, hair long with strands of grey swept back over his ears and on to the collar of his shirt. He raised his hand, touched his ear, his brow slowly creasing. He was wearing cufflinks set with small red stones. I handed him the papers that were the gift of Gottfried and we stood before him. I saw in the mirror behind the desk the evening light fall on Angelina's face. The man looked from us to the papers and back to us again. His eyes were blue and watery. He smiled in what seemed a kind of recognition. Of what, though? That we were doomed? That we were fools? That we were lovers?

I was to learn that his name was Piotr.

He led us up the stairs and along a corridor and opened the door to a room where we were to begin this new time, a time we could know nothing of. I can bring this room before me now. Photographs of men in uniform and of weddings. Rows of books with broken spines. A floor of wood, small rugs placed around it. A round table by the window covered with candles and broken clocks, another by the bed with a lamp and more clocks. The window was covered by two heavy velvet curtains, one green, strange to say, and the other black. A wardrobe with a mirror set into the door reflecting the bed. The bed was high and made of wood, heaps of white pillows rising up the headboard, a cover of lace. Did sea captains bring their mistresses here? The man parted the curtains and looked out for a moment at the sea. He bowed once then and left. Angelina untied her blue scarf, let it drop. We moved towards each other like wisps of fog.

On the morning of our fourth day I went out and bought two gold earrings set with tiny pearls. The money I was carrying had become like gamblers' money, something to keep in the game, nothing to do with the purchase of train tickets or shoes or food. Nothing to do with survival when our days ran out. It was Piotr who told me about the earrings. The old man who sold them to me took them out of a drawer wrapped in an old piece of newspaper. What desperate story lay behind them, I wondered? I pictured them in place above her long neck, strands of dark hair falling over them. I looked at my watch. Twenty-seven minutes since I left the room. That plus the forty-five minutes or so when Angelina went one way looking for apples and I another looking for wine – the whole of the time we had been apart since leaving Berlin.

I went up the stairs two at a time and into the room. Angelina wasn't there and I felt an ache. I took off my jacket, sat, looked at the earrings. I looked towards the window then and saw her foot resting on the railing of the balcony. I walked through the shadows and stood by the black curtain. She was in a chair leaning against the wall looking out towards the sea. She was wearing a shirt of mine, trousers of hers, no shoes. The buttons of the shirt had been put in the wrong holes. She didn't see me, or if she did it was not my presence that was drawing her attention. She looked down, then out again at the sea, pushing her hair away from her face with her hand. I watched her eyes narrow as she looked at the horizon. I looked out too, but could see nothing other than water and sky. I followed her eyes down and saw a sheaf of papers on her lap. She had a pencil in her hand and on the top page was a drawing of a horse moving over the water from right to left, its head high, its mane flowing, its legs stretched to the limit as it ran. I saw the veins in its flank, the muscles of its neck, back and legs, the look in its eye of clarity and decision. This was another chapter in the biography of this horse. Where was it going with such strength and desire? I moved into the folds of the curtain and looked at Angelina's face. Her breathing was short. Her lips were forming fragments of words, her hand went up in the air and then back to the page as though she was trying to take hold of something out of reach or out of sight. There was in her face no guile or restlessness, there was just the whole of her looking for a single necessary line somewhere out there in the clouds and milky light and rolling water. She would never, could never, love me like that, I thought, as her hand dropped to the page.

'Where do you think it's going?' I said.

'It's difficult to know,' said Piotr.

We were sitting on a low wall looking out to sea at a boat moving away from us, thick black smoke rising from its chimney. It was late afternoon, the last afternoon, the last boat, the last talk with Piotr, for on the following day we would have to leave this place. The boat sounded like a dog groaning in its sleep.

'Could it be Stockholm?'

'No. Stockholm would be more to the east.'

'Do you know much about the boats?'

'Not much. But I talk to the sailors sometimes.'

'It seems to be swinging off to the left now.'

'Yes.'

'It could be going anywhere, I suppose.'

'Maybe it's for Travemünde, or Copenhagen.'

I took in the names. What kind of life goes on there, I wondered? I looked at Piotr. I saw marks on the side of his face I had never noticed before, small dry pits, maybe from some fever he had as a child. What was that? I tried to form a picture of him from that time, his home, his parents. Even then, even when I had graver things to occupy me, my curiosity was there like rheumatism. But I let it pass.

'I didn't see you yesterday,' I said.

'No. I had a day off.'

'How was it?'

'Good.'

'Did you rest?'

'I went for a walk.'

'To another town?'

'I went out along the beach under the dunes, then up a trail.'

'Where does it go?'

'To a forest. Haven't you been?'

'No.'

'That's a pity. You should try to see it.'

'The time is short.'

'Well, yes. Holidays come to an end. But if you have a chance, go in the morning. I always go when the leaves are still wet. You can see the sun burning off the mist. The forest is full of animals – badgers, foxes, sea eagles, boar. And there are glacial lakes. I lived in a hole for two years, 1943 to 1945. In Wielkopolska. We moved by night, sometimes to another hole. You had to have another sense then if you were to stay alive. Then with the peace

I didn't need this sense any more. It went flat. I found that I missed it. That was something I hadn't expected. But I can get it back again if I go into a wilderness. It wakes up.

'Yesterday was good – soft, clear light. I walked for maybe three hours and then sat down by a lake. I had a sandwich in my pocket and I ate it. Just to be there is enough for me, to see that it is there, that everything in it is all right. The squirrels and birds call out warnings when you first get there, but then they stop. They get used to you. I suppose they forget you're there. After a while you're just one of the creatures. You could hear something, a fish on the surface of the water, a bee. There might be a sound like breathing from the swaying trees. But it's very quiet, very peaceful.'

He struck a match and pushed a cigarette into the bowl of his hands.

'Then I came back by bus.'

I imagined him there in the back seat, silent, back straight, hands folded on his lap, among schoolgirls singing camping songs.

'There was a band playing when I got there,' he said. 'Some people were dancing. I looked around but I didn't see you.'

'No. I wasn't there. I could hear the music through the window, though.'

'Did you like it?'

'There was a time when I couldn't stand that music. But I find I can like it now.'

'And your girl?'

'She was with me. We had a little dance on our own.'

He smiled. He seemed to like this picture. His eyes moved across my face, then back out to the sea.

'She's very beautiful,' he said.

'I know.'

'You shouldn't lose her.'

'No,' I said.

We watched the boat move out towards the horizon, very small now. We had the same view of the sea Angelina and I had from our room. I thought of the drawing I watched her make and placed the boat in it, just beyond the ear of the horse.

'Do you have a girl?' I asked him.

'No,' he said.

'Did you have?'

'I had a few, like most people. I also had a wife.'

'What happened to her?'

'I couldn't find her after the war. Later I heard she got to England, but I'm not sure that's right.'

He smiled, shrugged. He sent his cigarette somersaulting in an arc towards the sea. I looked at him – the long fingers, the slow, watery eyes, the hair rolling over the collar of the white shirt he wore when he sat behind the desk in the hotel.

'Have you always done this?' I asked him.

'What?'

'Working in a hotel.'

'No.'

'What were you doing?'

'I made trumpets.'

'Only trumpets?'

'Yes.'

'Did you like doing that?'

'Yes. It was good. I liked the people there.'

'Why did you stop?'

'I got tired. I couldn't concentrate.'

I looked at him again. I tried to see past the weariness and delicacy, but nothing was clear. Could he help us? Would he? Those were the days, the long decades, when you were not to ask the wrong question of the wrong man. We had all learned, even those with power, to measure every gesture, to have the cunning of the smuggler. But I was in a place now where those skills could not help me.

'Tomorrow we must leave,' I told him.

'I know that,' he said.

'Angelina wanted to cook something for me. Fish with grapes. But we never got around to it.'

'I could let you into the kitchen,' he said.

'It's all right. We haven't the grapes.'

'No. I suppose you wouldn't have.'

I took a long breath.

'When we leave here, we don't know where we will go,' I said.

'No?'

'No.'

'There are many fine places,' he said. He was alert now, his speech slow and tight.

'Yes,' I said. 'But we haven't permits. Our papers say that tomorrow we must return to Berlin.'

'And you're not going to do it?'

'No.'

'That's very risky.'

'Yes,' I said.

He turned to face me. The sun poised just above the sea struck his face, his eyes turning gold.

'I was wondering . . .' I said.

'Yes?'

'I was wondering if you might know a place. A place where we might go for a while.'

'A place where you can hide?'

'Yes. I suppose you would have to call it that.'

'And you came out here to ask me this?'

'No, I didn't. Angelina was in the room, drawing. I saw you from the window. I just came to talk. I didn't think of it until a moment ago.'

He turned away. I could see that this weighed heavily on him, and I regretted it. He had no means of knowing what to do. It was like playing chess in the dark.

'There's a house in the dunes,' he said finally. 'I have a key. I can take you there.'

The house was set into the side of a hollow behind the range of dunes that faced the sea. A path of sand wound down from the door through trees and out between two dunes to the beach. The dunes were huge, like the bows of two liners face to face. The sand was cool and soft. We sank in it to our ankles when we walked to the beach. Everything was slow there. I had never known time to move like that. From the house we heard waves rolling into the shore, birdsong, leaves clattering like applause in the wind. There were white linen curtains at the windows, holy water fonts and pictures of the Sacred Heart on the walls. Just inside the door a sack of cabbage and carrots and potatoes Piotr had brought us. We had been up to the lake and carried back buckets of water which we had heated in a kettle over a gas ring and poured into a bath. We went into the bath in the afternoon, when the sun was still high over the dune. I could see the table in front of the house, coffee cups, a pot of jam, a bird picking bread from a plate. I saw the paraffin lamp hanging from a hook in the ceiling, the curtains billowing in the light wind, the lamp swaying. I saw Angelina's drawings and her pencils, the high bed with the iron railings at the top, pillows pushed through the gaps, sheets falling to the floor. Her blue dress hung by a strap from a chair. We lay in the bath, her back along my chest, the sun dropping from the sky, through the trees and down behind the dune, the light moving from blue to grey. We spoke in whispers, the water slowly cooling.

We had a rhythm of a kind. We woke around nine when the sun rose over the dune and hit our window. Got up after ten. We walked up through the trees to the lake to get water. Breakfast. Then I read or washed clothes or cut wood and Angelina painted. She was painting a vine with tiny white flowers on the beam that ran across the centre of the house. There was a clock ticking somewhere, there were people asking questions, messages were being passed to the police, there was a reckoning, I knew, on its way to us, but I drove all of this away. We walked down to the beach and swam. I watched her move through the water, her black hair flowing behind her. There was a time in bed usually in the afternoon when everything was still outside, and then we made dinner. Dinner was long, hours out at the table in the sand with candles in the cooling air while I told her the stories I have been relating here, about Pan Kazimierz and Jerzy, the train to Germany during the war and Renata with dreams so heavy in her head I thought they would drag her to the ground.

One day when evening arrived I left the bed and walked to the front of the house and sat in the sand. Angelina was still sleeping. The sun fell to the top of the dune to my left and filled the house and the valley it was in with an orange light so powerful that it made of the air a lens. I saw the edges and veins of the leaves, the patterns in the boards that made up the house, the metallic rainbow colours on the wings of insects, vivid and elemental. She was in the air between me and these things like an electrical charge. I felt something I didn't know very well, something that seemed to draw me to fall into it, something like gratitude. Then the light weakened and faded away.

Angelina came out and lay in the sand with her head in my

lap. I looked down at her face. I saw no effort there, there was nothing hidden, there was just peace as she listened to the rolling of the waves and felt the cool sand shaped around her body. There were parts of her that I could not enter. The place of family. The place of the past. The place of the horse. It was not that she denied me. It was that I hadn't yet found the means. But there were times when I was with her when I believed that all I saw of her was mine. And there were times when I brought her peace – a little fragile maybe, but peace nevertheless.

I saw a man with a sack round a corner of the dune from the beach. He walked towards us, kicking up waves of sand with his feet. He was the first person to pass through that gap in five days. He had on a red shirt. His sack was in one hand and his shoes were in the other.

The sun moved into a break in the line of dunes and threw orange light like an unrolling carpet across the sand in front of us. When the man reached the light I saw that it was Piotr. He was smiling, unshaven, a little breathless, his hair falling down around his eyes as he trudged through the sand, a different being from the clerk with delicate gestures in the white shirt behind the desk in the hotel. He dropped the sack, sat down with us.

'I have presents,' he said.

He took from the sack four bottles of wine, three trout packed with ice into a towel and a bunch of green grapes.

Angelina laughed.

'That's my only dish,' she said.

'I thought it might be,' said Piotr.

'Why?'

'It was a guess.'

She lifted the grapes and smelled them.

'They're wonderful. How did you get them?'

'Through trade.'

'That's abolished,' I said.

'Not in Szczecin. A Danish boat came in. I'd met the purser before. He's a Pole. His liking for vodka, you could say, is stronger than average. He has a particular nostalgia for Polonez, and I brought him some. They were carrying a shipment from Portugal. Ham, herbs, lemons and so on. Such wonderful smells! He gave me a choice and I picked grapes, for you.'

We dug a hole in the sand and built a fire. Angelina peeled the grapes and cooked them with the trout. Night fell and we ate the trout and drank the wine by the light of the candles and the moon. Piotr drank faster than us, though Angelina had nearly a bottle to herself for it was the red wine from Hungary which she favoured. He started off the meal very grand and ceremonial, pouring the wine out like a waiter and making toasts to youth and beauty. He even put French words in them. But then I saw the drink pushing him this way and that. He told a long story in which his cousin came out of a bath and saw a page of his schoolwork blown by the wind and stuck to a tree outside his window. He reached for it, fell to the ground, completely naked, and after running here and there found himself in a courtyard. 'It was a convent,' said Piotr. 'There was a nun's face in every window!' He laughed loud and long then, a mad, shrill laugh, like a cockatoo. When he was quiet again he looked at us, his eyes like blue flames until they clouded over. Then he passed into a long silence. I didn't like what was happening. Angelina was beginning to drift. I couldn't see where any of this was going. And the world we'd made there in the dunes was like none I'd ever known, but it was poised as if on a needle. I feared a fall. 'I should be dead,' said Piotr after a long while. 'The rest of them are.' He looked up.

'When something like that happens, all the chords break,' he said. 'Don't you see? All the chords inside.' He fanned the fingers of both hands out over his chest. 'The instrument will no longer play.'

He dropped his head.

'Sorry,' he said.

'You're all right,' I said.

'I can't drink any more,' he said. 'All of a sudden. I don't know why.'

Angelina smiled, reached her hand across to his.

'I like you this way,' she said.

He sat up, ran his hand through his hair.

'I'm afraid I bring you bad news along with the fish.'

We looked at him, waiting.

'That's what I came with. Bad news. That's me today.'

'What is it?' I said.

'It's why I wanted to bring the grapes.'

'Yes,' I said. 'And the news?'

'You can't stay here any more.'

He waited, but nothing was said. I saw Angelina look up into the trees, as if she'd heard something there, as if the conversation no longer concerned her.

'An official is coming from Pila. Head of education for his district.'

'To Miedzyzdroje?' I said.

'To this house.'

'When?'

'Two weeks. And then after him another and another. Officials of middle rank who have earned a reward. Until the autumn.'

'And we have to leave before this one from Pila arrives?'

'No. You must leave the day after tomorrow. Workmen are coming to make the house ready.'

I looked at the house. The moonlight was shining pale and white along the side wall. It looked like frost.

'I've let you down,' said Piotr. 'I know it.'

Angelina was smiling. She reached across with the bottle and poured him more wine. I felt it all running away from me then. It was as though I was trying to carry sand and it was falling down around my arms and through my fingers.

'Do you know anywhere else we could go?' I said. 'Somewhere like this?'

He shook his head.

I turned to Angelina.

'Maybe we could go to Naklo,' I said. 'There would still be people there I know. Or back to Berlin. They break through there all the time and we could—'

'What would you do?' said Angelina to Piotr.

'Me?' he said. 'You ask me? That's curious.' He laughed a little, then looked at me. 'You remember how it was, don't you? People here laughed, loved. We had a life inside us. Before all those things happened. Remember? Now we're in the last place. Windows closed, door bolted, air stale. None of us are worth anything to anyone. But the strange thing is, everything is watched! Every footstep. You'd think we were made from jewels. So we hide the inner life. I hid mine so well that now I can't find it.' He took a long drink of wine. 'Well, what loss to anyone?' He turned to Angelina, took her hand. 'What would I do? I don't know. But then I don't know anything. I don't think very well. But there are people who are strong. I'm sure of it. If you could find someone like that they could help you.' He drank what remained in the glass. 'I like to come up here to the forest. That's what I like.'

He dropped the glass then, looked down into the sand. 'I'm sorry,' he said. His eyes fluttered, he let out a long sigh. 'Fish with grapes,' he said. 'Very beautiful.' I saw Angelina turn away from him, and from me. She looked out towards the sea, the moonlight bright on her face. She looked as she did when she was trying to find the lines of the horse as it ran westwards across the water, intent, unreachable, everything moving inside her like a flock of birds rising from a field.

I lifted the bottles and the plates from the table and brought them into the house. Angelina walked barefoot across the sand towards the sea. I could see the moonlight shining on the water through the gap in the dunes. I touched Piotr on the shoulder and he looked up at me, his eyes red and wet. 'I wanted us to have a happy night,' he said. I tried to raise him from the chair but it was only his arms and shoulders that moved.

'I'll make a bed for you on the floor,' I told him.

'No, no,' he said. 'I'm going back.'

'But you can't,' I said.

'Look,' he said. 'I can do it.'

He rubbed his hands over his legs, and stood.

'It was just that the legs were stiff.' He walked in a circle to show me. 'Where's Angelina?' he said.

'There,' I said, pointing, her figure a pale smear against the dark horizon.

'I will say good-night,' he said.

We walked together towards the sea. When we reached Angelina he shook her hand and began to bow but she raised him up and kissed his cheek. We watched him walk in the direction of Miedzyzdroje along the beach near the edge of the water, arms still and at his sides, bow-legged and cautious, something military in his step. He knew we were watching him. He did not want us to trouble ourselves any more. We watched until he moved into the darkness.

We went into the house and I stood in the room with the bed, waiting. Outside all was silent, even the sea, though I could feel its dense, heavy presence, the way it cooled currents of air, the smell of salt. I heard Angelina moving in the other room. She turned off the paraffin light. All this arrives very clear and heavy to my mind now, the way her eyes were slow and bright, the way her hands rose as she came into the room and moved over to me. 'You have everything now,' she would say later, and I would believe her. I cannot, will not, wish anything to be otherwise or regret the knowledge she gave me or the distance she carried me, though afterwards everything changed and all was lost. Yet why do I do it? Why do I call this forth? Because it is there, it insists. And I have no final defence against it. What matter the pain, at my age? It's better to feel than not, no? I felt her hands on my back. She took everything slowly and I followed, for she was to lead me down her way into the heart of this moment over which a kind of doom seemed to hang. We moved to the bed. I saw her in the moonlight, a cool marble white over her brow, trails of hair across her eye. I felt her skin warm and animate now, her hand delicate as an alighting bird, a beauty too great to absorb. We flowed like water all around each other and I have to see these things, I have to take and hold the pictures knowing that I will return to them in this wheel of yearning and loss that will turn through the years, her fingers around the iron railings at the top of the bed, her silver rings, her arms slender and brown from the sun, the veins and the bones moving in her hands, her calls and whispers and I trying to bring her all that I was with logic and need and what force I carried. I knew that in all the world there was nothing singular in her or me or in what we felt or did, but I knew too that out of all the certainties I searched for with such steadfastness and devotion in texts and in churches and in heroes this now was my rite and she now was my creed.

After, the room was like a boat drifting on a lake. I saw her dark eyes in the moonlight. 'You have everything now,' she said. She took her gold chain from around her neck and fixed it to mine. I felt her skin, her breath. I felt gratitude and a great wonder and then rising through it all like an acid the terror of losing her.

15

The Roads of Europe

M. replaced the receiver back on to the telephone. He stood still and thought, Where has she come from? What story will she tell? What will it mean? He walked back into the bedroom. Eleanor was rising from the pillow on to one elbow, her eyes still glassy from sleep. 'I was dreaming,' she said. 'I was deep in the sea with hundreds of blue and silver fish.' She flapped her hands like a bird beating its wings to show him how they moved through the water. She smiled. She sat up a little more, the sheets about to fall from around her breasts. He turned away, looking for a shirt. 'I have to go,' he said. 'There's a conference. They need me to translate a report. It's an emergency.' He found the clothes, made for the door. He heard her call to him from the bed. 'I'll buy you dinner,' she said.

On the street the evening light hit M. like a wave. He seemed to hear drumbeats as he ran. I don't know that Spanish city where all those things happened to him, but I have here beside me a guidebook with photographs and a map and I picture him as if from a cloud moving among the cars and workers and promenaders with their dogs down along the avenues and into the entanglement of streets near to the sea. He bought roses from a woman with a wooden cart. He stepped slowly then as if on to ice into the plaza in front of the cathedral. He picked a spot and waited. He was a tiny figure there solitary and still among the crowd beneath the huge grey stones and vaulted entrance to the cathedral. Could it be true, he wondered? He looked at the door and offered a prayer a little self-consciously in the direction of the altar that she would arrive. He looked for a clock. He clutched his roses. He turned slowly around to check each of the entrances to the plaza. He didn't know, I suppose, the peace that can come with simple words spoken to God. I didn't either, though I know a little now.

Finally then he saw her. She had come around the corner out of a narrow street and was walking towards the centre of the plaza. Her pace was steady and serene, her arms were folded in front of her. In this large arena mendicants were holding out their hands, traders were making offers, tourists were consulting brochures. There were roller skaters, mobile phone users, guitarists, mothers with children, worshippers moving with small steps towards the cathedral. Some, thought M., were preoccupied, some confused, some bored. None were at all like her as she moved forward at her unvarying pace, looking at nothing, it seemed, except what was within her, her long legs like scythes cutting grass. He walked towards her. She saw him, slowed, and then stopped. She was very close to him as they stood there in the centre of the plaza. She studied his face, then looked into his eyes.

He handed her the roses.

'I had some for you before,' he said. 'But I couldn't find you.'

She took them, smiled, her eyes still on his.

'I thought I lost you,' he said.

'Well you didn't,' she said.

Blue morning light came in through the window and moved like smoke along the floor. He heard the rattle of a motorbike, the lifting of a shutter from a shopfront. They were the sounds of those who must rise before others. He was in Hanna's bed lying next to her among scattered pillows, his limbs still and heavy as though the blood moving through them had thickened. He thought of the story of the night – of how she looped her arm through his as they stepped away from the cathedral, of their long walk through the narrow streets, of the bar with caves underground, the white-faced mimes on the steps of the restaurant, the waiter who referred to her as his wife. He bought a cold bottle of wine and they brought it with them up into this room where she put the roses into a glass and her hands on either side of his face and kissed him. He could see now in the morning light the bottle still nearly full and the spent candles with pools of wax running off the plate. He rose a little and looked along the bed. He saw her thigh, the curve of her hip, hair fallen across her eyes. The room turned from blue to rose, and brightened. Everything was new. It was being made as he looked at it. Golden light ran over him and her.

When M. returned home he found Eleanor sitting on the floor, her legs splayed beneath her, her nails digging into the rug. Around her were telephone books and balled, wet tissues. 'I was calling the hospitals,' she said. 'And the police.' She looked up at him, her eyes red and wet, her breathing staggered, her hair in knots. He saw her suitcase by the door, the bed in the room beyond neatly made. 'You don't deserve this,' she said.

He stood in the doorway, one shoelace untied, his hair like a trampled field. Bright yellow light filled the room and the sound of traffic rose as if from a single engine. He felt her pain there too but it seemed far away. He watched her get to her feet. He wished that she didn't feel that way. He wished he could reach her, bring her comfort. But he knew that could not be. He stayed in his place by the door, the room before him brightening to white and then vanishing. Then in front of him he had only the picture of Hanna above him in her bed, balanced on her fingertips, the red and gold of the candlelight moving over her skin, her head thrown back, a long, meandering note, full of breath and a little helpless, rising slowly from her throat. This was all that he could see.

M. watched her. It was enough for him. He watched the way her head turned at a certain sound, her fingers slid along her lip as she listened, the way she went up on her toes to reach something. He watched her lean in close to the mirror to draw a line on her eyelid, the way she cut the flesh of a peach, the arrangement of her rings, the shifting of her weight while she watched something cook, leg to leg, the hip pivoting, the way her foot rolled to music, her slow wink, the dimpling of her cheek, the way she reached behind her to fasten her dress. He loved these things. He tried to embed them in his memory. He watched the slow rise of her eyes to meet his, her stillness in sleep, the way the shadows fell on her flesh, the opening of her arms to draw him to her.

He was making a new world, particle by particle. It grew larger, more real, than the world he had known. When he left this world to enter the other it was like the rending of a membrane.

M. entered his home with a loaf of bread. It was during the afternoon, three o'clock. From the bathroom he heard the radio, the sound of falling water. He saw her jeans on the bed, one leg crooked at the knee. Her shoes were on the floor, one of them tipped on to its side. This too became a picture. He placed the bread on the table, and sat. He heard the water from the shower stop falling and then listened as she moved around the bathroom. The door opened and a cloud of steam smelling of soap billowed out. She walked towards him. She was wearing a T-shirt and her legs and feet were bare. She left footprints made of mist on the floor. She smiled, kissed him. He reached up to draw her to him but she stopped him.

'A second,' she said, and turned.

'What?'

'Just this.'

She upended the loaf of bread.

'Why did you do that?'

'It's bad luck to keep bread upside-down in the house.'

'I didn't know,' said M.

'Well you wouldn't,' she said.

She sat astride him on his lap, the T-shirt rising up her leg. Her skin was still cool from the water. She looked down at him through lank strands of dripping hair, her arms around his neck. She moved down to kiss him. His hand moved over the slope of her hip and on to her back, her skin warmer there, smoother. He felt her ribs contract with her quickening breath. He saw the muscles flex in her leg, her hips slowly circling. There was the vapour of soap and skin cut by the rising heat. She slipped the buttons on his trousers, reached for him. He heard the notes of a violin on a radio. She rose a little from the chair and then descended driven by muscles of leg and back and hips and he was inside her, charges running up his spine and detonating deep within his head.

He watched her. I could have told him that this alone would be enough to plague him. But he wanted all of what he could see then, and for the times to come.

It was a hot night. M. and Hanna were on the rooftop of his home under a half-moon. There were pale stars, clouds gliding past like swans. Far below were the night sounds of the street.

They were lying on their backs side by side, looking up.

'. . . I was driving to my aunt's house the day after his funeral,' M. was saying. 'I was in his car. It's much bigger and smoother than mine. It was more like being in a house than a car. It seemed a waste to only go as far as my aunt's. I thought, Maybe I could just keep going. Across Ireland, over the water, on into places I didn't know. I could go on for months. It wouldn't matter where I went or what I saw, it was just the idea of moving through a world I didn't know and nobody knowing me. I pictured a burnt landscape without trees, the big yellow car rolling along, the tyres hissing. I'd drive for as long as I felt like it and then stop. That was the idea, anyway.'

'But you didn't do it.'

'No.'

'Why not?'

'It passed – though there were times when I thought of it again.'

She rolled over onto her side to face him.

'Why don't you do it now?' she said.

'What?'

'Get into your car and drive.'

'Do you mean it?'

'Yes.'

'I'd miss you,' he said.

She touched his face.

'I'd be with you,' she said. 'If you'd invite me.'

'Yes?'

'Yes. I like that picture. To see those places without trees, to be where nobody knows us.'

He looked into her eyes. He pictured the sunlit road, her beside him.

'Will we do it?' she said.

'All right,' said M..

* * *

I take down the map of Europe from the wall and stretch it out on the table. I bring from the library picture books from the countries M. and Hanna are to travel through. I see him carrying a small pile of boxes full of paintings and books along a narrow street, her taking her things from the drawers in their bedroom and arranging them in a suitcase. Her movements are slow and light. It seems she is thinking of nothing other than this task. Miedzyzdroje and the sting it carries drift away from me as I watch. I see M. run to a machine and take money from it, folded notes thick as a fist. She arranges the sweep of her hair in the mirror, paints her lips a pale pink. M. comes in and watches her through a gap in the door.

Wladyslaw taught me how to drive in Chicago, but I never had a car. I never had enough money to think about being without work for more than a month, maybe two, nor a girl and an open road ahead of me that wasn't shrouded somewhere along its way in darkness. I look at pictures of the Spanish coast in the books I have brought and see M. and Hanna climb towards the mountains, the coves and the villages, the heaving rock. They cross over into France and keep to the shore. I see the white-masted boats, the girls on the beach, a little hotel on a hillside at the edge of a village, painted pink, bougainvillaea pouring from its veranda. Maybe they passed some nights there behind a window I like the look of on the second floor. I never saw such places and won't ever, I suppose. I don't want a ride on a boat. I don't need to see bougainvillaea, though I never saw it nor heard of it before. I don't even want that girl who would stop your breath walking alone at the edge of the water – well, maybe for a little while, if she was kind, and interested, and didn't laugh. It's just these pictures I begin to long for before I wake, this idea of freedom, M. and Hanna in the car, the rippling heat and the cooling breeze, this journey that I, like M., can believe for a moment has no limits and no end. Freedom. A word that changes at borders of place and time. Jerzy looked for freedom and I looked over his shoulder, but the more we struggled to find it, the tighter grew the ligature.

They drove on through heat I've never felt, aromas I've never known, across borders I would never have been given permission to cross, through vineyards and sunflower fields, around hillsides terraced with citrus and olive trees, Hanna lying across the seat beside M., her head resting at the edge of the window, her bare feet tucked under his leg, sea breezes and the aromas of salt and pine circling around as the wheels rolled and the music played and she told him stories about this woman whose life had been a single long journey towards him. The roads of Europe were their roads, the lights over the doors to restaurants and hotels were shining for them. All along the way M. went to machines and took money from them, the scientists and poets and poten-tates of the different countries they passed through looking up at him from the bills. He put them in his pocket. He paid no attention to them. Her soft voice and the feel of her near him and the way she placed him at the centre of her world obliter-ated prudence and duty and commerce and all that was not of this everlasting now the way the sunlight blanched the land. I see M. there at the wheel of his car, radiant, self-absorbed as lovers are at times such as this, her eyes on him as he drives, her feet moving under his leg to the rhythm of the music. Never had the air borne such colours or wine tasted like that or shapes been assembled so beautifully. No one could touch him. Those were his days, the music passing through his mind playing perfect notes at the perfect pitch, each one a surprise when it was struck yet inevitable as it faded. Each day, each hour, he cut away the tissue that connected him to his past and he fed himself to her as she fed herself to him. It became too late to find a way back from this feast. He knew this. But he didn't care. He spent himself as he spent the money. There could be no measuring in this, no equivocation, for this was real, this was the truth, this was the new world, and his discovery of it was as it had been for Galileo in his tower, Kepler at his blackboard and Newton finding the numbers for gravity – all that was came into its light and all that had been was now pale and far away. He drove on over burnt red lands rising from blue water, the sun caught on his skin and hair and eyes, the smells rising from him those of the earth. Then they turned to the north. She was beside him at every moment of this journey and at no time did he wish for the soft sounds of her voice to stall or the charge in the air around him to diminish. He could not grow accustomed to her. 'The man who is loved by this woman is blessed,' he remembered thinking. How, he wondered, had it come to pass that it was him? He was like a gambler whose every throw of the dice brought him victory. They took rooms for a night or a few days and did not leave them sometimes until the shadows began to fall as he moved around her trying to know all that she was. Then again when they left they got into his car and looked at maps as I now am looking at mine and he drove, she close to him, her head on his shoulder, speaking softly, almost whispering. His desire grew and he let it, he played it out as she did according to the rhythm of the day and the silent language they made between them that at times like that could be without flaw, they drove on or walked among trees or sat in chairs outside a little bar, their fingers moving over each other's skin in the delicate night air until the time came but even then a little further they went making wagers with this yearning of body and soul that seemed without limit, another glass of wine maybe or a little more walking through the trees taking in their aroma before climbing the stairs with a slight ache and a liquefying mouth and currents flickering around them as they entered the room and the white rectangle that was the bed where the gates that they had held closed could open and they found each other again in this act which never seemed to carry the pattern of any other, and yet this was as it was in every room and every bed of this journey, for this was how they were, they were free in this, they had found that the act of love was not an event that repeated but was instead a single story made up of speech and gesture and light and dark, the varying notes of peace and hunger and urgency, folding and unfolding through their days without ever finding an end.

I see them walking along a sand path, a late evening sun lighting their faces. A small cove is behind them, waves rolling in. They sit on a rock. They are so close it seems they've been stitched together. He reaches up and takes something from her eye. He looks as if he could be broken by a whisper.

'You won't leave again, will you?' he says.

He felt it before he woke, a force rising in him as if out of the earth. He opened his eyes. The doors to the balcony of their room were open, the sky dark, just a thin line of pale light along the rooftops. He saw a cat walking there. He reached behind him and found that she was there. He turned to face her. And he found that she too had wakened, she too felt it, for she drew him to her, her body moving, her knee rising up his leg to his hip, her hands racing like small animals up his chest, her mouth searching for his. She guided him upwards and moved beneath him. Her legs fell open like the wings of a butterfly. They were there in the night, held in a dream yet alive as never before.

Later then her cry, high and pure before it descended. It rang in his head. She was beside him, her eyes closed. He looked at her ribs moving as she breathed. Then she laughed. He turned and kissed her from shoulder to neck, lifted the hair away so that he could look at her face. There were streaks of colour in the sky, the light flowing over her. How long can they go on, he wondered, living like this?

They got a corner room in an old stone hotel looking out over the ramparts of a medieval wall to trees and a river. They walked together through the streets. People looked at them. He was unshaven, his hair long and bleached, his skin dark from the weeks in the south. People looked at her everywhere they went.

They went into a bar. It was still light, a cool summer evening. There was a pool table there. M. wanted to play with her but there were men at the table and others waiting. 'Play,' said Hanna. 'I'll watch.'

In another room a guitar player and a violinist were placing their equipment on a small stage and tuning their instruments. It became M.'s turn at the pool table. He was awkward and tentative but the other man was worse and M. won. In the next game several balls struck by M. went in in succession and by the third he was in a rhythm, the balls finding a true geometry as they spun around the cushions through narrow corridors into pockets. His shots grew more outlandish and yet they went in. The music started. She got out of her chair and stood at the back of the crowd facing the stage. M. won games four, five, six and seven. He couldn't miss. More people arrived to watch the band. They closed in around Hanna. M. could just see the glow of her hair in the overhead light, her head moving to the music. In the ninth game there was a long tactical battle over the last ball. M. could not see her at all now. He thought of missing deliberately and leaving the black ball over the pocket, but could not bring himself to do it. Yet he felt a great need to know what she was doing in the crowd. He tried a wide angle shot off a side cushion into a corner pocket but missed. The balls fell awkwardly for his opponent and he too missed. The black and white landed against the end rails opposite each other and at an angle. He hit the cue ball with hard right-hand spin, sending the black ball off the side rail, the end rail near him and back up the table into the corner pocket.

'Excuse me for a moment,' said M.

He went into the crowd. He couldn't find her. He moved all around the bar, the music loud and hateful to him at this moment. He went out into the street. It was dark. He ran along the street in front of the bar in both directions. People watched him. He tried to think of a method for covering the area but couldn't. There was an intersection with several roads radiating off it and he ran a little way along each of them, then back. Nothing. He was out of breath. Many possibilities of where she was and what she was doing moved through his mind. He had drifted a little way from the bar. Maybe half a kilometre. He thought of the man he was due to face at the pool table, thin, weak-chinned, a chaotic brown moustache and enormous eyebrows. He would have already racked the balls and be waiting. Somehow M. could not tolerate the thought of forsaking his place at the table. He headed back towards the bar and then immediately saw her. She was at a telephone, her back towards him. He watched her weight shift from foot to foot as she nodded and listened, her hand rise and sweep through her hair, then emphatic gestures as she seemed to try to be understood. She reached into her pocket and put more money into the slot. He moved to the cover of a building and watched a moment longer, then moved on.

He arrived at the bar. The men were waiting at the table. They were silent, their expressions sour. Blue smoke enshrouded them. The thin man with the moustache was standing with his arms folded around a cue. He gestured with his head towards the table.

'Sorry,' said M.

He stepped up and broke. The balls had been racked too loosely and did not scatter well when he struck them. The cue ball slid off the side of the pack, sprung off two rails and disappeared into a pocket. Two shots to his opponent. M. could see as the man crouched over the ball that he was a poor player, and very ponderous. His eyes moved along the table to the object ball as though he was following the progress of an ant, and then back. He did this six times and then struck the cue ball with terrible violence, sending it whirling around the table and unsettling a line of balls along the end rail. When everything stopped moving the congestion of balls around the spot remained intact but there were three of solid colour left hanging over pockets for him. They were unmissable.

Hanna arrived, calm, smiling, newly lipsticked. She kissed M.

'You're playing again?' she asked.

'I haven't left the table,' he said. He didn't look at her.

All M.'s balls were either trapped behind his opponent's or in the group around the spot. He couldn't find a shot. The other man went 5–0 up. Finally M. saw an obscure possibility of a four-ball combination coming out of the pack. He struck it severely and the object ball went in, but so did two of the other man's balls. The black ball slid to rest over a side pocket. The man tapped it in.

M. sat down. She leaned against him.

'Bad luck,' she said.

M. entered the room carrying breakfast for him and Hanna on a tray. All through dinner after the pool game he had tried to drive out of his mind the picture of her speaking on the telephone. It took him more than four hours, but he did it. Now he felt well. He listened to the water moving through the heavy stone walls of the room. The bathroom door was half open and he could see through the mirror her form behind the white curtain as she leaned over to turn off the taps. He saw her step from the bath, a towel held in front of her. He looked at the morning sunlight coming in through the windows and filling the room. He felt light, easy, complete. Hanna saw him in the mirror, stopped, smiled.

'I met some people,' said M.

'Where?'

'Downstairs, where they have breakfast. They're from Finland, a couple, very nice. I thought you'd like to meet them.'

She turned away, opened her bag of make-up.

'Aren't we leaving here?' she said.

'I thought maybe tomorrow,' said M. 'We could have dinner. I said to them that we'd see them in the bar downstairs.'

'Yes,' she said, her back to him. 'That's fine.'

Later that morning Hanna came into the room. M. had been to collect their laundry and she to buy shoes. How would she look in this moment? Preoccupied? Poised? Perfectly groomed, at any rate, I would say.

She stood still and looked at M.

'Did you find anything?' he asked her.

'No,' she said.

Still she did not move.

'Are you all right?' said M.

'Have you seen the car?' she asked.

'No.'

'You didn't pass it?'

'No.'

'The window is broken.'

'Which one?'

'The front. There's a hole and hundreds of little pieces of glass. I could see a stone in the front seat.'

'Is there anything missing?'

'I don't think so,' she said.

'I'd better get it fixed,' said M.

'Yes,' she said.

16

A Dream

I woke. I could see that it was early, the leaves still wet, wisps of mist still turning in the pale light high above the house, everything still.

Angelina was not in the bed. Did I wake as she left it? I looked at the twists in the sheet where she lay through the night. I lay on my back listening for her.

I got up. I moved through the rooms and did not find her. I went out to the table, around the house and all the way up the trail to the lake to see if she had gone for water. I didn't see her there.

In the house I found her clothes hanging on the rail, her bag, the box of paints she was using on the beam. I sat. I made tea. I waited.

I walked down into the valley and out between the dunes to the sea. The water was still and gleaming like mercury under the morning sun. I looked right and left along the beach but I didn't see her. I sat for a while watching a fishing boat cast nets, then I walked back to the house.

After a while I went back out and sat on the slope of a dune between the house and the sea. The sun made its way across the sky. Around eleven o'clock, I thought to myself, Now she would be painting the beam. A little later, with the sun directly above me, it would be the swim. Then bed. You have everything now, she said. I went into the house and tried to eat soup and bread but I couldn't. I looked on every shelf, in every drawer and all around everything that was there but found nothing either missing or added. I lay down on the bed. I got her smell. I said prayers to saints to bring her back to me. Then I went back out and sat on the dune. She could be coming just now, I thought.

Long after darkness fell I got up. I put all our things in cases and made the house ready. What would I do with her dresses, her shoes, her drawings? I put the picture of the horse running across water in one of my bags and the rest of her things in hers. I found I couldn't carry everything for there were three of us taking it all when we came here and so I put her bags in some low bushes out behind the house near the trail that went up to the lake. Then I went back along the beach to Miedzyzdroje.

When I got there I sat on a bench near the bandstand and waited until there was a trace of light in the east. I watched it fall across the sand and the empty promenade and over the façade of the hotel. The green and black curtains were drawn across the window of the room where I stayed with Angelina. I went into the streets then and to the house where Piotr had his room. I had to knock three times before he woke. He looked behind me for Angelina and then let me in.

'They've been asking about you again,' he said. 'They came to the hotel.'

I waited through the day in Piotr's room while he worked in the hotel. When he finished he went by train to Szczecin. I slept some but I could not say how much. He had left me food on the little table by his window but I didn't eat it. I thought all day of Angelina. I felt her moving through me.

It was dark by the time Piotr came back from Szczecin. He

took a bottle of vodka down from a cupboard and we sat at the table. I ate a little of the food and drank while he told me what happened in Szczecin. I listened very carefully to everything he said but all those things about cars and boats and cities and officials seemed to be happening to other people, far away.

'I talked with people around the town,' he said. 'Some of them I can trust and some of them I don't know. It's confusing. Maybe some of what they said is real. One said he saw someone like her walking on the deck of a boat in a blue dress. She has a blue dress, no?'

'She does.'

'Was it in the house after she left?'

'I don't know.'

'But you can check. You packed the bags.'

'Yes.'

'Well, he says he saw her very early in the morning – that's this morning now, not yesterday. She was on the deck of a freighter. It was not long after dawn. There was no one with her. There was no one around at all. She smoked a cigarette and then went below. The boat sailed at midday.'

'Where did it go?'

'This is it! There were two big boats docked there, one for Russia and the other for Norway. He can't remember which was the one where he saw the woman.'

I chewed Piotr's bread and followed the story as far as I could, Angelina down among the ropes and boxes in the hold of the boat on a rolling sea, sailors bringing her food.

'Anyone else?' I said.

'Different people saying they saw her drinking coffee or getting on a bus or entering a church. None of them were sure. Then there was another one. I'm uncertain of him. I never saw him before. He heard me ask a woman I know there in a bakery about Angelina and he said he saw someone just like that coming out of a public building yesterday afternoon wearing a grey raincoat and getting into the back of a black car. A car for officials. Now the only thing we can know for sure is that I have become such an idiot that I forgot to speak quietly about things like this in front of strangers. But I tell you anyway. You should know everything.'

'Piotr,' I said.

'What?'

'Stop.'

'What do you mean?'

'Forget this.'

'Why?'

'It's dangerous.'

'I don't care. And the longer we delay the further she will have travelled and the less likely it will be that we will find her.'

'And it's stupid.'

'Why?'

'I'm not going to look for her,' I said.

'Don't say that.'

'I'm saying it.'

'But you *must* find her,' he said. He brought his hand down on the table. The glasses shook but did not fall, little rings forming on the surface of the vodka. His face was contorted and red, his eyes wide. I could see there his own loss and his pity for me and the way we in our weakness look for others to complete the stories we have been unable to complete ourselves.

'She's gone,' I said. 'I'm never going to see her again.'

He held his position, then let it fall. He dropped back into his chair. He let out a long sigh.

'Why did she go?' he said.

'Because she could,' I said. 'It's something she has a skill for.'

* * *

The boat rocked in long, slow strides through the Baltic towards Copenhagen. I thought of a fat man on skates. It was night. I was in a pine box meant for a bass drum down there in a world of iron and oil. Next to me were tubas, cellos, clarinets, violins. A little box for the triangle. I heard footsteps sometimes, the engine grinding on like someone mourning a death. I got bread, coffee, ham, smoked mackerel. One sailor brought me boiled eggs for breakfast and a picture from a magazine of Rita Hayworth in a bikini. Piotr was not so weak as he said he was. He informed his supervisor at the hotel that he was ill. He travelled to the factory in Wielkopolska where once he made trumpets. He worked his way delicately through everyone he knew there and those known to them. Finally he found the manager of an orchestra based in Poznan that was about to travel to France. This was a man he had once encountered during the war as he moved from hole to hole. Piotr gave him what money he had and the promise of more from me when I would be earning in the West. He came back then to Miedzyzdroje and we walked out at night to the house in the dunes to bury Angelina's bag in the sand. The next day we went to Szczecin and I got into my box.

From Copenhagen the boat would go to Calais. I had the address of an office in Paris written by the orchestra manager on a piece of paper. Poles there would help to find me work cleaning plates in a hotel kitchen and then a place on a boat headed for Montreal via Cork. After Cork we would put in during a gale in Sligo. There I would collect the pictures I would use when thinking of M. in his home in Ireland. I would be separated from my bag with Angelina's drawing of the horse in it while getting out of the boat at night in Calais. I would never see it again. Her gold chain I would leave behind in the shower room of a boarding-house while travelling to Renata in Chicago.

There on the boat moving through the Baltic I dreamed of Angelina. I saw her as I did from the rooftop outside our room in Berlin rounding a corner way down in the street into the sunlight in her yellow dress, her black hair flowing, her face held up to catch the sun. She went through the door. I heard her footsteps running up the stairs. She came in then smiling and fresh and free from all past and all burdens and all sorrows, her step light and quick, her arms out to reach for me. I ran my hands through her hair and over her face. I felt her beating heart. I got the aroma of sun and skin. I held her in my arms shaking and laughing with a happiness that seemed sent down from the heavens and with a golden light flooding the room around us. This is her, I thought, this is truly her. Lost, and found again. I have her now. I have her.

17

Fire

'I have to leave you now,' wrote Hanna. 'It is because of problems in my family which are too complicated for me to explain here. You are now with the car trying to get the window repaired. You will come back to this room expecting to find me and then for us to make plans to go on with our journey and with our lives together. Never have I had a time like this time with you and never will I again. Now you will find only this letter. It is something very poor, I know. I could not face you to tell you. I tried to make myself do it but I couldn't. I have tried to avoid having to leave you now but it is not possible. The time that I have to be away could be very long. I am so sorry, for you and for me. It is the destruction of everything I want in my life, but that doesn't matter. I do not expect that you can forgive me. If you hate me now I understand it. Goodbye, my love. I love you and I always will. Hanna.'

The pain was swift and violent. There was no part of him it did not wish to destroy. He stood in the room holding her letter – the smooth, sloping words, the lines so perfectly even. The same hand that filled in forms, that made lists, that left him notes if she would not be at home when he arrived. How could that be? All passed in this instant from light to darkness. He already knew that it would break him. It had to. There was nothing to relieve it. He had cut himself off from everything because of her. How could he gather himself up? How could he remake himself? He couldn't. He had nothing. He knew this.

He looked at the clock. It had taken him two and a half hours to find someone to repair the window of his car, to get the car there, to make himself understood. He looked out each of the windows of the room. He didn't see her. It had begun to rain. He put his things in his bags and went down to pay the bill. He asked at the desk if they had seen her. No, they had not. Was there a train station there? No, they said. The nearest was forty kilometres to the north-east. Buses? Yes, of course. He ran out into the rain and through the streets. Bus? Bus? he asked. People pointed. He got to the station and looked at the board with the schedule on it but nothing made sense to him. How many buses have left here in the last two and a half hours? he asked the man selling tickets. He looked at M. through the glass. He did not understand him. M. tried the sentence four different ways, pointing at a clock and at a bus parked in the station yard. Nothing worked. The man continued to stare at him. M. tried again to understand the schedule on the board. Finally he was able to determine that according to what was written four buses had departed from this station since he went out to get the window repaired, two of them to the town where the railway station was located. That was the route he chose to follow. He wrote down the names of the towns the bus passed through on the way. He ran back out into the rain.

He found that the garage where he had left the car was closed. There was a shop next to it selling meat and M. asked there why there was no one in the garage. The man behind the counter shrugged his shoulders. M. did not know if the man had understood his question or if he could not answer it. He went around to all the eating places he could find in the vicinity but he did not find the man who was to put the glass in his window. He waited. The hopelessness of all this filled him like a congestion.

When after nearly an hour with the sky darkening further under the rainclouds the man returned to his shop, he refused to give M. his car. He pointed to the broken windscreen, he walked all around the car gesticulating, he waved papers in the air. M. had no idea what he was speaking about. Had he forgotten him? Did he think M. was a salesman, or someone who hadn't paid their bill? M. pointed to the clock on the wall, he held up his hand and rotated it to indicate a key turning in a lock, he pointed to his car and then to himself, he took out his wallet and showed the man his credit cards. The man ignored him. He held papers up in M.'s face and shouted, pointing at different names and numbers on them, his jowls working, his voice rising in a thunderous outpouring that M. could not imagine the end of. He left the garage. The rain was heavier. He ran back through the streets looking for an agency that would rent him a car. He found nothing. He returned to the hotel. His clothes were drenched. His dripping hair fell down around his face.

At the hotel they hired M. a car. They regretted that they must give him one from the most expensive category because none of the others were available. He drove back to the garage. The man there allowed him with a dismissive wave of his hand to remove his bags and hers from the boot and transfer them to the car he had rented. He looked through her bag in a search he knew was hopeless for her passport. He cursed himself for never having done it before. Nothing. He looked at a map. He found the route. He headed out.

Pictures of her passed through his mind. His lungs constricted. Let this be a dream, he thought.

By the time he arrived at the station it was eleven o'clock at night and all the trains had gone. There was a woman with bandages around her ankles drinking beer on a bench. A man was sweeping. The ticket office was closed. What else, he thought, might he have expected to find? He took the photographs which I have here on the table beside my books and maps and he showed them to the man with the broom. The man lifted his eyes to look. It seemed to take a great effort. He shook his head. No, he had not seen her.

M. got back into the car. He had the feeling that he must continue to move, but for a time he could not. He slid down the seat and closed his eyes. The pain moved into him like a storm entering a valley, acute, vicious, enduring.

He turned the key in the ignition. He began to drive. He had no plan of where to go. He turned on the radio but the laughter and the speed and the loudness of the speech that came out of it oppressed him. He listened to the wheels moving over the wet road. He looked at the silhouettes of the trees. He passed through towns. Everything there looked malignant to him.

He saw a hotel set up on a hill above the main road. He pulled over. He opened the boot and reached for the bags, but then left them. He went up the hill and asked for a room.

He had a shower and got into bed. She would have liked this place, he thought. The beamed ceiling, the paintings and pencil sketches, the big wooden bed and linen sheets. The thought of where she was fluttered like a bat around the dark room.

His head ached when he woke. He went downstairs and took a little breakfast. He went to the desk to pay his bill. He put his hand in his pocket but did not find his wallet. He remembered then that he had put the wallet in one of his bags when he moved them to the other car.

'I'll be right back,' he said to the clerk.

He walked down the hill and around the bend to where he had left the car. He saw it there ahead of him, pale sunlight

236

coming down through the morning haze and gleaming on its broad silver bonnet. Behind it was a red open-backed truck piled high with boxes and mattresses and bicycles. A small dark man with a moustache reaching out past his ears was leaning against the truck, his brown arms folded across his chest. There was a woman with a child in her arms in the passenger seat. M. looked at them rather than his car as he walked. He wondered how far they had travelled and where they were going. The man saw him and pushed away from the truck. M. took the keys from his pocket and turned towards the car. The man approached. He began to shout and wave his arms and point to the red truck. M. saw something then which at first and for long afterwards he did not understand. The rear windows of his car were black, the boot rumpled and half open, the paintwork blistered and scorched, the tyres blown and ragged. Parts of them had melted. Through the windscreen he could see that all that remained of the seats in the back were the metal frame and exposed springs. There was the stench of burnt rubber and leather. Had he made a mistake? Was this truly his car? On the passenger seat he saw the list of towns he had written in the bus station. He walked around to the back of the car. He saw then that the grille and bonnet of the red truck were bent badly out of shape. Scorch marks ran up the bonnet towards the windscreen. Blackened pieces of metal that seemed to be from the engine of the truck were lying on the pavement. The small dark man shouted at him continuously. M. tried to open the boot but it was stuck. Finally he kicked it and it sprung open. Everything there – bags, credit cards, receipts, documents for banks, storage, car, his clothes and hers – had been destroyed by fire. He had no money or the means to get it. He could not reach anyone who could help him. No one there understood him. He saw one of her shoes, a belt, the arm of a pair of sunglasses, the sleeve of her white linen shirt, burned and blackened. Things familiar and now distant. He seemed to see all of this from a great height and far away, the hill, the bend in the road, the elderly man who was making his way past him with two walking sticks, the mangled vehicles, the owner of the truck pointing and shouting, his wife and child motionless and looking on, the trees, the playground where children were running, the sun pouring down and lighting the edges of the clouds white and gold and himself there small from this distance, bent over and looking into the man's brown and yellow eyes, understanding nothing.

For days when he woke M. did not at first know where he was. He saw the green Chinese pattern on the sofa he was lying on, the tiny pink flowers on the wallpaper. He rolled over. White sheets covered tables, chairs, mirrors, lamps. They were like ghosts about to walk. His aunt had put them there after he had last left this house after his father died and he had not removed them. This was his world. He lay on his back and it assembled around him.

He drank cold water from the tap and walked out on the road beside the beach to the thin neck of sand that led out to the graveyard at the end of the bay. It was summertime, caravans packed like fallen boulders into coves, the doors and windows of the houses wide open to let in the air, radios playing, people calling out, dogs and children running along the sand. M. didn't know them. He walked among the gravestones and the flowers and then down to the ruins of the monastery at the foot of the graveyard and sat at a wall looking out over the bay. He hoped for something there, from the play of light on the water or the wild colours or the stones where the monks had prayed.

He went back to the house. He ate something. He spread documents in different languages out on a table in the kitchen.

He made telephone calls to brokers and bankers and lawyers. He moved money from place to place. He counted what money remained. He tried to repair the damage he had done. He tried too as he walked the roads or sat in the house or drank in the bar to put a shape on his life, to find a direction in which to face, and he tried to hold his attention there until something was revealed, but he could not, for in his weakness it slid off, and each movement of his mind hurt him, as movement hurts the skin of a person damaged by fire, for everywhere he turned she was there.

When all this tired him M. walked the roads watching men bring in the hay or stood at the back of the church staring at the statues or lay down on the green sofa. He turned the pages of old magazines. He listened to the radio. At times he looked at a book he had found, its covers grey, its pages yellow and stained with blue ink, something from the schooldays of his father that told of galaxies and planets, the laws of heat and motion and the shapes and movements of atoms. He liked to see the way his father's hand formed words then, the drawings and obser-vations he made in the book's margins. He liked too this picture of spinning spheres and orbits and everything in its place. Was that how the world truly was? If he started from the beginning, moving from the smallest thing up to the largest, could he make the world for himself again and find . . . ? But his mind could not hold the thought.

When night came he walked to the bar. He sat in a corner behind a wall pretending to read. The passing of time made him find more things that he had lost. It shamed him that he could think of nothing else. He tried to keep his face out of view.

The day came then, a dank, warm day without wind and with heavy grey clouds spilling down the hillsides, when he drew the curtains, locked all the doors and took his father's long yellow car out from the barn where he had stored it. He packed it with clothes, maps, sandwiches. His father's book with its diagrams and formulas. Another by Werner Heisenberg with the title *Physics and Philosophy*. Her photographs. He drove out along the road climbing the peninsula, the colours deep grey and green. 'No one would know him in these places,' he remembered saying to her. He was moving. The sound of the tyres on the road calmed him. 'And no one would know where he was.' Not all of the stories she told could be true. He knew this. That was not her nature. To expect them to be true would be to misunderstand her. But there were events, records, people. Everyone born leaves a trace. He pulled over. He wrote down a list of places – Isle of Wight, Barcelona, the town where he met her. That was just the beginning. Then Turku. Finally he would go to Turku. How easy it would be to find her mother with her ballet school or her man Ritso with his wild hair and strange clothes. He looked at a map of Europe, the entanglement of roads like a basketful of river eels. What matter to anyone if it was fruitless? If he could not be with her he must know why. Maybe he could save it, maybe not. But at least to know. He drove on into the failing light.

18

Three Clues

'I'm shrinking,' Renata tells me on the telephone. 'Wrists, ankles, hips, cheeks. You could hold me up in the crook of your arm. The nurse's assistant does it when she comes to wash me.'

When she hangs up I telephone Jacob.

'Would you like to meet my sister?' I ask him.

'I would, of course,' he says.

The next morning we set off by train, Jacob wrapped in his bright red coat, the two of us drinking tea from his flask as we roll southwards towards Krakow. Nothing much stirs on the land, just a few cars from time to time slithering in the icy lanes between the snow-covered fields. He hands me a sandwich from his pocket, the sun a pearl globe just above the treetops. Finally then the train slows as we pass behind the houses of Krakow.

'I should be kinder to my sister,' I say. 'But something seems to stop me.'

We ring the bell of Renata's home and stand in front of the door. It is answered by a small round-faced girl, a fringe of dark hair on her forehead which then falls and hooks around her pink cheeks like parentheses. She gives a little bow in a country style.

Jacob tells me he thinks it better that I go in first on my own, so I follow the girl into the bedroom. I find Renata there in a bed jacket and starched white nightdress propped up against a

241

slope of satin pillows, her fingernails and lips painted red, her tiny hands sparkling with rings and bangles, her hair dyed the colour of rust and lacquered stiff as a bird's nest around her face. I squeeze her hand and kiss her cool dry cheek and see that the cover of the pillow under her shoulder is worn away, the broken satin stretched across like the strings of a guitar. I stand by the bed and look at her. I don't know how to begin. She is so tiny, so frail, like a figure in a catacomb.

'You needn't look so pitying,' she says. 'Or so smug. Maybe one day you'll be held together with string and bandages. Maybe you'll have to be carried to the bathroom.'

'I don't doubt it,' I say.

'Here,' she says. 'Hand me over the bottle in that drawer there.'

I go to where she points and find a bottle of vodka. I pour her a glass.

'That's new,' I say. 'Isn't it?'

'What?'

'Drinking in the morning.'

'Yes,' she says. She drinks in rapid sips until the vodka is gone. 'Since I've been stuck in the bed. I haven't the concentration to read, the television is monstrous, no one visits. I lie here wondering what would happen if there was a fire and every now and then I take a glass of vodka. You think I should deny myself?'

'No.'

'Then give me another.'

She takes her glass from under her pillow and holds it out while I pour. Then she throws it down like a cowboy in a single gulp. Her whole face collapses, eyes and mouth both disappearing, as the drink scalds her throat. She looks for a moment like a walnut.

'I look every day for the grace to bear this, but I don't find it,' she says. 'I know a sour old person is one of the plagues of the earth. I don't like to be sour. I pray to avoid it. But it's a terrible struggle. I don't find a single compensation for old age.'

'Maybe we're free to do what we want.'

'We're free to do what we're no longer able for.'

'There's that,' I say.

She looks around the room, her fingers picking at stray threads on the sleeve of her dressing-gown.

'Nearly everyone I know is dead,' she says. 'There's one old lady down on the first floor. We used to go out on Wednesdays to the cinema and then for a hot chocolate after. But that's finished now because we're both stuck in our beds. We speak by telephone. We talk about grandchildren and visits from doctors. We get the same magazines sent to us and talk about the dresses. Then at some point she'll tell me about the cow that's living with her in her bedroom. She wouldn't mind, she says, because when she was a little girl she liked cows. But this one is too big. There's barely room for the bed now, she says.'

We both laugh then, and I feel better.

'There's more,' she says. 'At the age of eighty-seven she has a project to change her name to Zbigniew!'

'I'd like to meet her,' I say.

'I'm sure you would. I'm told she's still very well presented.'

I notice then on a dresser a small plastic Christmas tree with pink branches, its lights blinking on and off.

'You've decided to mark the season,' I say.

'Bobby brought it to me. Or I should say Ryszard. That's how he prefers to be known. He says, "We've no need to be ashamed of our Polish names," very dignified. He gets ideas about what will cheer me up. He brought the Christmas tree last week and the month before it was a picture of a dove in flight. "Positive images", he calls them.'

She tries to prop herself up but her arms won't support her weight and she slips down into the bank of pillows, two of them at her shoulders pushed forward and up like a pair of folding wings before dropping down on her face. For a moment I can see only her hair.

'That girl,' she says from under the pillows, 'doesn't know how to fix a bed.'

I clear the pillows away and follow her instructions until she is upright again.

'Where did you get her?' I ask.

'From the priests. She cleans their house. But don't say anything to her about the vodka because she'll tell them and they'll interfere.'

The mention of the girl makes her think of the occasion.

'I thought you said you were bringing someone.'

'I did.'

'Well where is he?'

'He's waiting outside.'

'Call him, please,' she says. 'That's rude.'

I lean out the door and call to Jacob and watch him advance along the hall on the tips of his toes. He dips his head, enters, and stands in the centre of the room. I see he has a box of chocolates and feel foolish for having brought nothing. Renata has drawn the sheet up to her chin, two skeletal hands folded in front of her, her little head among the pillows like a raspberry set down in a basket.

Jacob leaves the chocolates on the table beside the bed and goes out for a chair. Renata puckers her lips, then wets a finger and draws it over each of her eyebrows. 'He's a fine-looking man,' she says gravely, leaning over a little towards me. She's trying to get a look at herself in the mirror. 'Wonderful set of shoulders.'

We're all together then in the room, Jacob and I in our chairs, the girl from the country coming and going with tea and cakes. Renata has Jacob up near her head, drawn in close to the bed. I watch her primp and trill and cajole, laying her hand on his for emphasis, all the gestures except certain more intimate ones a little outsized, as she asks him all about his studies, his family and how he likes our country, especially its girls. I watch her throw her head back, clasp her hands to her chest and let out a long tinkling laugh like a run of notes on a xylophone over something that Jacob has said. She's lost none of her skill, I think, even if she never uses it.

She pushes herself back up the pillows and adjusts her bed jacket. She looks over to me as if to include me once more in the gathering, then back to Jacob.

'Do you know what the difference is between a man and a woman?' she says.

We do not venture an answer.

'I will tell you. In the mind of every man there are six monkeys sitting on chairs. And in the mind of every woman there are six monkeys sitting on chairs, with another one watching.'

Jacob is looking at the floor, taking this in, nodding. I thought I'd heard most of her thoughts on these matters more than once, but this one is new.

She looks at us and laughs.

'Now it's time for a story,' she says, 'before you go. Which of you will tell it?'

It is a long while since I have heard anyone ask for a story. Whenever it happened to me it was a request that came from a woman, a woman I was pursuing and who was allowing herself to be pursued, and it always filled me with fear and a wish to escape. I never felt that I had anything ready. I thought I would disappoint them, and there would be a cooling. I turn to Jacob and find that he is looking at me. I know it is I who must do it. So I tell her about M. I tell her of how I met him in the Stary Rynek and of the story he told me that night, of how he risked everything for that beautiful woman he knew so little of and of how then he lost her. I tell her how he looked as he told this story. 'He's driving around looking for her,' I say. 'Here. This is her.' I show Renata a photograph. 'What do you see in her face, Renata? In the middle of their rapture, in the highest point he had ever reached, she left him. No explanation, no trace. He loved her with all that he was. This cannot be doubted. Then she did that to him. Can you think why?'

Renata raises one brow as if to ask if I have reached the end. There is something caustic in this, I think, and it makes me nervous.

'Is that how you see it?' she asks. 'That this was done *to* him?'

She looks from one of us to the other, stopping at me. 'Is that the opinion of both of you? Has it not occurred to you that there could be things in her life which have nothing at all to do with him?'

Her mouth snaps shut, like a purse closed with drawstrings. Her eyes do not move from mine. It is a look that seems made from ice.

That was not the first time Renata had left me feeling chastened, but afterwards I began to think of Hanna in a new way. She gave me the first of the clues.

'How many times do you think a person can fall in love?'

I am walking along the river with Jerzy. We have been talking about the poor quality of the sausages being produced by a new factory in Wroclaw, and my question startles him. He stops and pushes his hands down into the pockets of his jacket. He looks over at the trees on the other side of the river. It could be that he would like to ask why we have changed course in this way, but he does not. He is thinking instead of an answer.

'If you are Chopin,' he says, 'maybe not very often. But if you are Charlie Chaplin, maybe every day.'

He looks at me.

'Why do you ask?'

'It's that young man I met in Krakow.'

'The one who has you reading about the physicists?'

'Yes.'

'What of him?'

'It's his anguish. And the thought that it could have no end.'

'Maybe it will be the making of him,' he says.

'That's the sort of thing said by people far away from the feeling itself.'

He ignores this. He turns me by the arm towards the bridge we always aim for, and we begin again to walk.

'He should look down at himself as though from a distant star,' he says. 'Sometimes you have to make of your pain a small thing.'

'And that is an operation for heroes.'

'Well then at least he must let it find the way to its own death. He must not grow attached to it. He must be patient. He must believe that one day he will be well again.'

This appears to bring the matter to an end for Jerzy. He now begins to speak about the greatly superior sausages his sister has sent him from Ostroleka. 'Hunters' sausages,' he says. 'From her own butcher.'

'But Jerzy! Think of it. To have so much and then to lose it. To be able to think of nothing except finding it again. All the clues impossible to follow. Maybe never again to be able to feel anything.'

I sense him looking at me out of the corner of his eye. He

knows well of my long wintry bachelorhood. And the reasons for it.

'Do you know where he's gone?' he says.

'Finland, I think. That's what he said.'

'Is there a phone number, or an address? Maybe you'd be more peaceful if you could communicate with him.'

'I haven't even got his name! We talked the whole night and he told me all those things about himself. We drank enough to lay waste to a regiment. And then he was gone. I kept three photographs by accident which must be precious to him. I get the idea sometimes that I should bring them to him. What do you think? I know the city he was heading for, the story he was following. You could come with me.'

'Wait a minute. Why Finland?'

'He has the hope that he will find her there. Or at least someone who will be able to tell him where she is. Her mother, as it happens.'

We have still to walk eight hundred metres to the bridge and then back again so I tell him the story of the ballet that came to Rouen, of Paris and the naval attaché, the island in England, the student of engineering from Finland on the beach and then the aspiring theatre director who moved in with her mother and who once fell off a roof.

I feel some sense of agitation in Jerzy. He stops, and lays a hand on my arm.

'But what are you saying?' he says.

'What do you mean?'

'This is the plot of a novel.'

'Well I know it's melodramatic, but—'

'No, no! It actually exists. It's called *Her Bright Shining Eyes* or *The Shining Star* or something like that. By Malgorzata something, I think. One of my daughters read it when she was a teenager. I picked it up one day and even though I didn't want

248

to read it I was driven along by curiosity. It starts, let me see, in Zamosc, or maybe Chelm, then it goes to Warsaw, and it finishes on the sea at Gdynia. Very popular with Polish girls, my daughter told me at the time. There was the older military man, the student who gambled, the ballet school . . . I don't remember anything about a theatre director . . .'

And all the rest of the way to the bridge and back along the footpath I listen again to this story of the little girl and the dream of the dance that never left her.

That was the second of the clues.

I am given the third clue right here in this room where I began to think of all these things and to make sense of them after coming back from Krakow and where now this work is soon to come to an end. It is New Year's Eve. I have balloons on the wall and a bottle of champagne in a bucket with ice and three glasses because Miss Zelenska who lives on the floor below and who prepared a carp for me for Christmas is coming up to join Jacob and me for this drink. Then we will all go down to the town hall to hear the orchestra and maybe dance a little and welcome in this new time into which none of us can see. But I don't care about that now, for the labour has been long and the end of it is soon to come and I feel a lightness and a thirst and a feeling of expectancy as I wait for their arrival and for this night to begin. It is Jacob who arrives first, his shoes newly polished. He is wearing a red tie with white stripes, for Poland, he says. He is carrying a book with the mark of our library on it, a book with pictures, for he has something to show me, he says, something about that photograph of Hanna, something that made him think. Finally it came to him, he says, for it made him remember a photograph of his father standing in front of a statue when he was a young man.

So he wrote to him in Africa asking him about it and waited for the reply without saying anything to me for he wanted to know for sure, and now he has the letter, and he can tell me. I take Hanna's picture as he asks me to from the drawer, the one of her in the turquoise coat smiling in the snow, and he opens the book to a page he's marked with a little strip of paper where there's a creased black and white photograph of Jacob's father in a dark suit standing in front of the same statue in nearly the same place as the girl and, printed in the book, a close-up picture of the statue itself. Look, he says to me, here it is, the same statue in all three pictures, a statue not from Finland or any of the other places in her story. It is of someone you above all should know well. And as I hear Miss Zelenska come up the stairs and pause at the door to arrange her hair maybe before knocking, I get this clue from Jacob which, had M. known it, would have made his journey shorter and very different, but no more heartening perhaps, for I can see as I look from the picture in the book, a serious picture without people in it and with exaggerated colours such as might be found on a postcard, to the picture of Jacob's father stiff-shouldered and nervously smiling and finally to the picture of M.'s beautiful girl that the position of the trees and the arrangement of streets and windows and bricks of the clock tower are the same, and that the pale blue-green statue of the powerfully built man dressed in robes and with long hair curling above his shoulders, the index finger of one hand pointing to the heavens and the other holding an astrolabe, commemorates someone whom I have studied, whom all of us have celebrated and that each year at Christmas Grand-Uncle Zenon praised with such zeal and pride for his discovery that the sun not the earth is the centre of our system and that the planets move in circular orbits around it. But above all he praised him for his nationality, for this was a statue of our own Nicolaus Copernicus.

19

Starlight

We set out in the morning on the nine o'clock train, Jerzy, Jacob and I. We've cakes and a flask of tea for the journey. We even have blankets for our knees in case the heating fails. It's cold and radiant, the shadows from the trees long over the glittering snow, children racing in the lanes. We are four days into this new year which I had awaited like a man hiding from gunfire behind a wall. It started well, as it happens, for at the New Year's Eve dance Miss Zelenska went up on her toes and kissed me on the cheek. She is fair-haired and laughs in a way that sends her back on her heels. When we met on the stairs one day before Christmas and I told her about the last time I tried to cook the carp she laughed and laid her hand on my arm and said that she would be pleased to cook it for me. Tonight, when we return from our excursion, I am to prepare her dinner.

We are making for Torun, birthplace of Copernicus. Jerzy, I would guess, is coming to humour me. Jacob is coming to see the statue before which his father once stood. I am here in order to say goodbye, I think.

I say to them on the way that I am going to tell them about Copernicus.

'We already know about Copernicus,' says Jerzy. 'We know about him like we know about our own grandmothers.' His arms are folded across his chest. He looks like a citizen complaining about dogs at a town hall meeting. Yet in his aspect there is the suspending of his authority for the day and a passing of it to me. 'Well, I suppose Jacob doesn't,' he says.

'That's correct,' I say. 'And maybe there are some things about Copernicus that you haven't heard. Or if you heard them once you may have forgotten them.'

'That's possible,' says Jerzy.

'For a Pole, Copernicus was a lucky man,' I tell them. 'I looked in the books of the library for signs of struggle in his life, but I couldn't find any. Maybe some nervousness about the Church's reaction to his ideas about the solar system, but nothing more. The best education, the finest comforts, security, servants. Aren't these our national aspirations now? Well, most of us would be willing to forgo servants, I suppose. But the rest, yes, that is what is called for. How did it happen that Copernicus came by these things? He was ten when his father died. His great fortune, and the fortune of science, was that he and his brother then came under the protection of their rich Uncle Lucas, Bishop of Ermeland. What would have become of him were this not the case, we of course cannot know. But Torun was then still a small medieval city. What could he have expected of life? Maybe writing by day in a ledger and at night dreaming and gazing out of his window at the stars? As it was, Uncle Lucas sent the boys to the university in Krakow, where Nicolaus developed a passion for astronomy. This did not seem to be a suitable occupation to Uncle Lucas, and the boys were therefore sent to Italy, where they studied law and medicine. Italy then was experiencing the Renaissance. Nicolaus was exposed to ideas and to people he could not previously have imagined. His brother stayed on in Italy to serve the Church, but Nicolaus returned to Poland. He was excited by what he had seen and sought his mother's counsel about what he should do with his life. "It is your Uncle Lucas who has provided for you," she said. "You should do what he says."'

Jerzy unfolds his arms and moves to the edge of his seat. He looks at me intently. 'And then?' he says.

'Lucas got a position for him as the canon of Frombork. This is where he had the servants. He also had plenty of time. He practised medicine, law, architecture. He was a civil servant. He even had a spell in the military when he organised the defences at Olsztyn. But of most importance to him, and of course to us, was the interest in astronomy which he had first discovered in Krakow. He gathered together a large library and commissioned the building of an observatory in the grounds of Frombork cathedral. And from here he made the calculations and did the thinking that led him to the conclusion that the sun rather than the earth was at the centre of the planetary system.'

Jerzy raises a finger in the air.

'Excuse me,' he says.

'Yes?'

'What was the work he did as a civil servant? Do you know?'

'Yes I do know,' I say. 'He worked with currency.'

'I thought you were going to say that,' he says. He shakes his head in wonderment, an unusual gesture for him. 'That's remarkable.'

'I think so too,' I say.

'You don't suppose it could be a coincidence, do you?' he says.

'I would doubt it,' I say.

'Yes,' he says. 'I also.'

'You don't think that what could be a coincidence?' says Jacob.

Jerzy turns around to face him.

'It's that girl who made such a mess of the young man our friend here met in Krakow,' says Jerzy. 'It seems that everything she told him about her home life was an invention. Her mother came out of a novel for teenage girls and now we learn that her stepfather, or whoever he is – a Finn named Ritso who had an obsession with theatre – has been based on the life of our Nicolaus Copernicus. You just switch plays for astronomy and disregard various details and there he more or less is.' He leans back in his seat. 'She's more intriguing than I thought,' he says.

'Yes,' I say. 'I would say that too.'

'Why do you suppose she did that?' he says.

'I'm not so sure,' I say. 'Why do *you* suppose she did it?'

I can see that this sort of pedagogy could irritate him were it to go on, but for the moment he appears to accept it.

'Perhaps she had something to hide,' he says. 'Some betrayal, or crime.'

'Well, yes, perhaps,' I say. 'But she needn't have something to hide simply because she does not wish to reveal herself.'

He looks at me sharply. I can see in the way his lip curls a little and his face greys that a thought is beginning to form within him about Moscow and the conversation we had by the river when I came back from Chicago. He is unsure of his bearings. I could press him and wait to see what would happen. Perhaps I might even obtain his forgiveness if it all played out in the right way. But this is not the moment for that. There is no moment for that at all unless he wishes it, this fine man.

'Maybe she just did it to entertain herself,' I say. 'She liked stories. That torments him now because he realises he hasn't much of an idea of who she is. But it was also something that drew him to her. That mysterious air she had when she told them. He went into some of them himself. They made them together. And this thing of Copernicus and the romantic novel, that's one of the ways that stories are made, isn't it? A piece of something from one place, then another piece from somewhere else?'

'Do *you* know who she is?' says Jacob.

'No,' I say. 'There is someone I have in mind when I think about her. Sometimes I have the feeling that I know all there is to know of that person – I mean about how she moves, the sound of her voice, her moods. But really I haven't an idea. That's just the person I make when I think about her. She could as easily be any other way. I never met her, as you know. But I think I know something about her that the man who loved her did not know.'

'What's that?' says Jacob.

'That she has not been living in Finland.'

'Why do you say that?' he asks.

'I have the idea that the time was going to come when she would leave him. Maybe that time was imminent. She made a telephone call the night before she left. She seemed a little agitated during the course of it. Perhaps she was under pressure from someone. But I think she was forced to leave when she did because he had arranged a dinner with a couple from Finland and she was afraid she would be exposed as not knowing the language. I think she broke the car window herself so that he would be occupied when she got away.'

'That's conjecture,' says Jerzy.

'Perhaps,' I say. 'But I also think I know where she is from.'

'Where?' says Jacob.

'I think she's a Pole.'

'Why?' says Jerzy. 'I can see now that you say it that there is some evidence that points that way, but it's not conclusive. That novel about the ballet dancer, for example, was probably available in other countries.'

'I imagine so,' I say.

'And even the photograph,' says Jacob. 'We know it was taken here, but my father was also photographed in front of that statue. Maybe she was a visitor, like him.'

'That could be.'

'What, then?' says Jerzy.

'There are two things,' I say.

'And the first?' he says.

'What she did with a loaf of bread.'

He looks at me suspiciously.

'What would that be?'

'She righted it when it was the wrong way up on a table. She was superstitious about it. "It's bad luck to keep bread upside-down in the house," she said to him.'

'That means she's a Pole?' says Jacob.

'It's true that that's done here,' says Jerzy. 'My wife does it. It used to irritate me but now I find I do it myself.

'And the other?' he says to me.

'That's something that only came to me yesterday. I was thinking about the days when they first met. They were alone one night together in the bar and she poured him a drink. She lifted her glass and said something to him. She said it was a toast. He didn't understand it, but he was so fascinated by her that he took everything in. When we were in the bars that night in Krakow he toasted me in the same way, or tried to. It was just a sound. I didn't pay attention to it. But it came back to me yesterday. I'd been doing all that work in the library, and all that thinking about him and about the past, and I'd got to the end of it. I felt the work was over. It was a strange feeling, like nothing I'd ever felt before. If I'd ever in my life finished a long piece of hard work I do not say that I had a feeling of triumph, no, that would be ridiculous. I never did any such thing that would merit a feeling of triumph. But maybe there was relief. And even satisfaction if it seemed to have been done well and I'd spent myself in the doing of it. Anyway, I'd long been looking forward to finishing this work. It's not that anyone was making me do it, of course, or that there was anything much to it. It was only something for an old man who had nothing else to do. But it seemed a burden at times. I looked forward to the feeling of relief I might get at the end of it. And so then there came the time when I had read about the physicists and I had passed through once again as though in another life all those things that had happened to me and also to that young man and his girl. I knew it would arrive all at once, the end, and as I moved towards it I was already thinking about the sweetness of that relief. And maybe I'd get even more if I was lucky. But it wasn't like that at all. I just felt it all running out of me. I felt an urge to hold it in, to keep it a while longer in case more could be made of it. But I knew that wasn't right. I knew I had to let it go. And it went. I'd been carrying it a long while, from long before I met that man in Krakow. And now I no longer had it. I looked around the room. There were just walls, tables, chairs, things. They seemed naked there. I knew I wasn't going to see and hear again all the things that existed between me and the things of the room, all those people and their voices and what they did. I had a feeling that already they had an existence somewhere outside of me, but I didn't know where. And if all of them together as I had thought about them and pictured them had any feeling about me then and in time to come it would be the feeling of indifference. That was a kind of sadness, yes, but it also made me laugh. So I went into the kitchen and poured myself a drink. That picture of my young friend and Hanna together in the bar where she worked came to me and I said her toast out loud. There is something strange in that, I said to myself. So I wrote out the way it sounded on a piece of paper and said it again. Then I had it. "Lykniem bo odwykniem" – "Let's drink or we will forget how to do it." A Polish toast, as you no doubt know.'

The train comes into the station at Torun then and we collect our flask and blankets and make for the street. I say to them that

I think we should walk everywhere here today, for this place is not so big and the day is so bright and alive. And that's what we do. We pass through a tunnel and along the streets to where the road begins to rise to the river, the walls and the steeples of the city of Copernicus before us.

'When he lost Hanna,' I say to them as we walk, 'my young friend began to read about physics. He was hurt. And he didn't understand what had happened. The feeling became so strong that it began to spread to everything around him, so that the world outside too was drained of sense. He couldn't find a way to change this. So he set out looking for her. And he began to read about physics. He wanted to feel connected to the world, to find the fundamental things. And he wanted it to make sense again.

'He thought physics did that. He thought it classified and explained the biggest and the smallest things. I also. And for a very long time that is what the physicists did. They allowed us to look out at the world and see and understand where and what all the things in it were, how they worked and how they fit together. But then there was a change. I have a great many holes in my knowledge. In fact I have a knowledge that you could say is mostly holes. This change that happened in physics is one of these holes. And it was a very big change, and fundamental. For what the physicists began to discover when they looked into the world of the very small was that it bore no relation to the visible world, even though the visible world is supposed to be made from it. Up here planets and billiard balls and bicycles obeyed the laws laid out by Isaac Newton. But down in the world of the very small everything was different. You couldn't make sense of it. You couldn't get a picture of it in your mind. They found that instead of those very small things moving continuously, the way a ball rolls down a street, they jumped. They found that something could be two contradictory things at once – that light, for example, could be both a particle, or a substance, and a wave, or a pattern of energy. It was whatever you wanted it to become. If you set up an experiment to show that light was a particle, it would prove that light was a particle. If your experiment was designed to show that light was a wave, it would behave like a wave. They also found that there was something in the very nature of this sub-atomic world that made it impossible for it to be known fully. When I saw that young man in the square in Krakow he was reading a book by Werner Heisenberg. It was this German who discovered that if you want to know both the momentum and the position of a particle, you cannot do so, for the act of measuring one of these characteristics changes the behaviour of the other. The original information required cannot be got. Newton's laws cannot be applied.

'The more the scientists looked into this world, the more it disappeared. It seemed to be without things as we understand them. Einstein was the first to put forward this idea when he said that matter was energy. And when they looked at atoms, those tiny impenetrable things said to make up matter, they found that they were composed of almost nothing at all. If an atom were the size of the dome of St Peter's Cathedral in Rome, then its nucleus would be the size of a grain of salt and its electrons all but invisible motes of dust. There was the idea we had as children in school that the atom was just like the solar system, with the electrons rotating around the nucleus as the planets do around the sun. Then Niels Bohr said that no, this was not correct, electrons jump in and out of orbits at varying distances from the nucleus according to how much energy they get. A French prince named Louis de Broglie then said that in this world particles and waves were interchangeable and Erwin Schrödinger refined this further by finding a mathematical formula that demonstrated that electrons are standing waves, like a clothesline between two poles set in motion. Finally Max Born destroyed the atom altogether by demonstrating mathematically that these waves are not real things at all but rather what he called probability waves, things of statistics rather than of reality. Atoms do not exist. They are numbers used to make sense of what is happening in experiments. All is number then, as Pythagoras once said.

'Sometimes the physicists suffered when they discovered these things. It was not a picture of the world which pleased them. When Max Planck presented his paper contending that things in the sub-atomic world moved in jumps instead of smoothly and continuously, he hoped that someone would successfully contradict him. Einstein laboured for decades to prove the quantum physicists wrong and was called a fool for it. Heisenberg walked under trees through the night asking himself how nature could be so absurd.

'My poor young friend. He looks for a Pole in Finland and for certainty in physics!'

Along the bridge a little way we stop to look down at the river. Wind runs over the water, the light hitting it in explosions of silver and white. We watch a boat pass beneath us, two men sitting on crates holding fishing lines. The city is there before us. I see smoke rising from chimneys, a round white face in a window. Jacob begins to walk and I follow. Jerzy pulls away from the wall with what seems a kind of grief and falls into step beside me. He leans his head towards me but it is a while before he says anything.

'You've been speaking a lot today,' he says.

'Yes I know,' I say. 'I'm sorry. I'll be silent now.'

'No, no,' he says. 'Don't. I find it interesting, and . . .' – here he pauses and grimaces a little as though he is having problems with his digestion – 'admirable.' Giving praise, I know, embarrasses him. But so does receiving it.

'Thank you,' I say. 'But that I speak of it does not mean that I understand it.'

'Well no, perhaps not. You would need to know more about numbers. But I was thinking just then of what you said about the sadness of the physicists, and their distress. I think that . . . well, I believe, that the breaking of a belief long held by new evidence, a belief about which certainty has been felt – well, this is a process that can be painful.'

'Yes,' I say.

His jaws are working as though he is trying to chew something intractable.

'This pain has its own laws and clock. It must follow its own course. Eventually it passes. And what I want to say is this – no one outside can do anything to affect it. It would be unreasonable to expect them to try. I believe this utterly.'

I stop then and turn to face him, but he does not want this, he just nods once to say that the subject is now finished and leads me on until we reach Jacob, his step lighter, his face assuming again the contours I have known. In this world which the physicists say is all approximation, he has offered me at least a piece of what I have long wished for from him.

We enter the city through a towering arched gate and walk along under the walls and through the cobbled alleys and lanes, the shadows of the ancient houses around us like diagrams laid out on a page. I step out ahead of them holding a guidebook open at a map and I lead them into a quiet street with trees and then through the door of a hotel. We take our seats in the dining room, Jerzy and Jacob on one side of the table and me on the other, a high beamed ceiling above us, waitresses in starched uniforms speaking in whispers. Beside us are two of our new men ingratiating themselves with each other, briefcases at their sides, nails polished, hair arranged like American senators'. Whenever they move, clouds of cologne billow towards us. I can see from the way Jerzy looks at them that the political beliefs which his mind long ago abandoned still remain in part within his viscera. But we will not let these men interfere with our lunch, this lunch which I tell myself marks the end of my labours, even if those labours may not yet be entirely over, for one act yet remains to be done. Afterwards we go out into the now truly dazzling afternoon light which sweeps across the square towards us like a herd of galloping horses. I lead them up into the high tower there and we look down on this city unknown to us all, yet where the air seems curiously concentrated for each of us, where there is a sense of something being prepared. We look all around and then at each other and Jacob begins to laugh. He laughs all the way down the stairs and across the square to the statue of Copernicus, the laughter fading as he stands there but a smile remaining while he looks from the robed figure of the astronomer to the spot where his father once waited to be photographed and Hanna smiled at someone we can never know. I lead them to the house where this great Polish hero of the heavens was born and I leave them at the door, for I have an errand, I say, an errand that could take perhaps an hour.

Later then we stand together on a low rise in the land, Jerzy, Jacob and I. Below us brown grass and grey flats and the blinking sign of a video shop. Just next to it a pharmacist's. The light is fading from the sky, a pale blue. Each of us is silent as we look out. We are waiting. I hope the wait will not be long. I feel the air growing colder now. I think of M., and wonder how he is. Packing his bags, maybe, in a Finnish hotel. Is there anywhere left for him now? She told stories to beguile him and please herself and keep the truth at bay. I have told these for the company and now they are passing and soon I will be alone. But no matter. I feel well and strong this night. I feel a power moving around me and wish I could pass some of it to M. I think of a physicist from his country I would like to tell him about were he here. He could help him, maybe. His name was John Stewart Bell, and he was from Belfast. When studying the separateness of things Bell found against all sense that things were not separate, that if you took two paired particles and set them far apart from one another, even at opposite ends of the universe, they still had the means to communicate with one another within the same moment, so that if you changed the condition of one the other would react instantaneously, in that very instant of time, not through some signal sent at the speed of light, and that therefore all is somehow of the same fabric, all is one. This makes me laugh, though I didn't laugh when I first read it. I watch the print of my breath vanish from the air. I look above the rooftops and the line of black naked trees to the sky and the slender pale moon like a trail of powder, the first faint starlight beyond it. I think of all those men of numbers down through the ages breaking their brains in a search for something they would never quite reach, the whole of the universe written down in equations on the page, all that was and all that will be, all together in a perfect, harmonious unity. This is M. and me, and Jerzy and Jacob, for have we not all been tried and convicted as we made our way along this same futile road? We have sought what cannot be granted, the inner life never finding its match outside, mysteries never revealed, love transported here and there in search of completion but ever denied. We stand together side by side on this little hill, our shattered beliefs lying like heaps of dust at our feet. This too makes me laugh. I feel Jerzy stir beside me when he hears this, but then he settles back in to his watch. How rich seems the air this night, how alive and full of movement! Einstein said that the physicists' efforts to understand the world resemble a man guessing at the workings of a watch he cannot open, but just here and now in the twilight in this city of Copernicus I feel it all churning and boiling and dancing around me, all the many billions of tiny particles, creation, then annihilation and then creation again, this world which just now I meet and feel again where nothing is lost and everything is changed. There are no things, there are only forces, processes, movement. I know this, and I get some taste of the loveliness of it. You cannot hold a single thing to you for it must break and fall away. That is its nature. And I understand now too the idea of the physicist Dirac who found that for all matter there is antimatter, for each particle an antiparticle, where the play of energy and matter is carried out, where creation is destruction and destruction creation, for I see what is high must fall and what is broken must find form, for each thing holds its opposite, and that already in exaltation is despair and in despair exaltation. I feel something stir and rise within me, a cleansing and an opening and the flow of raw power such as I felt long ago in the hotel room in Erfurt, that whirring of a hundred dials, that laying waste to what I have known followed by another birth, but all of it a little slower and sweeter and sadder maybe, for I am old now and even the blood too is hobbled a little. All is one, even in this decrepitude. It is just a moment, this little miracle, a moment for which I am grateful, and before it passes I seem to hear at the very limits of what can be heard a voice saying, 'Goodbye . . . goodbye . . . Say goodbye, goodbye . . .' trailing off as in the last notes of a song. And then I feel Jacob reach his hand around the back of Jerzy and tap me on the shoulder. He turns his face from the street to me and on it is a look of wonder. It was not difficult work nor long in the doing to move around the city of Torun with some questions and photographs while he and Jerzy were looking at the gyroscopes and sextants of Copernicus. The questions were few and they were simple, for I could see then that in the story of Ritso a real person began where Copernicus ended, a person known to Hanna, linked to her by bonds and by fate. So I asked the people moving around in the streets of this little city if they knew of a man, maybe a little fat, lame after a fall from a rooftop, an almost bald man with a badly trimmed beard who wears mismatched clothes. Perhaps he has an interest in the theatre. Perhaps he knows about remedies. Had they ever seen this beautiful girl here in the photographs? I was not long in getting an answer, and nor are we long waiting on this hillside before we see the light go out in the pharmacist's below us and the upraised front of a wheelchair appear in the door. In it is a large smiling man with a red face, a green scarf and basketball shoes. He holds the hand of a little girl who walks beside him, laughing as he whispers something into her ear. I see a woman's hands on the back of the wheelchair then as she manoeuvres the wheels over the ledge of the door. These are the hands of the man's wife. They move towards us, father, daughter, mother the three points of this triangle. The pale light of a streetlamp falls on this face I now know better than Angelina's, the bones wide around the eyes, the neck long and slender. This is the face that M. never wanted to lose sight of. She walks as he said she walked, as though on small skis, pushing the wheelchair and looking at nothing or maybe at something else beyond what can be seen in these forsaken streets known only to those who live among them. When will come her next time of release from them? Whom will she beguile with her knowledge and beauty and stories? And do they cost her, these acts of mind and passion played out in places far from her home? How I would love to see what is behind those green eyes and how well I know that I cannot. The man who is loved by this woman is blessed, thought M. She loves this man,

265

I think, this man in colourful clothes who drinks wine and smiles and each time she ventures out welcomes her home with a glass of vodka and a ceremonial cake with a strawberry on top and who asks no questions. And I think she loves M. But out of pity or hopelessness she will spare him the blessing of this love the next time she gets away, but of course he does not wish to be spared it, even though he might know that it is written that he will lose her again and suffer again. If I take a few steps down this little rise in the land I could touch her as she passes. Think not badly of her, M. Her skill is great as you know, and a skill unexpressed is an anguish. It is freedom that she lacks. So think not of the harm she brought you, for that is past, and think no more of certainty, for certainty is for fools and zealots and provincials. The world is bigger and harder and more wondrous than our attempts to ensnare it. All is one, theories and tracts and stories, a girl in a banana grove in Africa, another in a house in the sand and this one here moving away from me with her long strides. Say goodbye. All is one and all is change. And you too M. must say goodbye, for you will not walk with her now. Say goodbye to that wheel of yearning and sorrow. Say goodbye, all of us, for all is passing and all is being made.

She grows indistinct now, the darkness taking her. We turn away together on to the path, the cold air on our skin, starlight above.